A WINTER'S KILL

THE KILLING SEASONS
BOOK 1

JK ELLEM

To my father Noel
8/8/32 – 11/13/18

I wrote a lot of A Winter's Kill with my laptop balancing on my knees while I sat in the corridor outside my father's hospital room waiting for the nurses to finish, or inside the darkened confines next to his bed while he slept peacefully, or on the sofa in his apartment while he dozed watching old John Wayne movies on cable. Many hours were spent in silence, typing away, while all the time I kept a watchful eye on someone as they slowly died.

There were good days, and there were bad days, rays of light and laughter, and deep, dark places of despair and regret. But through it all, the time I did get to spend with him in his final weeks were the best moments I had ever spent with him as a father and as a son should. It's just a pity that we don't come to realize these precious moments we have with someone until time starts to run out.

I traveled to some very dark places during this time, and perhaps it is reflected in my writing in the book. But I have no regrets.

Our time on this planet is short. The clock is ticking, and we don't know when or how the clock will stop.

So make the most of it. Don't waste any of your time, and do what you want to do and not what others think you should be doing.

JKE

March 2019

A WINTER'S KILL

1

If her parents were lucky, they would find her in a few days. If not, then the wildlife would have something to keep them fed during the long winter months ahead.

He reached for her, then paused and sniffed the air. There was something there, subtle but distinct. A fragrant scent had separated itself from the other smells, and now rode a cold breeze toward him.

He stood among a myriad of white pine trees, their branches caked and heavy with snow. Petals of white drifted gently from the dull, muted sky above, the sun just a watery haze, the forest silent and still.

He turned his head, his nostrils flared. He sniffed the air again trying to pinpoint its source. He was standing downwind. The scent teased him, like the invisible caress of a past lover, their lingering smell on your skin, in your memory, long after the sex had ended.

He stood perfectly still, contemplating what to do next.

Then it was gone, carried away on the breeze. Nothing there now.

He shook his head, clearing his mind, shaking off the distraction and focusing back on the task at hand.

A wide tree trunk rose in front of him, a huge eastern white pine, as old as the forest itself. Redness was seeping around its base, warm liquid feeding the rootball. Crimson on a field of blinding white.

Reaching out, he twisted, pulled, wrenched, tearing flesh, ripping muscle, splintering bone. Finally, twenty inches of carbon shaft came away in his gloved hand. Duct tape across her mouth stifled whatever sound she would have made. A feeble moan escaped her lips as he peeled the tape away.

She didn't want to give up the bolt easily. This one must have nicked a rib on the way in before it lodged behind the bone itself, and the blades of the arrow snapped open.

All his kills were at less than thirty yards, so he chose mechanical broadheads. They maintained their kinetic energy in flight, offered a wider wound channel and a shorter blood trail while still making it a quick kill. It was ironic that the hunting magazines considered it too harsh, too raw to describe it like that. So they used the term "fast expiration" whereas in fact what they really meant was "a quick kill."

He took a few moments to examine the bolt, making sure it wasn't damaged. For him it was as much about the end result as it was about perfecting the mechanics of the kill. Just as a dedicated sporting shooter studied the penetration depths, trajectory lines and expansion patterns of bullets in ballistic gel, he studied the devastating impact his weaponry had on human flesh and bone. There was, however, no practice, no paper targets or foam shapes. Humans *were* his practice.

Ribbons of flesh clung from the broadhead, and part of the Mossy Oak finish on the shaft was coated with blood, thick and slippery. He'd used slightly heavier bolts this time, preferring penetration over speed.

Satisfied, he wiped it clean with a rag and fixed it back into his quiver then berated himself for getting carried away. It was the first kill of the season after all.

He looked up and regarded her as she hung there, limp, head down, straw-colored hair covering her face, droopy like a rag doll.

The first shot was just for fun, deliberate, but not fatal, just enough to bring her down. The second and third shots pinned her to the tree like an insect to a corkboard. One bolt through a lung, the next through her stomach, the broadheads burrowing deep into the rough bark behind her.

Then he took his time and watched her slowly suffer and slowly die. He took out his thermos from his backpack and drank some coffee while she withered and gasped, all wide-eyed, crimson bubbles slowly forming on her lips, her chest cavity making sucking noises.

After his second cup of coffee, he'd seen enough.

The last bolt finally killed her: a heart shot, the bolt passing left of the sternum in between the intercostal cartilage of the fifth and sixth rib.

Slowly and carefully he packed up his gear. The snow around him resembled the floor of an ER theater, mushy and red.

All summer long he'd been hibernating, just like the bears do in winter. Working hard at his job, head down, tail up. Long hours, little sleep, countless demands placed on his skills and expertise. People depended on him, trusted him, never questioning. An elevated position of authority and standing in the community granted him that luxury. He liked not being questioned. That was important to him.

During the fall he spent his months preparing, getting ready, making sure this season would be his best ever. He spent weeks poring over maps, searching for a new hunting ground, one that best suited his tastes and the risks he was willing to take. He needed a new field to plow and sow, a new location to harvest his crop, preferring to only spend one season in the same place before moving on to the next the following year.

Less chance of getting caught or leaving a trail for others to follow.

Familiarity within a small town often led to sloppiness or recognition. Townsfolk would remember a face from last year. Maybe the make and model of a car or the numbers and letters of a license plate. These small details seemed to stick in people's minds in small towns. Perhaps because nothing much else happened that was worthy of note. The pace was slower, the texture of daily life more distinct compared to life in the city. But it was a risk he was willing to take if the hunting was good. It heightened the experience, the thrill. Everything was planned and calculated to cover every possible contingency, even fleeing the town quickly if needed.

It was a long trek back through the forest to where he had parked. The hood and roof of his car were covered with a light dusting of snow. He swung out the tailgate and threw his backpack and crossbow inside, covering everything with an old tarp.

He climbed in, started the engine and hit the gas. The tread of the wheels slipped then gripped solid ground, throwing up tufts of snow and frozen mud as he drove off.

Moments later, he turned off the woodland dirt road and back onto the main highway into town.

The car was a rental; they all were. A Jeep Wrangler fitted with big, meaty winter tires that made light work of the snow and icy slush. By the time he'd finished with the car and had left town, it would be driven far away by someone else to another town or city. Another layer of DNA and other trace evidence would be added to the concoction already inside. The laziness in cleaning a car properly between rentals was his good fortune. It made his vacation less worrisome.

Ten minutes later, a sign appeared on the side of the highway. "Welcome to Willow Falls, Iowa. Fields of Opportunities."

He smiled as he drove past.

Can't argue with that.

2

The gathering went as well as could be expected for the funeral of one's mother.

The mood was appropriately somber and sullen, with just the right amount of remorse in the offers of condolence for such a loss.

People ate when they weren't hungry. They needed something to occupy their hands and eyes, to hide the discomfort they felt when compressed together in a small room.

Nothing quite ruins one's appetite like the cold, harsh reality of death masked under the pretense of a celebration of life. Thoughts of the deceased were soon replaced by thoughts of oneself. Of wondering when their turn would be. Or who would come to pay their respects when it was them in the casket and not the recently departed. It was a known fact that a sudden spike in health checkups often followed in the footsteps of a good funeral.

Where were all these people when *my* mother lay alone in the care facility in Salt Lake City? Carolyn Ryder thought to herself as she stood in the small, cramped living room of her mother's house watching people she didn't know. Where were they as her mother lay wheezing and coughing in her bed? In those final moments when her lungs were slowly collapsing from the onslaught of respiratory failure?

She stood five feet nine inches tall, with a lean, athletic build, shoulder-length chestnut hair, and bright blue-gray eyes that missed nothing. The people around Carolyn reminded her of cattle in a pen. The vacant stares, the shuffling feet, the occasional glance in her direction, a nod here, a forced smile there.

She could forgive them for not recognizing her or knowing who she really was. She had not been home to Willow Falls—her hometown and the home of her mother—for ten years.

And those who had reluctantly approached her were unsure of what to do or what to say. They fidgeted, stared at the carpet or at the ceiling as they offered their heartfelt sympathy. These people were more familiar with Jodie Ryder, Carolyn's older sister who had never left Willow Falls. Jodie had stayed behind, got married, and then divorced just as quick. Thankfully, there were no kids involved, just the baggage of a failed marriage to a man who had run off with a piece of young skirt, who twiddled her hair behind the front counter of a local tire store.

Carolyn often wondered what would have happened if Jodie had had kids. While on the surface her sister appeared calm and in control, she tended to be more emotional when things got difficult or stressful.

She shouldn't be so judgmental, Carolyn reminded herself. She pushed off the wall she had been leaning against for physical and moral support for the last ten minutes and surveyed the room. She was stuck in a roomful of complete strangers, some of who eyed her like she was some kind of vagrant who had wandered in through the front door on the promise of food and drink and a warm place to shelter from the bone-cold and swirling snow outside.

In the kitchen she found Jodie keeping company with a spread of frozen food on metal baking trays. A hot oven behind her yawned wide, radiating heat into the cold house. She had a rumpled dish cloth over one shoulder and a matching scowl on her face.

Carolyn readied herself for what might follow. Since she had arrived a few days ago, she had barely seen her sister. The air between them seemed colder than outside.

Near midnight, while she was filling up her car in a freezing gas station forecourt somewhere in Nebraska, Carolyn's cell phone had rung. Carolyn was driving the nonstop trip, all eleven hundred miles from Salt Lake City. She knew her mother was close to passing. That's why she was making the mad dash across four states so she could be by her bedside and say goodbye. Jodie had called Carolyn a few days beforehand to forewarn her.

But she was too late. While at the gas station, Jodie had called to say their mother had just died.

Carolyn calmly finished filling her car. Replaced the hose. Went inside and sat alone in a cubicle in the restroom that smelled of urine, and cried.

Ten minutes later she emerged, got in her car, and kept driving east.

When Carolyn finally arrived in Willow Falls, she was greeted with the news that the funeral, the wake, the church, and the guest list had already been hastily organized by Jodie without even waiting for her younger sister to be consulted.

Jodie looked up from sliding appetizers onto a ceramic serving platter. "You shouldn't be in here. You should be outside talking to people, reacquainting yourself with them." Jodie always had a way of making Carolyn feel like she was an eight-year-old instead of a twenty-eight-year-old. Like she was constantly being scolded for doing the wrong thing. The same was whenever Carolyn asked her older sister a question. Jodie's typical response was as though it were either a stupid question or that she had already answered it before, neither of which was true. Carolyn put it down to jealousy and wanting to bring her younger sister down a peg or two, despite her occupation and title she held.

Carolyn took a deep breath. She could feel an argument brewing. This wasn't the time or the place, but it was all her sister's making if she wanted to finally vent herself in front of a houseful of guests on the day they had buried their mother. "Reacquaint with them? I don't know even know who these people are."

Jodie loaded up another baking tray with more frozen food to heat up, then slid it into the oven and slammed the oven door just a little too forcefully. "That's because you've never bothered to come back, to visit, to stay in contact with anyone at home."

Carolyn leaned her back against the counter, a kitchen island separating the two of them. This wasn't her home. She was born here, spent her childhood here, but she had lost all connection with the place. "That's because I live and worked in Salt Lake City," Carolyn replied. "Where mom was originally in the care facility I had placed her in so she could be closer to me. I saw her nearly every day when I could."

"Worked?" Jodie wiped her hands on the dishtowel and wound a loose strand of hair behind her ear.

Carolyn nodded. She hadn't told her sister yet. But now was as good a time as any other. "I resigned two weeks ago." Carolyn was planning to return to Willow Falls and stay awhile, spend more time with her mother. She just thought their mother had more time.

Jodie gave a smirk. "Little late for that now, isn't it?"

Carolyn stepped forward, her anger simmering, the sarcasm in her sister's voice clear and cutting. Through gritted teeth came Carolyn's next words. "I was there for her, until you decided to shift her back here."

Jodie folded her arms defiantly across her chest, her face all frowns, furrows, and harsh angles. "It was Mom's wishes. She wanted to come home, see out what little time she had here, to be buried with Dad. Don't act so surprised."

Jodie had moved back into her mother's house to tend to her.

Louise Ryder was expected to live for a few more months, but the illness had taken an unexpected turn and suddenly claimed her.

"I had every intention of coming back here sooner, to look after her, to help you." It was no use. Carolyn couldn't appease her older sister. Jodie had always seen herself as a Florence Nightingale. She relished playing the role, using their mother to garner leverage and sympathy from her friends and those in town who knew Louise Ryder and her ever-present daughter Jodie.

This wasn't going to be a pleasant homecoming for Carolyn. She had known it as soon as she'd turned onto I-80 and headed east. The prodigal daughter of the family was returning.

Carolyn believed that Jodie was instrumental in planting the seed in their mother's half-lucid mind to die at home and not in the care facility in Salt Lake City where she could have continued to receive the proper medical care and attention that she needed. Instead, in Carolyn's opinion, she had died an undignified, painful, and uncomfortable death in a bed in the house she had lived in all her adult life without doctors and nurses on hand to ease her through the end-of-life stage.

Jodie had to become the martyr, the one who went against Carolyn's wishes of leaving their terminally ill mother where she was, with Carolyn close by. Instead, Louise Ryder was dragged a thousand miles east and across four states from Utah to Iowa, back to Willow Falls, farther away from where Carolyn worked. Carolyn had been outvoted, "two to one." She had always been outvoted two to one for as long as Carolyn could remember.

It was Jodie who the townsfolk knew and loved, not her distant and seldom-seen sister.

"Look, I didn't come here to argue," Carolyn said. That was the truth.

After a while, no one spoke, just two sisters from two different worlds in a standoff in the kitchen.

"Which motel are you staying at?" Jodie finally asked.

"The Boulders Inn. Nothing special but it's comfortable and

close by." Despite the offer from Jodie to stay in her mother's house, Carolyn preferred to wait until after the funeral. She knew they would come to blows under the same roof otherwise. Then two sullen sisters would have sat in opposite pews inside the church under a cloud of whispers and curious stares.

Carolyn changed the subject. "When this is over, we need to go through the house, the estate."

"Does it have to be all formality with you, Carolyn?" Jodie said, throwing the dishcloth on the counter.

"Not right away, but sooner rather than later. I need to sort everything out with the house, her possessions."

Jodie shook her head and offered a sour smile. "That's right, sis, mom made you sole executor of her estate." It was a sore point that niggled at Jodie. "The big FBI agent is somehow more responsible and mature than her older sister," Jodie mocked.

Carolyn couldn't believe it either when Jodie had begrudgingly informed her when she had arrived. Apparently, the family lawyer had called Jodie when he couldn't get hold of Carolyn. Their mother had said nothing to either of them, had been keeping it a secret.

It was the only win Carolyn had over Jodie. A significant one nonetheless. "As you said, sis," Carolyn countered, "I'm just following her wishes." Carolyn made for the door then turned back. "I'm going back to the room full of strangers. They seem friendlier."

3

The next day, Carolyn decided to move into her mother's house after all. Despite their differences, Jodie thought it would be a good idea. She needed to go back to work, and Carolyn needed the time to go through their mother's things and take care of the formalities of the estate.

The only parts of town Carolyn had seen since arriving were the motel, the church where the service had been conducted, and her mother's house. She wanted to take a drive around and see how much Willow Falls had changed, but that would have to wait. So she checked out of the motel and drove to her mother's house again.

Pulling up at the curb, Carolyn paused for a moment to gather her thoughts.

Everything was blanketed with snow. Rooftops, gutters, parked cars. Trees lined each side of the street, dark limbs caked in white, arthritic fingers reaching for the sky. The street itself was a mush of deep ruts and tire tracks. People bundled up in thick winter clothing staggered around in their front yards shoveling snow from driveways and paths.

Carolyn looked up at her mother's house to the small gabled window high on the roofline, where her childhood bedroom was.

Last night, she had stayed back to help Jodie clean up after the last of the guests had gone. She had been tempted to go upstairs, climb the creaking treads of the old staircase to the top floor, and see her old bedroom. But she thought better of it.

Carolyn took a deep breath, her gut knotted and tight, then climbed out of the car. She pulled her small suitcase out of the trunk and made her way up the driveway and up onto the front porch. Jodie had given her a spare key last night and said to let herself in.

By her very nature, Carolyn was a loner, used to the solace of her own company where she rarely felt lonely at all. While others needed people constantly around them, or a pet nestled at their feet. She didn't.

Carolyn had disciplined herself over the years to be self-sufficient, to not need the company of others, to be independent. She had made up her mind a long time ago that she didn't need anyone else. She trusted her own instincts and her own judgment. Any action that she took was the result of her own conclusions, not blindly following what others told her.

There was only one other person, however, she did trust. But he was somewhere else, on a road or on a bus traveling the vast expanse of the country. She could rely on Ben, but he wasn't here.

She almost wished he was.

As Carolyn stood staring at the front door she had never felt so hollow and empty in all her life. Impulsively, she straightened the crooked and tattered Christmas wreath that hung there. Cheap "Made-in-China" plastic, Carolyn thought.

She pulled the wreath from the door, went back down the porch steps, around to the side of the house, found the trash bin, opened the lid, and threw the wreath inside. With Christmas just a week away, she would find something better.

She went back up the porch stairs and pulled out her key.

It was a small start, but a start anyway.

It was time to purge.

She unlocked the front door, stepped over the threshold and faded into her past.

WHAT WAS it with people as they got older? They seemed to become hoarders of all things domestic.

Carolyn stood in her mother's kitchen looking at the dusty collection of cardboard boxes lined neatly on top of the kitchen cabinets. There were coffeemakers, toasters, waffle machines, all unused and still in their original faded boxes, covered with dust and images of domesticated women, massive hair, and big-patterned dresses from the 1970s.

Everything she saw, touched, felt, and smelled was permanently tethered to the late memory of her mother. No legal document could ever transfer those deep-seated emotions or cut those ties. She'd become the caretaker of a dead person's life and all the possessions they had left behind.

As she stood there, she couldn't help but think about her own mortality. Who would be there for her? Would she have any regrets? Who would pack up her life's possessions and sell them or throw them in the trash?

Even though she was dead and buried, Carolyn would always think of this as her mother's kitchen, her mother's house, her mother's ten spray bottles of all-purpose cleaner that Carolyn had found scattered throughout the house. It was as though the older you got, the more worried you became about running out of everyday household essentials. Carolyn found cupboards piled high with rolls of toilet paper. Drawers packed tight with tubes of toothpaste and bars of soap and a myriad of bottles of cleaning chemicals crammed in under countertops and under sinks.

Moving upstairs to the second floor, Carolyn found that Jodie had moved into the guest bedroom. Maybe she needed to exorcise the ghosts of the past from her own bedroom.

There were three bedrooms on this level: her mother's, the guest bedroom, and Jodie's old bedroom.

On the third floor there wasn't much space except for a linen cupboard and Carolyn's bedroom.

She felt a mix of trepidation and guilt as she climbed the final flight of stairs that took her to her bedroom door.

Inside, she found everything exactly how she remembered, and Carolyn felt herself transported back to her early childhood and teenage years before she had left for college. Even at that young age, she had displayed a need for order, a sense of control. It gave her comfort, certainty. Everything would be fine, OK, if her room, her small desk, her drawers and dresser were neat and tidy, unlike her sister, Jodie, whose bedroom reflected her life: chaos, mess, and mayhem.

Looking around, Carolyn noticed that someone had kept the room exactly how it was: her mother, no doubt, a shrine to her youngest. Maybe hoping one day her daughter would return to the small, stifling town she had so willingly fled when she was eighteen years old.

The town seemed so innocent now, so quaint and picturesque. But back then, Carolyn likened it to quicksand. As a young woman, she had felt its grasp. And once it took hold, you couldn't move, couldn't leave, would soon join the others you knew who were already drowning below the surface. Each year she had spent here, she felt herself sink a little lower, felt the town inch up a little higher, felt her mind succumb a little further.

She walked over to the small window and pulled up the blind. She could see her car on the street below, her footsteps in the snow. She made a mental note to shovel the path to the porch.

It was then she noticed someone else's footsteps, a muddle of dark indentations, following hers right up the path and to the front porch.

4

I t was a part of the forest Mitch Bowman had never explored. This was only the third time he'd taken out his new Polaris snowmobile.

The overly cautious salesman at the dealership warned him to break in the engine first, to go easy and not to over-rev it.

And he had.

On the two previous rides, he had treated it with kid gloves. Taking it slow, getting used to the steering, the weight of the machine and the powerful engine. But now Mitch wanted to see what the five-thousand-dollar machine was capable of. He was itching to shred the forest hillside even if he was a little inexperienced.

How hard could it be?

And he'd seen enough YouTube videos to know what to do, and those FailArmy videos were just idiots trying to jump across frozen creeks or tackle steep hillsides.

Much to his wife's scorn, Mitch had bought the snowmobile with his Christmas bonus as a treat to himself. And why not? He busted his chops last quarter, hit his sales target, and earned the bonus through nothing but hard work, dedication, and relentless focus. That and listening continuously to his collection of Tony Robbins CDs in his car every day while on the road selling medical supplies for a company in Des Moines. After all, Tony had said you should reward yourself whenever you reach certain milestones in your life plan. So what better way to reward yourself than buying a brand new, two-hundred horsepower Snow Raptor.

The hard work had certainly paid off, Mitch thought as he coasted the snowmobile along, the powerful engine purring under him, ready to be unleashed.

Christ, the vibration of the engine was almost giving him a hard-on, better than his wife, Sandra, ever could.

He pulled up alongside the base of a snow-covered ridge and sat for a moment, contemplating which trail to take through the snow. There had been a fresh fall late last night, and Mitch was keen to be the first up here to take advantage before the rest of the snowmobile fanatics got out of bed and ruined it for everyone else.

To hell with what the salesman had said. He was probably just some stooge who'd never owned a snowmobile like this one.

Mitch opened the throttle slightly. The machine responded instantly. The track bit deep into the snow, throwing up a flurry of white behind him as he took off around the base of the ridge.

Moments later, the ridge fell away, and a stretch of pure white virgin snow opened up before him. He felt a twinge of apprehension, then the adrenaline kicked in, and he opened the throttle a little more. The snowmobile growled and responded, increasing speed, tearing through the layer of white effortlessly like a sprinting snow leopard.

What had Tony said? You need to get out of your comfort zone, take risks if you were going to take your life to the next level. That's exactly what Mitch wanted, to take his life to the next level. Sure he was never going to be seen on the X Games or be featured in the next Red Bull TV commercial. But he was going to tear up some of this snow and have some fun while the weather was clear. That was for damn sure.

Up ahead, maybe half a mile or less, Mitch could see the start of the forest, a spread of tall white pines caked and glistening. He knew there was a large flat plain on the other side that would be perfect for testing the snowmobile to the max.

He could go around, and not through, the forest, but that would take extra time. He was in the mood for exploring as well and what better way to practice his maneuvering skills and throttle control than to thread his way through the pine trees in the forest.

With his mind made up, he angled the snowmobile toward the forest, his scarf drawn tight across his face, hiding the wide grin he had.

This was a day he was going to remember for a long time. Something he would tell his friends and family about on Christmas Day.

But for all the wrong reasons.

ENTERING THE FOREST, Mitch was cautious. He took it slow. After all, he didn't want to wrap himself around a tree.

Pine trees spread out in all directions, and he easily maneuvered the snowmobile, leaning into each twist and turn, weaving a path through the trees and rocks. Quickly his confidence grew, and he soon became bored with the slow pace. His ego demanded he go faster. So he opened the throttle a little more.

The snowmobile whined and growled louder. The big track bit harder into the snow as the machine sped up, his turns coming on faster.

Mitch yelled with glee. It was like a drug. The speed. The noise. The power at the tip of your thumb. It made him feel strong, in control, a man.

The trees thinned, and Mitch powered on, throwing caution to the wind that whipped past his face, cold but invigorating.

Adrenaline flooded his bloodstream, and Mitch's ego began to invade his thoughts. He saw himself getting Salesman of the Year. Then getting a personal invite to a one-on-one coaching session with Tony Robins in Fiji. Spending some time with Tony in his Jacuzzi sipping cocktails and comparing teeth whitener. Serving divorce papers to his wife. Partying on a luxury yacht in the Bahamas, surrounded by an entourage of bikini-clad women. A supermodel for a wife. Another as a mistress. There was no limit to the possibilities Mitch saw spreading in front of him as he roared through the white wilderness.

Then something ahead came into view. Harsh reds and dark crimsons stood out against the backdrop of white-and-black verticals.

At first, Mitch thought it was a small deer, nailed to one of the trees, with its throat cut and its belly sliced open, glistening red entrails hanging out. Maybe some kids getting their kicks, playing some sadistic game with a young buck they had managed to bring down.

Then as he drew closer, he felt like he'd just been punched hard in the gut. He released the throttle, fumbled for the brake, almost colliding with a tree trunk.

The snowmobile swerved then skidded to a halt in a spray of icy churn. Mitch only just managed to rip his scarf away from his mouth before bending over to the side and puking up his breakfast in the snow.

"Jesus..." he whispered as he wiped his mouth. He lifted his ski mask and set it on the top of his helmet.

He wanted to look away but he couldn't. He was in a trance, a mix of macabre fascination and complete revulsion at what was skewered to a large tree trunk.

It wasn't a deer.

It wasn't a bear.

It was something much worse.

5

Carolyn thought twice about opening the front door.

How did he know she was here? He hadn't shown his face at all since she'd been back.

No doubt Jodie would have texted him where she was now staying.

Let's just get this over and done with, Carolyn thought as she opened the door.

On the porch stood a slightly sheepish Tyler Finch, dressed in his Willow Falls police uniform. Finch was the same age as Carolyn and slightly taller. He had smooth, short black hair, dark eyes, and an angular face. He'd put on a few more pounds since she'd last seen him. But that was ten years ago. Everyone changes.

"Hello, Carolyn," Finch said, unsure of what he was going to say after all these years.

Carolyn took a deep breath, her body tense and coiled. "I was wondering when you would come looking for me. News must travel fast around here."

"You just upped and left town," Finch retorted. "You didn't say a thing, told nobody."

"Sorry to hurt your feelings," said Carolyn, her tone cutting and acidic. "You slept with my sister, for Christ's sake!"

Finch's eyes went wide.

Carolyn nodded, seeing his expression suddenly change. "That's right, you prick. Didn't you think I would find out? The very next argument we had, Jodie threw that little tidbit of information in my face."

Looking at the floor, Finch took a deep breath and let it out slowly. This wasn't the reception he was expecting.

Jodie had vowed to him never to tell her sister about what had happened. It was their secret. It was just a one-off Jodie had later explained to Carolyn. Jodie was drunk, and Carolyn had knocked back Finch a few days prior because she was having her period. That's what he had complained to Jodie about. Christ, they had had sex plenty of times before. Couldn't he just go without for one week?

"It was a weak moment. I was at a low point," Finch said, still staring at the floor, wishing he could just squeeze through the cracks of the wooden planks and disappear under the front porch, dig himself a hole. He looked up. "I'm sorry, really."

Carolyn regarded him skeptically. The apology sounded heart-felt, but in the two years they had gone out together in high school, she'd come to know that Tyler Finch could be very smooth and very charming when he wanted to be. When he wanted something, that is. And that little "something" almost ten years ago had been to get into Carolyn Ryder's gym shorts at every opportunity he could.

"Please don't hold a grudge." Finch offered his hand. "It's been ten years, Carolyn. Water under the bridge."

Carolyn looked at Finch's extended hand. She never held grudges. Only against criminals. "Sometimes it takes a long time for that water to reach the bridge before it can pass under," she offered, enjoying the rare moment of weakness from him. Tyler Finch never apologized for anything. Carolyn stepped forward, batted away his hand. "Come here," she said, grabbing him in a hug. "It's ancient history." She hugged him tight. "It's good to see you." Carolyn meant it, thinking that Finch was perhaps the only friend right now she had in town even if he had cheated on her with Jodie.

They moved inside and into the kitchen. Finch perched himself on a stool at the counter while Carolyn busied herself refilling the coffeemaker.

"I just came by to say I'm sorry about your mother. I heard you had moved back in here to sort things out."

Carolyn scooped coffee into the filter, filled the water reservoir, and switched the machine on. "The service was yesterday. It was nice." Carolyn really wanted to say that she had felt awkward standing in a roomful of strangers, all of them looking, judging, whispering.

"I was on duty; otherwise, I would have been here. By the time I came off shift, it was too late to come by anyway. I didn't want to intrude."

More like you were trying to avoid running into me. "Thanks," she replied instead. "It was a difficult day yesterday. I needed some space and was surrounded by people I didn't even know."

Finch just smiled and nodded.

Carolyn sat down on the stool next to Finch, the coffeemaker doing its thing in the background. "I'm really proud of what you've done, Tyler, honestly," she said, nodding at the uniform.

Finch looked down at his uniform. "I joined the police pretty much straight out of high school."

"I know," Carolyn replied.

Finch gave a wry smile. "So you've been keeping tabs on me?"

"No, not really. It's called Facebook," Carolyn replied, slightly amused.

Finch gave a hopeful look. "I just use it to keep in touch with everyone, guys and girls from high school, workmates, family, and the like. Send me a friend request."

"No way!" Carolyn replied. "I hardly use it personally, mostly for work. You'd be surprised what people post on their page that gives them away."

"But look at you!" Finch exclaimed. "FBI Special Agent and everything."

"I left the bureau a few weeks back," Carolyn explained. "I wanted to come home and look after Mom, give Jodie a hand. I thought I had more time, but I was too late."

"I know. It was sudden, I heard."

It was obvious to Carolyn that Finch and her sister were still on speaking terms, had remained so after all these years. It was a small town so Carolyn expected it. She just had to be careful what she told him; otherwise, it might find its way back to Jodie.

The coffeemaker gave a final splutter, and Carolyn poured two cups and brought them back to the counter.

"So tell me what's happened around here since I left," Carolyn said, handing Finch a cup of steaming fresh coffee.

Finch smirked over the brim of the cup. "I'm still here. My folks are still here. My brother, Seth, is still here, works at a local garage. He became a mechanic. What's there to tell? A few more large chain stores moved in, and a few of the older stores closed down. But the town and the people are still the same."

Carolyn had expected as much. She had come home to bury her mother and then spend some time by herself, to think, to ponder what she was going to do next. She wasn't thinking of adding to the permanent population of Willow Falls anytime soon.

"So how long are you going to be in town?" Finch asked.

Carolyn was noncommittal. "As long as it takes." She waved her hand around. The house was silent except for a wall clock ticking in the hallway. "There's a lot to sort out and Jodie had to go back to work. She's done a lot in my absence and I'm truly grateful for that."

Finch said nothing, just quietly drank his coffee.

Truth be told, Carolyn really didn't know how long she was going to stay. She couldn't see past today, was happy to just take it one day at a time.

"What about the police department?" Carolyn asked. "How many of you are there?"

"It's small, just three of us. Why?"

Carolyn shrugged. "Just curious."

"Thinking of joining up?" Finch gave a lopsided grin.

Carolyn looked at him. He had still retained his boyish good looks. The police uniform just enhanced it a little more, gave him an air of authority that she knew he would have enjoyed.

But he did nothing for her. He had once, but that was then and this was now. "Not a chance," she replied. "I've done my time. I need a break.

"I thought you were all career?" Finch said. "You know, wanting to go as far as you could."

Carolyn rolled her eyes. "I can imagine where you heard that from." It was something Jodie would often say to Carolyn, that she was too busy lately with work, to see their mother, to come back home to visit, that Carolyn was a cold, career woman who wanted to rise as fast and go as far as she could. "I loved my job, Tyler; don't get me wrong. It's not a crime if you're good at it and others recognized that fact as well."

"So why did you quit, then?"

"I didn't 'quit' as you put it." Carolyn didn't like the term, sounded too much like "gave up." "Like I said, I wanted to come home and be with my mom. I was just too late." Carolyn got up and poured herself another cup. "So how's your job? I'm curious to see what you get up to in a place like this."

"I like it. I like being here, the town, the people. It's a great community. But nothing really much happens. Just the usual traffic violations, maybe a DUI or the odd domestic. Haven't had a homicide for about eight years now."

In Carolyn's mind, Finch was always a hometown boy. He would never leave Willow Falls. "I didn't exactly get a warm reception yesterday," she said.

"They'll come around, Carolyn. Just give them time. No one

knows who you really are except that you're Louise's daughter who left town ten years ago for the big city and bright lights. They're used to seeing Jodie's face around town, not yours."

"Well, I'm certainly not going to run and hide," Carolyn replied. "I'll take a drive through town later and take a proper look. See what's changed."

"Like I said, not much has." Finch finished his coffee and placed the cup on the counter. "Nothing much really happens here in Willow Falls. And that's how we like it."

Just then Finch's two-way radio crackled to life. Unclipping it from his belt, he stood up, smiled apologetically, and walked out into the hallway.

Carolyn looked around the kitchen, not really in the mood to rifle through cupboards and boxes of her mom's stuff. Maybe she'd head into town and take a quick tour.

Finch came back a few moments later, a frown on his face.

"What's up?" Carolyn asked.

"Nothing. Just a call that came in. Probably a false alarm or something." Finch looked around like he was unsure of what to do next. "Look, I need to go," he said hastily. "Maybe we can catch up later or something."

"No problem."

Carolyn let him out the front door, and as she watched him go, she couldn't help but think that the water had well and truly passed under the bridge many years ago on that day she'd left Willow Falls and had never looked back. And she certainly wasn't going to reverse the flow of the river any time soon either.

6

Structure and order were what was required.

Carolyn felt she needed the focus, create a routine for the days she was going to spend in Willow Falls.

First she took a large trash bag from under the sink and promptly emptied out the fridge. Her mother hoarded jars of food, opened one, used a little, then promptly forgot about it until the expiration was long past. God knows what Jodie had been doing here all this time.

There were a few frozen dinners in the chest freezer in the laundry room, which Carolyn left, thinking they belonged to Jodie who hadn't stocked up in the way of fresh produce. Obviously, their mother wasn't eating much in the final days of her life.

Next Carolyn went up to her bedroom. She paused at the door, building up the courage to do what her mom couldn't, something long overdue.

She pushed the door, and with trash bag in hand, quickly, efficiently, and ruthlessly set about tearing down her past. Nothing was spared. The drawers were pulled out and tipped onto the floor. So were the contents of the small closet. With one sweep of her arm,

Carolyn cleared the entire surface of the dresser into the trash bag, the makeup old and out of date.

She stripped the sheets, balled them up, and added them to the growing pile in the middle of the floor. She ignored the temptation to pause and reminisce over a much-loved jacket or well-worn pair of jeans, content with the knowledge that most of her teenage garments would probably still fit her today. Anything worthwhile she had taken with her ten years ago.

The past needed to be purged, bagged, then tossed.

In the linen cupboard in the hallway, she found a clean set of sheets that were more appropriate and promptly remade the bed and then went downstairs to grab some coffee.

She wasn't ready to enter her mother's room, so she left that area of the house undisturbed.

Coming back up the stairs, with coffee cup in hand, she noticed that the door of Jodie's room, the guest bedroom, was slightly ajar so she firmly closed it, not at all interested in taking a look inside. It was someone else's life that had already encroached on hers, thanks to Tyler Finch. Things like that were best left alone. Carolyn had moved on from that incident. Her old bedroom and the rest of the house had to as well.

Spurred on by her new-found determination to rid herself of the past, she put down the cup and began decluttering the rest of her bedroom, throwing out anything that was old or remotely tied to her teenage years. She swapped around the chest of drawers with the small desk, placing her desk beneath the window so that it looked out onto the front yard and street below.

Taking a bucket of hot soapy water she scrubbed blue tack marks off the walls–from old Katy Perry and Taylor Swift posters, no doubt—and wiped grubby fingerprints off the walls. She got down on her hands and knees, wiped clean the dusty wall trims, windowsill, and cleaned the surfaces of the furniture she wanted to keep.

Finally, she slid up the lower sash of the window, pushing it up as far as it would go.

Cold, bracing air wafted in, and Carolyn stood for a moment and just breathed. It was the final detox of the room, symbolic as it was rejuvenating. Out with the old and musty. In with the new and the fresh.

By the time she was finished she had four full trash bags that she tied off and carried downstairs and out to the large polyethylene trash cans that sat along the side of the house.

In the garage she found an assortment of tools and garden implements. She took a snow shovel and a tub of ice-and-snow melt then spent the next twenty minutes clearing then treating the driveway and the path from the porch steps all the way back to the street.

The last thing she wanted was for her or anyone else to slip and land on their ass. She left the shovel and the tub next to the bottom step of the porch as a reminder to repeat the chore each morning.

By late morning she was happy at the progress she had made. There was still a lot more to do.

She went into the kitchen and after thirty minutes of sorting through the cupboards and filling three packing boxes, she'd had had enough for the morning. She decided that she would take a break and take a look around the town. The huge task of wading through the contents of the rest of the house could wait.

She stripped off her dirty clothes, took a hot shower, dressed in fashionable but functional clothing she'd brought with her, including a knitted cap and scarf, and a pair of stylish snow boots.

She regarded herself in the mirror and thought she was a bit overdressed for Willow Falls but didn't really care. She didn't want to blend in anymore, to go unnoticed.

The time for that was over.

The house had no alarm system, so she doubled-checked that all the doors and windows were locked and secure before she went out to her car on the street. She preferred leaving the garage empty for storing boxes and other items until she and Jodie had decided on what they were going to split between them before discarding the rest.

Out of habit, Carolyn did one final lap of the perimeter of the property. Satisfied that everything was locked, she climbed into her car and headed into town.

THE CALL HAD COME in garbled. A rapid burst of blubbering words and broken sentences that seemed to echo from far away.

The caller hadn't identified themself, making the task of verifying it, whether it was genuine or just a crank call, almost impossible.

Then the words, "body" and "woman" and "so much blood" came through, and the dispatcher suddenly sat up a little straighter, pulled her headset a little closer, strained her face a little tighter, and began punching her keyboard as fast as she could.

It had taken Tyler Finch the best part of twenty minutes to drive to the location after leaving Carolyn's place. It was ten miles out of town, up in the foothills. The dispatcher had given him directions as best as she could interpret from the caller who had abruptly ended the call.

Finch followed a dirt road that was nothing more than a ribbon of frozen, rutted, mud speckled with stones. He followed it through cold desolate fields before turning east then along the edge of a spread of pine trees that led up to the foothills. It was a common drop-off point for snowboarders and snowmobile enthusiasts.

Finch saw the shape of a large boxy pickup truck ahead and slowed. There was no one else around. The pickup had a trailer attached to the rear, ramps deployed. He called in the license plates and the identity of the driver came back moments later. Mitch Bowman. Forty-three. Male. Married. Current resident of Willow Falls. No priors, just two speeding tickets and a parking violation.

Finch climbed out of his SUV and pulled his jacket collar up. His feet sank immediately in the soft snow. "Great," he muttered. The pickup truck was empty and locked.

Cutting a furrow through the snow, Finch recognized the familiar churn of a snowmobile track. The track snaked away up the slope before fading into the distance, a tall dark wall of forest beyond.

There was no way Finch's police SUV would be able to go any farther. He would have to go back to the police station, hook up the trailer, and bring the police snowmobile back with him.

Finch silently cursed. Then came the growl of an approaching motor.

A shape appeared out of the tree line up ahead, fast and low, cutting a sway through the snow. A snowmobile was hurtling down the hillside toward Finch. It wobbled and pitched, like the driver was either insane or drunk or both, Finch thought as he watched.

Finch waved his hands frantically above his head, signaling the rider to slow down.

But the snowmobile kept on coming fast, making a direct line to where Finch was standing. Suddenly it pitched violently sideways, the rider only just managing to recover and not topple over.

The snowmobile came to a violent halt, thirty yards away, burying the front skis in the snow and nearly throwing the rider off.

Mitch Bowman tumbled off the machine, stumbled, staggered, fell, then gathered himself, and stumbled some more straight toward Finch, almost colliding into him at the last moment.

"Whoa, slow down," Finch said.

Bowman wriggled in Finch's grip like a slimy fish he'd just caught. His face was wild with panic, wide-eyed and fearful. His head swiveled left and right, looking over his shoulder back up the hillside from where he had just come as though Satan was chasing him.

"Girl...dead...up in the forest..." Bowman spluttered.

Finch held on to him firmly. Bowman smelled of vomit and

sweat. The usually calm and confident salesman was reduced to a blubbering mess.

"Where?" Finch demanded.

Bowman shivered but didn't answer.

Finch shook him hard. "Where is she?" he yelled. Maybe she wasn't dead. Maybe she could be saved. But he needed to act now.

Bowman squirmed and kicked, trying to break free.

"Knock it off!" Finch yelled, getting annoyed. "Or I'll cuff you."

Bowman mumbled something that made no sense.

Finch pulled him back toward his police SUV, pushed him into the rear seat and glared at him. "Stay here and don't move," he ordered.

Glancing over, Finch saw Bowman's snowmobile. It sat idling. He would take it and follow the trail back up to where Bowman had been.

As a precaution, Finch took Bowman's car keys from him. The man was in no condition to drive. Finch locked the doors of his SUV, trapping Bowman inside like a prisoner before trudging back up to where the snowmobile sat.

Finch climbed onto the saddle, revved the engine, then performed a tight turn and roared off back up the hillside, running in the same furrow Bowman had made in the snow on the way down.

Mitch Bowman sat huddled and shivering in the back of the police SUV, staring through the side window, watching Finch ride off. He mumbled something under his breath, the glass fogging with each word he said, thinking that Finch could still hear his warning.

"A man... up there...in the forest...watching...his eyes...saw me."

7

The town, the stores, the streets hadn't changed.

There were some new additions like a Dollar Store, a small CVS, and a massive Walmart superstore that Carolyn had passed on the way in from Salt Lake City. But apart from that, Willow Falls seemed caught in its own time warp.

Carolyn slowed her speed as she drove down the main street of town, tires crunching as she navigated through ruts of snow and ice.

The sky was clear and blue, everything in sharp focus. A few large pickup trucks hugged the curbs, big meaty tires, jacked-up suspension, light bars, decked out for the hunting season, she guessed.

Olsen's Coffee & Bakery loomed on the right, a favorite haunt of hers back in the day. It was an institution in Willow Falls. She'd spent countless hours there drinking coffee and planning her escape from the town. Now, years later, she was returning, like an escapee taking a tour of Alcatraz. It seemed surreal. Somehow the older parts of the town appeared a little smaller, a little more faded, a little less appealing. The bakery looked as though it had been given a face-lift though. Gone was the old yellow façade, replaced now with a rendered brick exterior, brown and beige, contemporary stone edging, new dark green awnings, and huge bay windows.

Carolyn pulled into the parking lot and headed for the front door.

Inside it was warm, cozy, and filled with the wonderful smells of freshly baked bread, cookies, bagels, and ground coffee.

The faces behind the counter were new, young, all smiles, but the atmosphere was the same old place that Carolyn remembered, a place where she had felt safe, grounded, and at home whenever she was here. The inside had been completely refurbished as well. Dark brown wood veneer, rustic brickwork, wooden floors, and chalkboard menus now hung from the ceiling. A long glass display cabinet dominated the front counter and was filled with a billion calories neatly stacked in white plastic trays. Cookies, brownies, muffins, bagels, and pastries, with cardboard labels in neat hand-written script.

Carolyn ordered a large coffee and couldn't resist the massive cheesecake brownie that promised to deliver nearly all her daily allowance of sugar in one indulgent hit. What the hell, she thought. It had been a rough twenty-four hours and she needed comforting.

She sat down at a long wooden bench with metal high stools. A flat-screen TV on the wall was tuned to the local news channel. An unnatural-looking middle-aged woman stood in front of the weather map promising a clear wintry day with the possibility of snowfall at night. The woman's face should come with a "wrinkle-free" label like a dress shirt, Carolyn thought begrudgingly as she watched.

From where she sat, Carolyn had a clear view of the parking lot and the street beyond. The traffic was light, and she noticed a few men, hunters mainly, dressed in heavy jackets of earthy tones, with mossy camouflaged ball caps on their heads, walking the streets.

The front door opened and Carolyn turned to see a man enter. He glanced in her direction and smiled, a warm, confident smile.

Unable to help herself, she took a mental snapshot. Old habits and all that. All she needed was a split second and she was done.

She turned away and stared at the TV screen again, processing the details of the man in her head. Maybe a tad over six feet tall, short dark wavy hair, dark eyes, just the right amount of stubble across his jaw, older than her, maybe mid-forties, rugged, vintage-looking, a man who took care of himself without being obsessive or vain. Despite his obvious good looks, he still retained some rough and frayed edges, which Carolyn found appealing. He wore functional but stylish clothing, muted woodland colors, quality without being excessive, base layers, well chosen and matching. Definitely not a hunter. He reminded Carolyn of an older version of someone she knew, someone she held dear to her heart. How he would look perhaps twenty years from now. It was that likeness that made Carolyn take note of the stranger as he walked past her.

The man ordered at the counter then walked and stood watching the weather forecast on the TV screen, his back to Carolyn, and just a few feet away from her.

Under the layers of clothing he appeared lean, strong looking, with good posture.

"Looks like we'll get some more snow tonight," he said to no one in particular.

Carolyn looked around, wondering if he was talking to her.

There was an older couple at a far corner table and two teenagers nearby, glued to their cell phones, thumbs scrolling furiously, blank expressions on their faces.

The man turned and looked straight at Carolyn.

She suddenly felt her face prickle and flush, and it wasn't because of the heating system in the store. "Apparently, that's what the woman with the botox face reckons," she replied, referring to the animated weather woman who was strutting across the TV screen, fake smile and exaggerated hand gestures, hoping some major network executive would save her from her tedious, mundane life on the local channel news and catapult her into prime time stardom.

The man laughed, deep and gravelly.

Carolyn found his laugh and warm smile extremely attractive.

He smiled again, unwound his scarf, and placed it on the bench where Carolyn sat. "Do you mind?"

A bit presumptuous, Carolyn thought. She really didn't need or want any company. She was just happy to sit, drink her coffee, and plan out what else she needed to do today.

The man pulled out a stool and raised a questioning eyebrow.

Direct and assertive, qualities that Carolyn liked. "Sure," she relented. She could do with a friendly face in the town, an ally.

Carolyn's coffee arrived, and much to her sudden embarrassment, so did the huge brownie she ordered. It was the size of a roof tile with a side of whipped cream.

Great, she thought.

"What are you celebrating?" the man said as he sat down opposite her, looking at the brownie. It was a good-natured comment.

Carolyn felt truly embarrassed now, which was unusual because she didn't really care what people thought about her. "Nothing really, I just missed breakfast." It was a lame excuse and she knew it.

The man's coffee arrived and he extended his hand. "I'm Michael, Michael Ritter."

Carolyn took his hand.

Another click of her mental camera.

His hand was cool, rough in parts, smooth in others. Firm grip, hands that didn't tap a mouse or punch a keyboard all day long. "Carolyn," she replied. Not eating the brownie would have been awkward. So Carolyn attacked it with her fork.

"Are you from around here?" Ritter asked. "I'm not, got into town a few days ago."

"I used to live here, a long time ago." Good, someone who doesn't know me around town. "My sister and mother live here."

Carolyn didn't want to explain the whole situation, so she used the present tense when referring to her mother. After all, he was a complete stranger, and she despised people who, after you just met them, insisted on telling you their whole life story, including the gallbladder they just had removed.

"So you're sort of a local and an outsider at the same time," Ritter said.

Carolyn nodded, her mouth full of cheesecake brownie. More embarrassment. Why is it that people always wait until you have your mouth full before they ask you something?

Ritter nodded toward the window. "It's a nice town. I like it, very pretty. Nice people, too."

Carolyn didn't see it like that. There were still plenty of old faces around town who knew who she was, and her mother, Louise, and sister, Jodie. She was probably branded the "other daughter," the one who had left, who hadn't helped her dying mother. Rumors spread thanks to Jodie who, no doubt, vented her discontent about her younger sister with the townsfolk at every opportunity she got. There would have been no mention of the fact that Carolyn was looking after her mother in Utah, all those previous months, visiting her almost every day.

"So what brings you back?" Ritter asked.

"Just family, Christmas, that time of year." Carolyn was noncommittal; it was just her nature, not overtly friendly. She was more used to questioning people, extracting information from them, not the other way around. She needed to be less harsh though. She wasn't at work anymore.

The man seated in front of her had a certain warmth to him, a genuineness in his eyes she could see. He was a stranger, but somehow she felt instantly comfortable, not threatened by him.

"Are you a doctor?" Carolyn just came out with it. It was his demeanor. Someone in control, confident, trustworthy.

"A surgeon."

"A surgeon?" Carolyn replied. "I'm impressed."

Ritter shook his head. "It's nothing, really. I usually don't start a new conversation with an attractive young woman by telling her that I'm a surgeon. She may think I'm trying to impress her and all that. It's no big deal."

Now the man definitely intrigued her. He was accomplished, attractive, self-assured without the ego and arrogance that typically went with someone like him. "So what brings you to the exciting town of Willow Falls?"

Ritter picked up the not-so-subtle hint of sarcasm in Carolyn's question. "Vacation, time away from work. Peace and quiet, I guess."

"Where do you work?" Carolyn continued as she ate, trying her best not to sound like she was interrogating a suspect. She wanted to know more about him and she wasn't afraid to ask.

"Chicago," Ritter replied. "Northwestern Memorial. Cardiothoracic surgery. Heart and lungs."

"I know what 'cardiothoracic' means," Carolyn replied. "So why here? Of all the places to go for a winter vacation, you picked this place?"

Ritter laughed. Small crease lines appeared around the corners of his eyes that only heightened his appeal. "Have I disappointed you? Should someone like me be skiing in Aspen or Jackson Hole?"

Carolyn felt her cheeks get hotter, a biological response that defied her usually cool and controlled persona. "Isn't that what all doctors and surgeons do this time of year?" she replied, trying to make light of the fact that he could probably tell she was blushing. "You know, drive their big gas-guzzling European SUVs to the ski resorts. Drink champagne, get in the hot tub together and compare suture patterns."

Ritter sat forward, his voice almost a whisper. "We mainly use skin glues and adhesive strips these days. Incision and wound closure techniques have come a long way." He paused to drink his coffee. "So what do you do?"

The question took her by surprise. No one yet had asked Carolyn since she had resigned from the FBI. She didn't really know how to answer it. While she was working for the FBI she'd say it without being asked. But that usually also involved pulling out her ID and thrusting it in front of someone's face with one hand resting on the grip of her sidearm.

In a social situation she was unsure what to say. Most of her friends were her work colleagues as well. Some people were put off when she told them what she did. Maybe they were worried that she would come knocking on their door and demand to search their home. She wasn't sure. It just seemed like such a foolish thing to feel awkward about. So she decided the direct approach was best. "I used to work for the FBI," she replied. "But I resigned a few weeks back." Carolyn carefully watched Ritter's reaction. To her surprise he didn't seem to react at all nor bombard her with stupid questions or run out the door either.

"Neat," was all he said. Like it was no big deal. "So what do you do around here for fun?" Ritter asked.

Carolyn shrugged. "The place hasn't really changed that much. There are a lot of hunters in town this time of year. Mainly for whitetail deer. I guess if you don't hunt then there's not much else to do." Carolyn wanted to ask, but the answer seemed obvious. She couldn't imagine he hunted, not based on what he was wearing anyway.

It must have been the way she looked at him that made Ritter answer an unasked question. "No. I don't hunt. I'm into saving lives not taking them even if they are just animals."

The more he spoke, the more Carolyn felt comfortable with him, and she hadn't felt comfortable about any man in a long, long time.

The next one would be different. There would be no public display. He would bury the next one deep in the snow, deep enough so the animals couldn't forage and dig to find her. Yet shallow enough so that when the snow and ice melted away in the spring, there was the slightest chance they would find her.

Maybe not this spring, and maybe not the next.

But eventually.

What was the point of taking the time, making the effort, and refining your skills if others weren't granted the privilege of seeing the results of all your hard work?

The young girl he had left in the forest was a Mona Lisa. A piece of art to be rightfully on display, to be a centerpiece, an exhibit for all eyes to gaze upon in silent horror.

In 2014 a homeowner in Toulouse, France had entered their attic to fix a leaking roof, only to discover an original and extremely valuable painting by the Italian artist Caravaggio. It was a rather grotesque painting entitled, _Judith Beheading Holofernes._

The next woman he intended to take would be just like one of those masterpieces that lay hidden, buried away for years in some dusty, damp basement, or leaking attic only to be stumbled upon then brought into the full light of day.

His next victim would be his Caravaggio.

She would rest in silent slumber below the snow and ice, never to see daylight.

Parents and loved ones would be left wondering, left to endure years of maddening torture of not knowing whatever happened to their wife, their daughter, their sister.

In the meantime, he had to decide who would be the subject of his next masterpiece. There were so many to choose from.

It wasn't like he had any compulsion against women. He just preferred them to men. Naturally, he found the male genitalia distasteful, unsightly, including his own. When he showered or when he stood in front of the mirror toweling himself off he would avert his eyes from the unsightly, crude lump of a thing.

The intricacies of a woman, however, he found most fascinating.

While they had less moving parts, those parts were exquisitely sculpted and shaped into something far more beautiful and elegant. Delicate, hidden, the closed petals of a perfectly shaped rose in hibernation, waiting to unfurl, to open, to relent.

Not the ugly, lumpy, hanging bits that a man had.

He had considered the woman at the restaurant right here in town who had served him just the other day. She had a lovely smile, and as she walked away to serve other tables, his mind clicked and ticked about what she would look like under the layers of her uniform, underwear, and modesty.

Perhaps?

The thrill of anticipation was always better than the eventual reveal, the uncovering. The more layers of paper, the more intense the expectation of the gift that lay beneath.

Then there was the woman he had helped on the side of the road just out of town, when her car had become bogged in a particularly deep rut of snow and muddy ice. He had helped push her out while she sat behind the wheel revving the engine. It was only when she was finally free of the slushy quagmire that he walked around the side of the vehicle and noticed the empty child seat in the back.

How delightful would that be? A young wife and relatively new mother plucked in plain view in the middle of the day, never to be seen again.

Then there was that repulsive, ugly, sea urchin of a woman who had tried to overcharge him for car rental insurance. She deserved to be rutted, gutted, and left for the animals to feed on. Maybe she was too close to home. His face, no doubt, would be on the CCTV at the rental counter, and his name on the rental agreement as well as her name as the person who had served him.

He sighed, undecided.

Another waitress had initially piqued his interest, thinking about it now. But taking her seemed predictable, trite even. He wanted a challenge, a candidate that would test his skills, not only during the hunt, but during the stalking as well.

Maybe he had made a mistake, chosen the wrong town this season. It seemed to be filled with either old, overweight, ugly women or young fickle mothers obsessed with their cell phones.

A tourist could be a possibility. Taking someone who was just passing through, visiting the right place at the wrong time. It did appeal to him in an unfortunate, ironic way.

Choices, choices, he thought to himself as he sat in the diner in the main street of Willow Falls, the lunchtime crowd all but gone.

He skimmed the local newspaper that sat open next to him. There was the chance of more snow later today he noted. And there was a sale on winter coats and jackets at the outdoor clothing store two blocks away. He didn't need to buy anything, had brought more than enough clothing and equipment with him. Still, browsing the racks of clothing stores did always afford the opportunity to judge the "other" merchandise on offer, not just the clothing.

Women often fell under his charm, especially when he

approached them holding up a size-four garment saying that they looked the same size as his wife and if he could just hold it up to them to compare.

Flattery was a powerful bait to lure the unsuspecting. It had certainly worked on that young mother in Illinois last season. He'd spotted her at the outlet mall. She was alone and had walked into a large clothing retailer. So he followed her inside. Outlet malls were such ripe pickings for him. Their patronage consisted almost entirely of women, with the odd bored husband or dopey boyfriend in tow.

He followed her at a distance across the parking lot. Then followed her as she drove to the childcare center to collect her young daughter. Then continued following her all the way home to her adoring husband and her two placid dogs.

It had taken him three days of watching and waiting before he moved on her. But that was the thrill of the hunt.

Once she was restrained, he'd driven her deep into a secluded part of the state forest. Then he let her loose and hunted her again, but a different type of hunting this time. She was given a small backpack with some supplies to keep her energy levels up. He didn't want easy. He wanted hard.

He gave her an hour's head start, and she ran like a frightened deer into ten thousand acres of rugged, lonely hopelessness. There was no chance that she would come across anyone else or make it to any road to flag down a passing vehicle.

She lasted four hours, which had surprised him. She was young, fit, and determined. He was older, fitter, and insane.

Maybe it was the image burned in her mind of her daughter waiting at home for her mother to return that had spurred her on. The will to survive for the sake of loved ones.

Sneaky, evil bastard, he grinned, thinking back.

The waitress returned and refilled his coffee cup. "Do you hunt?" she said. "Sorry to ask, but this time of year we get a lot of hunters in town. Some even travel from interstate for the deer season."

"I've noticed the hunters arrive in town over the last few days," he replied with a smile.

"Not that you look like a hunter," the waitress added hastily. "You look more like a businessman on vacation. Dressed casually though."

He held her gaze. He hadn't really noticed this one before. She hadn't registered on his radar...until now.

She was nice. Real nice. Straw-blonde hair pulled back in a bun, a few strands hanging down around elfin-like ears and small jaw, perfect little white teeth, a smattering of freckles under deep hazel eyes and a small nose.

She wore a name badge and he noted her name, *Alisha*.

Very nice indeed. Not in an attractive, sexual way. To others maybe. But not to him. He wasn't interested in her like that. He appreciated her youthful looks, her fine bone structure, and her sweet innocence. Like a ripe, furry peach, sweet and juicy on the inside, unblemished on the outside.

As he smiled and continued to study her, he saw the smooth brushstrokes of his Caravaggio materialize before his very eyes. The fine detail. The way the light played off her smooth skin, a human canvas he wanted to rip and cut and disfigure, to expose the sweetness underneath and then bleed away the goodness.

"So tell me," he said. "You look like you should be in college. Do you just work here during the holidays?"

The young woman rolled her eyes. "I wish," she replied. "I'm saving up to go to Iowa Western. It's a community college, but they have a really good aviation maintenance program."

How fascinating.

"I want to be a pilot someday, but it's expensive and I need to get my grades up, so I thought I'd enroll in that program as a starting point."

How delectable.

He raised his coffee cup to her. "Well, good for you. It's nice to see a young woman with the ambition to do something different."

And with that the deal was sealed. He had indeed found his hidden masterpiece, the one he wanted to hide, to bury away. It was valueless to take a valueless life. He could easily walk into a dark alley at night and stab to death a worthless street person.

But that would mean nothing to him.

No, he'd much rather take something of value, a person with dreams and aspirations. Someone who had a future. The prospect of destroying someone's carefully constructed future was what drove him to do what he did.

He marveled in awe at the tantalizing prospect that stood before him. "Getting back to your original question: No, I don't really hunt," he replied. "I can't really bring myself to kill an animal."

And that was the honest truth.

Humans, however, were another matter entirely.

9

When someone close to you dies, it brings into question your own mortality. Even though it was her mother's house, and Carolyn Ryder had lived there for all her childhood and teenage years, she still felt that she was treading through the fragile garden of someone else's existence.

Now it was up to Carolyn to pack up, box up, sell, donate, or throw them into the trash. And when it was all done, all that would remain was a cold headstone with wilting flowers. This is what your life boils down to. The bitter concentrate of emptiness. You fill a hole in the ground to simply replace the one you leave behind in other people's memories.

To take her mind off the melancholy she felt, Carolyn set up her laptop in the living room. On it she played episodes from her favorite binge series on Netflix. She'd seen all the seasons about a million times before, but the familiar voices and scenes that she could recite word for word gave her the comfort and certainty she craved as she performed the uncomfortable and the depressing.

When her father died, it had been her mother who had taken care of such things. Now it was left to her and her sister. Jodie had pulled a double shift at the hospital, had sent a text. She needed the money. So the lonely task was left to Carolyn.

She sat cross-legged on the floor surrounded by a stack of packing boxes, rolls of tape, and take-out cartons of food she had ordered.

She had arranged things into various piles: things that she and Jodie would want, things that no one wanted but would go to a charity store, and things that were just plain trash.

She felt sadness as she looked around. This is what someone's life had been reduced to. Slowly and methodically, she was erasing all physical traces that her mother ever existed.

She had contemplated calling Tyler Finch to come by to keep her company. Carolyn's close-knit group of school friends had dispersed into family lives of their own long ago. She didn't have the confidence to suddenly call them out of the blue, after all these years of not bothering to stay in touch and say, "Hey! I'm back in town; let's meet up!" It would seem fake, disingenuous. It was a sad fact that played on her mind as she worked.

Then common sense prevailed, and she decided against calling Finch. This was very much an evening of self-reflection for her, to collect her own thoughts, to assess where she was in her own life as much as it was the erasing of the physical memories of someone else's life.

The house creaked and groaned. It was dark outside and windy. Windows rattled in their frames. Wind swept off the edges of the gables and gutters, making hollow, mournful sounds.

Carolyn got up and stoked the fire, then padded barefoot into the kitchen, only to return moments later with her third glass of wine for the evening.

She settled in again in front of the fire, and arranged some cushions around her like she had built a fortress to keep her safe or to keep something out. As she gazed into the flames of the fire, her mind wandered aimlessly, unsettled, restless, a ghost roaming the empty house, looking for a place to occupy.

She was twenty-eight and alone, had no one.

The only decent man she had ever had in her life she had managed to push away as well, like everyone else who had shown a glimpse of interest in her.

That wasn't entirely true though. Neither of them had wanted to settle down. She was pursuing her career in Washington, and he wasn't happy with his job. Ben wasn't good with personal commitments. Even if Carolyn had wanted to settle down, he wouldn't. It was not his style. He was committed to her, when they were together. Totally loyal, unlike other men Carolyn had dated. Not that there had been many.

She knew Ben was a restless soul. They had agreed after a few years of seeing each other that they needed time apart. Working in Washington had that effect on you. It swallowed your life, became everything, no rest or respite.

Even when they were dating, Carolyn often felt in the relationship that it was her who was more committed, more invested, more engaged. It was strange. Despite her tough, uncompromising exterior, Carolyn was just as insecure, as vulnerable, as the next person. She just did a better job of hiding it.

She took another sip of wine, glanced at the TV show that was playing on the laptop next to her on the floor, and smiled. Dysfunctional families made for the best TV drama.

The front drapes were pulled open. She preferred looking out into the darkness outside.

Resolved to the task, Carolyn carried an empty packing box and her wineglass upstairs to her mother's room, unable to put it off any longer. Previously, she had decided on the top-down approach, to start upstairs and gradually work her way downstairs, packing, sorting, keeping, and discarding as she went with the living room as the staging area.

But the thought of going into her mother's room had laid those plans to rest, and she did all the other rooms first. Now, it couldn't wait. It was the only room in the entire house she hadn't ventured into. Outside the door to her mother's bedroom, she steeled herself then entered.

The room was still and heavy with the living scent of Louise Ryder. The walls, the carpet, everything physical seemed infused with a lifetime of occupancy. The photos on the walls. The toiletries clustered around the bathroom vanity. The perfumes, hairbrushes, and personal keepsakes carefully arranged on the dresser, all clues as to the daily rituals of someone else. An intimate look into how they thought, they arranged, they led their life: a life now gone.

Carolyn stood by the curtains next to the window and gazed out into the street below. Warm light pooled along the footpath under streetlamps. Slits of light could be seen through closed curtains and window shades of the houses across the street.

Snow had been falling steadily for a few hours now, covering the path that led all the way to the front porch.

Letting out a sigh, Carolyn went back downstairs and pulled on her jacket and boots. She didn't want Jodie slipping in the dark trying to reach the front door. She would just do a quick clearing of the snow and ice. The cold fresh air would do her good. The air inside her mother's bedroom was stifling and stale.

She opened the front door and went outside.

A gentle flurry of snowflakes settled around her as she walked down the porch steps.

She stopped.

The shovel and tub of snow melt were gone, not there.

She had left them at the bottom of the steps after she had cleared the path and driveway this morning. She was certain both were still sitting there when she had returned home a few hours ago. Weren't they?

Maybe she'd had too much wine. Maybe she had left them around the side, near the trash cans.

Carolyn looked around. Everything was layered with a fresh covering of snow, untouched. The outline of the garage loomed on her left as she walked toward the side of the house.

The side of the house was dark and gloomy.

Then she saw a man, his shape, crouching in the shadows, near a side window, like he was trying to look inside.

Her heart pounded. She had no flashlight, no weapon, nothing.

Slowly, Carolyn edged toward him.

He didn't move. Just kept crouching, trying to see inside, through a gap in the curtains.

She thought about going back, going to the garage, finding a garden tool, something, anything.

Carolyn was more angry than scared. This was her mother's house. She didn't need some voyeur looking through the windows at night, watching her or Jodie.

Searching the ground, Carolyn found a rock and lifted it.

She edged closer.

Still the man didn't move.

"Hey!" she yelled out. "What the hell are you doing?"

Nothing. No response.

She hoisted the rock, making ready to throw it.

Then she stopped and the shape became clearer.

It was the large trash can, the one she had thrown rubbish into earlier today.

She felt foolish. She let go of the rock and it thudded to the ground. Her cheeks felt flushed. Maybe she had had too much wine after all. What would her colleagues back at the bureau think? Ex-FBI agent mistakes trash can for prowler.

Carolyn let out a laugh. She was a little drunk, but it pleased her. She hadn't been drunk for a while.

She looked at the neighbor's house on this side. It was in darkness, no signs of life. Carolyn hadn't seen them at all since she moved in. Normally you would expect some noise, lights on at night, or a person in their front yard during the day, checking the mailbox, coming and going. But she hadn't seen a soul. Maybe they were away for Christmas.

On the other side of the trash can sat the tub of snow melt and the snow shovel. Carolyn picked up both and trudged back to the front of the house.

Maybe her memory was going. They say when you quit work or retire your mind begins to slow down; you become more forgetful. While working in a high-pressure environment, your brain is constantly active, being used every moment of every day. When you stop working, for even a short period of time, you lose that edge. Something like muscle memory. Use it or lose it, as they say.

And yet as she began to shovel and clear the path, Carolyn swore she had left the shovel and the tub on the steps at the bottom of the porch.

10

There was nothing there unless you looked really hard, let your eyes wander across the street then upward, up toward the jumbled roofline of the buildings that huddled in the darkness.

Something was there, hidden among the silhouette of air vents, ceiling exhausts, straight lines, and acute angles set against the backdrop of the night sky.

If you ignored the falling snow from above, the distracting glow of the streetlights from below, then you might see it. The overlay of foreground over background, blocking the natural palette of grays and blacks, an outline that was barely visible of someone crouching, watching, observing, contemplating.

Alisha Myers had finished her shift at the diner across the street.

He watched.

It was nearly midnight, the traffic minimal, the streets deserted.

She walked across the parking lot, a swirl of flakes around her, a small trail of footprints behind her and the prospect of a cozy evening curled up in front of a warm fire in front of her.

He watched.

Her face was shrouded, the hood of her jacket pulled up tight over her head. But he could tell from the way she walked—that same slow, relaxed saunter he had seen in the diner earlier today—that it was her. Her gait was both intriguing and annoying at the same time. Both innocent and provocative.

Then for no reason whatsoever, Alisha Myers stopped, pulled back her hood, tilted her face skyward, and caught snowflakes on her tongue.

He shifted his weight forward, and watched, his fingers gripping tighter the edge of the ornate fascia in front of him.

She continued her trek across the parking lot. When she reached the street corner, she pulled out her cell phone, her face now clearly lit from the glow of the screen. She scrolled and thumbed.

A message sent, the reply almost instant.

She stood on the street corner then waited: no hurry, enjoying the precious time outside in the fresh air.

He watched, wondering who would be coming for her. Who would brave the snow and icy streets, leave behind the warmth and comfort of home to make the trip?

A possessive boyfriend? An overprotective father to safely collect her, bundle her up, and take her home? Endless possibilities but only one possible outcome for the unaware Alisha Myers that he had in mind.

She would be missed. There would be plenty of heartache to fill the void he was going to create when he pulled her from this earth. And for the distraught parents and the possessive boyfriend, they would forever be staring into the hole in the fabric of their lives where she had once stood.

A car, a compact SUV appeared through the white haze, crawling and slewing up the street, headlights ablaze, making a beeline toward the diner.

Keeping his head perfectly still, he swiveled his eyes only, and refocused his attention on the SUV. Across the street he had a clear view of the driver's side window. A woman sat behind the wheel, not as young as Alisha. An older sister perhaps.

He watched the SUV pull up to the curb, the tires crunching to a stop. The driver climbed out. She was tall, full build, with light wavy hair that flowed out from under a knitted woolen hat. Definitely older than Alisha Myers. Late thirties, perhaps. She wore a stylish hooded jacket, tight black ski pants and sensible snow boots. The woman walked eagerly around the hood of the SUV and embraced Alisha Myers in the full glare of the headlights, a swirl of gentle snowflakes engulfing them both.

Then a kiss, as sisters would so often do—that continued into something that sisters would most certainly not do. It was long, deep, passionate. A kiss that carefree lovers often did with scant regard for old conventions or small-town prejudice.

He watched, licked his cold lips, and felt an instant, primal stirring deep in the pit of his gut. Like a hunger pain but for a different kind of food. This was unexpected but welcomed nonetheless. It added a different dynamic that he was keen to explore. The wheels and cogs of his mind began ticking over, digesting, formulating, and planning.

Both women finally untangled themselves and climbed into the car, all giggles and smiles.

Tires crunched, and the SUV pulled away, throwing up spurts of ice and grit in its wake. At the end of the street it turned then vanished in a flurry of white and darkness.

He'd seen enough.

Any doubt that he felt quickly evaporated. The scene that had just unfolded before his very eyes had confirmed in his mind what he was going to do. Uncertainty and hesitation had given way to clarity and purpose.

There was only one slight problem, not a problem really. There were never problems, only challenges. Now he had two candidates, a pair. They seemed inseparable, so why separate them? He had never done a double kill before, a double hunt.

The prospect was delicious, to say the least.

He slid silently from the rooftop and melted into the darkness.

11

The bruising would go down, eventually.

It was a good thing it was winter. She could wear long-sleeve garments, hide what needed hiding.

The house was quiet as Alisha tiptoed downstairs, every loose floorboard memorized, every dry door hinge noted.

Olivia would sleep in this morning. That meant she wouldn't rise until after ten o'clock, more than enough time for Alisha to do what was expected of her.

Unlike Olivia, Alisha wasn't allowed to sleep in even if she had finished a late shift at the diner last night, and they hadn't gotten to bed until well after midnight.

Alisha moved with quiet efficiency around the spotless kitchen, ticking off the mental list she had prepared as she went, a list that rarely altered. First, she boiled the kettle. Then she filled and turned on the coffeemaker. Next, she opened the dishwasher, carefully sliding out first the top rack, then the bottom one, checking that everything was stacked correctly: glasses, according to size; coffee cups, according to design; handles perfectly lined up, nothing stacked on top of one another, no overcrowding: forks, spoons, and knives all grouped together in the cutlery basket, not mixed.

Alisha frowned, her breath stuttered. A small side plate was jammed among the row of larger dinner plates, glaringly out of place, a temporary break in the pattern of flow and symmetry.

The bout of mild panic she quickly felt turned to genuine relief. She still had time to rectify the oversight. Alisha carefully shifted the side plate, placing it in its correct spot. She was certain it wasn't placed there the night before when she checked before going to bed.

Satisfied, she filled the dispenser with detergent, closed the door, and pressed the start button. Pots and pans cycle. That was important. The dishes and cups needed to be spotless, no coffee rings, no food stains. Pristine, like everything else in the kitchen.

It usually took Alisha just under an hour to finish her "rising chores," and when she was done, only then could she prepare her own breakfast.

Olivia would make her own breakfast during the week, preferred it that way. On weekends, Alisha was tasked with making Olivia's breakfast from a predetermined menu, a laminated sheet fixed to the refrigerator.

At first, Alisha had found it petty, ridiculous. Precise qualities, exact measures. Then after a few months she found comfort in the timetable of daily routine, a roadmap of domesticated certainty, expectation, and reward, if Olivia was happy.

Keeping Olivia happy was important, paramount.

Rewards included certain privileges, monitored freedoms, luxuries that Alisha had once taken for granted. Use of the car to drive to and from work. An unlocked bedroom door at night. An hour of monitored internet usage. The use of tampons when needed.

Alisha was reminded all too well when that particular privilege had been withdrawn a few months back. And to make matters worse, it had been a particularly heavy few days that month. The horror, the indignation she had suffered, when, partway through taking a customer's breakfast order in the diner, she had to suddenly rush off to the restroom. Thankfully, neither the customer nor the other waitstaff noticed the single line of red dribble that had slinked down her leg.

And the memory of scrubbing and washing her panties under the faucet in the sink, using nothing but soap from the dispenser, all the time watching and praying that no one would walk in and see her. She spent the rest of the morning shift wearing damp panties stuffed with toilet tissue, fearful of another leakage, resolute of making sure that privilege was never taken from her again.

At a small desk and chair in an alcove just off the kitchen, Alisha opened her laptop computer and ate silently while the machine booted up. She opened a file marked "AM," located her daily color-coded spreadsheet, and updated it for the chores completed so far.

Her progress would be tallied, scrutinized, and triple checked.

Her eyes tracked down a vertical column of cells on the spreadsheet. Brightly colored in orange, the cells represented blocked-out time each morning for the next five days. The word "Breakfast" was typed in each cell. It was her turn.

Alisha checked the time on the purple fitness activity tracker that she wore.

She closed the laptop and went back into the kitchen. She took out a plastic serving tray from the drawer then placed a plastic bowl, plastic spoon, and paper napkin on it. Everything lined up. Then she went into the walk-in pantry. It smelled of spices, flour, and dry goods. A row of sugary breakfast cereal boxes were lined up on a shelf, no cardboard edge too far forward or too far back. A row of perfect unhealthy breakfast flatness.

She selected a box, took it back to the serving tray, opened the lid, undid the rubber band, and unrolled the plastic bag that was inside.

Tiny colorful rainbows, unicorns, stars, blue moons, and hearts tumbled into the bowl. Alisha was extra generous this morning.

Anger and bitterness suddenly invaded her thoughts as she remembered back to when it was her who was getting served breakfast and the measly portions she had been given.

She placed a small creamer jug filled with milk next to the bowl on the tray. She checked that everything was neat and tidy before carrying the tray carefully to the staircase.

A key sat on a hook next to the door that led down to the basement under the stairs. Setting the tray down on a side table, Alisha took the key, opened the door, and flipped the light switch located on the inside at the top of the stairs.

A shaft of light covered the first few steps then faded into the darkness below. Careful not to spill the milk, Alisha descended into the basement, one step at a time.

At the bottom she paused, allowing her eyes to adjust to the gloom.

There was no point, really. She knew the warm, dark space intimately. Every rafter, every corner, every crack in the drywall and chip in the floor, the location of every window, blindfolded.

Alisha stepped forward, counted the exact steps, eighteen in total that took her nearly all the way across to the far wall. All the windows had been painted over and then boarded up with wooden planks. Fragments of dull morning sunlight seeped in through slits in the planks, where they had shrunk in places. It offered some reprieve from the total darkness.

Squatting down and facing straight ahead, Alisha placed the tray squarely on the dusty concrete floor. There was no sound except the ticking of water pipes and the hum of the boiler that sat in the far corner.

Slowly, she pushed the tray forward a few inches, the plastic underside scraping across the floor.

Nothing.

She shuffled forward some more then pushed the tray a little farther until it gently nudged something in the darkness ahead.

Two feet, perpendicular to the floor, side by side, bare soles, cuts, and abrasions.

No response.

Alisha nudged the feet again with the edge of the tray.

This time one foot moved slightly, followed by a stirring movement, then a faint groan, and the metallic clink of chains.

Alisha let out a sigh of relief. She had been worried, but everything was good now. It was a good sign, the movement. The tremors had gone.

Standing up, Alisha turned, retraced her steps, then climbed back up the stairs, out of the darkness and into the light again.

She closed and locked the heavy door behind her, then carefully placed the key back on the hook.

She diligently went back to the alcove, opened up the laptop again, clicked on the first orange cell in the column then typed a single word.

Done.

12

Carolyn was up at 7:00 a.m. the next morning. She quickly changed into running tights, a breathable base layer shirt and a hooded sweatshirt.

She had brought her running gear with her and wanted to keep up her fitness regimen, not turn soft and doughy.

She tiptoed past Jodie's room, not before opening the door a crack just to check in on her. Jodie had come home late last night. Carolyn had stayed up, and they talked for almost an hour. It was good, just to talk, to listen and to reconnect with her sister despite their differences and the harsh words that had been said. Carolyn could feel the fences slowly mending between them. It just needed time, and for Carolyn to forget, to let go of the past, including what had happened with Tyler Finch.

Downstairs, Carolyn slipped on her sneakers and slid her credit card into a zippered pocket along with her cell phone and ventured outside.

The snow shovel and the snow melt were where she had left them the night before on the porch steps, and Carolyn was thankful she wasn't losing her mind. She did some light stretching while watching the neighbor's house.

A compact SUV was now parked in their driveway. Carolyn hadn't heard it last night, only Jodie's car when she arrived home. The window shutters were still drawn tight, and there wasn't any obvious signs of life.

The air was cold and crisp, the sun blinding and the sky clear and deep blue. It was about two miles into town, a decent run there and back, so Carolyn set off at a steady pace, taking care along the footpaths that were frosty and snow covered in some places. At the end of the street she turned onto the main road that would take her right into town.

Traffic along the main road was light, and the footpath was wide and clear, so she pounded along, quickly falling into a familiar rhythm. No headphones. No distracting music screaming in her ears. Just the reassuring, calming beat of her feet on concrete and her steady breathing. She preferred it that way, eyes and ears taking in the sights and the sounds. You could learn a lot about a place by leaving the car behind, going on foot, running the streets or taking a walk.

Reaching the outskirts of town, the Willow Falls police department came into view and was exactly how she had remembered it. Some things never changed. It was a small low-squat building made of brick with three police cruisers sitting in a neat row in the parking lot at the side.

Carolyn stood across the street, hands on her knees, head craned looking at the building, contemplating if she should go inside and see Finch. She didn't want to encourage him. But she did need him as a friend in this town. Making up her mind, she crossed the street and went up the footpath toward the entrance.

The foyer was small, with a plain wooden counter, protective glass enclosure, a row of plastic chairs, and a soda machine in the corner. Despite growing up here, she had never, thankfully, been inside the place. It felt strange and somehow awkward. She had been inside many police stations in her job, but somehow this one felt different.

She looked at the corkboard on the wall. It contained the obligatory community safety posters and flyers and the ubiquitous local missing persons bulletin. Faces, some happy, most sad, stared back at her, vacant, disillusioned almost.

No matter where she went, people were always missing. From big cities, to small one-street towns. It made no difference. Normal, everyday people just vanished.

When she was a child, Carolyn couldn't understand how people went missing. Someone's mother, sister, brother, or son. Someone who was loved now gone, vanished, plucked off the face of the earth. They had lives, jobs, careers, someone relying on them, waiting at home for them. It seemed almost strange in today's society, with technology, CCTV, smart phones with built-in GPS, and social media, how anyone could just vanish.

Then Carolyn joined the FBI, and from that point on, she fully understood how it could be. Looking at the faces made Carolyn think about Beth Rimes, the police officer she had met, helped, then became lifelong friends with in Utah. She resolved to send Beth a quick email and find out how she was doing, if she was finally sleeping through the night, or if the nightmares were still there.

Maybe, if she had time, after her mother's estate was concluded, she would drive south to Florida, go and see Beth, see the new life she had made for herself.

Carolyn turned to see Tyler Finch standing on the other side of the counter.

"Hi, Tyler," she said. "I was on a run into town, and I thought I'd drop by."

Finch gave a weary smile. He looked terrible, like he hadn't slept in days, or if he had, it had been at his desk. Closer up, Carolyn could see his eyes were bloodshot, his hair was ruffled, and his uniform looked rumpled like he had definitely slept in it.

"What's wrong?" Carolyn asked.

"Just work," Finch replied.

He looked bone tired. Gone was his usual laid-back confidence, his lopsided grin, his quick humor. He seemed tense, strung tight like a bowstring.

Carolyn looked up and noticed the CCTV camera in the corner. The lens focused on her. It was strange for Carolyn, being on the other side of the divide. It felt foreign. She guessed she was on the other side of a lot of things these days, a different perspective, on the outside looking in.

"I thought nothing much happened in Willow Falls." Carolyn laughed, trying to coax a smile out of Finch. But he didn't smile. Something was wrong. "Did someone double-park?" Carolyn said jokingly.

No response. Just a tight line across Finch's lips.

"Sorry," Carolyn admitted. "I shouldn't joke. It's just that you look like hell."

"I feel like hell," Finch replied. He kept looking over his shoulder, behind him to the open doorway that led to the squad room in the back.

"So what's up?" Carolyn asked. She knew there was something wrong. Finch was serious.

Finch leaned in, lowered his voice, and spoke through the drilled holes in the plexiglass barrier. "Look, Carolyn, I can't talk now. Something's come up."

"Come on, Finch." Carolyn smiled. "You can tell me or have you forgotten? I'm on your side. I used to be in the FBI."

There was an awkward silence.

Carolyn could see Finch was wrestling with himself. He wanted to say something but couldn't bring himself to tell her.

"Carolyn, I can't. We need to keep a lid on it until we know more."

Now Carolyn was a little more than curious. "Finch," she persisted, "I might be able to help."

Then a booming voice came from the doorway behind where Finch stood. "We don't need your help."

A large man, another police officer, shuffled out and stood beside Finch. The man was older, ruddy complexion, wispy gray hair, and a saggy face from either heavy drinking or a lifetime spent frowning at people. He regarded Carolyn with a skeptical, almost sour look.

Finch turned to his senior officer. "This is Sergeant Bates."

Carolyn nodded. "I'm Carolyn—"

"So you're Jodie's sister, aren't you?" Bates cut her off, his voice gruff, condescending. "The one in the FBI." Bates made it sound like the three letters, when strung together, formed a dirty word. Forget the fact that Carolyn and her team in Utah had thwarted the largest domestic terrorist network in mainland America, that had been in the news for weeks a few months back.

"Ex-FBI," Carolyn corrected him.

A Mexican standoff ensued. Glares and stares. The air tense and uncomfortable.

Bates finally broke the silence. "We're kinda busy here at the moment, so unless it's urgent..."

Carolyn held his gaze. His expression didn't alter. He was looking down at her. No doubt Finch had been spreading the word about their history, how she'd left town and was now back.

Finch shuffled uneasily. He looked at Carolyn, and she could make out the minuscule shake of his head, like he was saying *just let it go.* Carolyn stood, contemplating whether or not to speak her mind. If she was still in the FBI, she would have put the old, grumpy sergeant in his place.

Carolyn regarded Bates coolly, and for the sake of not ruffling feathers and making it difficult for Finch, she said, "No. It's nothing important. I was just out on a morning run and thought I'd drop by." Carolyn looked at Finch. "I'll keeping running. Might drop in at the diner for a coffee."

Finch nodded, getting the hint.

Outside, Carolyn stood on the sidewalk and looked back at the building she had just walked out of, wondering what all that was about. Not exactly a warm reception. She set off again in the direction of the main street, wondering how many people in the town were going to treat her like an outcast, too.

13

I t wasn't that Carolyn was angry when she entered the diner and sat in a corner booth that looked out onto the street.

She was puzzled more than anything by the cold reception she had just received at the police station. The harsh reality was that she was now on the lowest rung of the ladder. Maybe not on the ladder at all. Just a civilian with no gun, no badge, no authority.

Not that she was arrogant nor flaunted her authority when in the FBI. However, it had given her certain power. Like being able to walk into any police department, sheriff's office, home, or place of business, flash her badge, and demand answers to her questions.

Some of her male colleagues in the bureau were certainly more temperamental. They would flaunt their authority. But not her. Carolyn was always conscious of other law enforcement agencies, would tread lightly, not ruffle feathers. Carolyn knew it was more effective to adopt a more subtle, cooperative approach than just barge into town riding on a high horse.

Slightly dejected, Carolyn flipped through the laminated menu as a waitress came over carrying a coffee cup and a glass coffee flask filled with wonderful-smelling black liquid.

Carolyn stared out at the street.

The old sergeant she could understand. Probably promoted sideways to a small town to see out what remaining years he had until retirement. She knew the type. Stubborn, not willing to change, a technological dinosaur. But Finch? Maybe it was payback for the last ten years.

"Hi," the waitress said.

Carolyn broke from her thoughts and looked up. The waitress had a nice smile. Pretty, too. Young, fresh college kid working here during the holidays, Carolyn guessed.

"Hi..." Carolyn glanced at the name badge on the waitress. "Alisha." She should be friendlier, Carolyn thought, more than the local police sergeant, at least.

The waitress smiled. "What can I get for you?" Alisha took out her order pad and pen from her apron.

Carolyn sighed and ran her eyes down the huge menu. She settled for an egg-white omelette.

"Been running?" Alisha asked, flipping her pen at Carolyn's attire.

"Just a few miles this morning." Carolyn drank her coffee.

"I wish I could run," Alisha replied. "Just don't get the time."

Carolyn noticed the purple fitness tracker Alisha wore on her wrist. "You probably cover about twenty miles a day running around here anyway. Do those things actually work?"

Alisha glanced at the silicon band on her wrist. "Oh, I mainly use it as a watch. Alarm clock as well so I don't miss my shift here."

As Alisha reached across and topped up Carolyn's coffee cup, the sleeve of her uniform rode up a few inches, revealing more of her wrist and forearm—and the dark bruising that was there.

Carolyn's eyes lingered just a little too long.

Alisha quickly pulled back the coffee flask and turned her body away. She hesitated for a moment then said, "I'll put your order in," before hurriedly leaving.

Carolyn watched her go, her mind thinking about what she had seen on the young woman's wrist.

The door of the diner swung open and Tyler Finch walked in. He spotted Carolyn in the booth, walked over, and slid in opposite her, unzipping his duty jacket.

Alisha came back. This time both sleeves of her uniform were rolled all the way down and buttoned at the wrist.

Carolyn could tell the waitress was avoiding her eyes. Instead, she turned to Finch and smiled, and filled up a fresh coffee cup she had brought with her.

"Hi, Tyler," she said, her voice overtly bright and bubbly. "What can I get you?"

Finch looked up and returned the smile. "Hey, Alisha. Coffee's just fine for now."

Alisha gave him another sweet smile, then sauntered off.

Carolyn noticed the little exchange and said, "So you're a regular here?"

Finch shrugged. "It's the only diner in town and I'm a cop. What would you expect?"

"Do you know her?" Carolyn asked, her eyes keenly watching the waitress as she flowed between the tables, serving other customers.

"Who? You mean Alisha?"

Carolyn rolled her eyes. "Yes, the waitress."

"She's a nice kid, been here for a few years." Finch drank his coffee. "Why?"

"No reason," Carolyn said. "Do you know her well?"

"Not really, Carolyn. Why? Where's this going?" Then Finch frowned. "I'm not sleeping with her if that's what you're thinking."

"That's not what I meant," Carolyn replied. She hesitated for a moment, thinking if she should mention the bruising on the girl's wrist to him. Then she decided against it. Probably just a disgruntled boyfriend. Still didn't make it right though.

Finch looked at Carolyn questioningly. "Then what?"

"Nothing," Carolyn replied breezily.

Finch leaned forward. "Look, I'm sorry about what happened before," he explained. "Let's just say it's been a rough twenty-four hours."

Carolyn gave a look of indifference. "Fine." She took out the menu again, held it up high, using it as a screen between them.

Finch could tell she was annoyed even though she wouldn't admit it.

"Look," he said. "I can't tell you anything. It's an ongoing case."

"Fine," Carolyn repeated, her eyes still on the menu, face totally hidden. "Wow. Look at how many different types of waffles they have," she said, her voice mocking astonishment.

Finch shrugged it off, slightly exasperated, liked he was boxed in at both ends. "Bates is old school," Finch persisted, referring to his sergeant. "He knew your mother and knows Jodie really well."

"Funny," Carolyn said from behind the menu. "So do I. Doesn't mean I have to be a rude prick."

"He's not like that."

"He must be new in town because I don't remember him," the voice still behind the menu.

Finch pulled the menu down so he could see Carolyn's face. "He arrived three years ago. You're being childish, now."

Carolyn's food arrived and she folded the menu back up. But she wasn't going to let Finch off the hook that easily.

Alisha and Carolyn locked eyes for a brief moment, but it was enough for Carolyn. She could tell there was something there, in the girl's eyes. Not embarrassment, more like fear.

Alisha topped off the coffee and was gone again. Carolyn watched her as she walked away.

"She's gay," Finch said, noticing Carolyn's keen interest in Alisha.

"Good for her," Carolyn replied in a flat tone, sprinkling salt on her food. "I'm not."

Finch watched as Carolyn ate. "There are people in this town who don't want you around. Don't like you."

Carolyn stopped eating and glared at Finch. "They don't even know me!" she said, raising her voice. "Unless you and my sister have taken it upon yourselves to fill them in on the last ten years of my life." She pointed a fork at Finch. "You don't even know me. People around here don't know me. You make it sound like I have some kind of reputation, no doubt concocted by you and my sister." Carolyn could feel her anger rising and started attacking her food with deliberate, exaggerated hacks of her fork.

"Look, it's a small town," Finch said defensively.

"Small minded, too." She placed her cutlery down, tempted to stab Finch with it.

"You can try and fit in," Finch offered. "Be a bit friendlier."

"Friendlier?" Carolyn said in disbelief. "I just walked into the police station to say hello, and I was treated like an outcast. Who have I offended?" Carolyn demanded. She couldn't believe what Finch was saying. No wonder she left the town all those years ago, got out. But now it felt like she was being drawn back into all the things she hated about the place.

Sure, on the surface, Willow Falls was a pretty town as Ritter had mentioned to her yesterday. But stay long enough, and you will soon discover the small-town paranoia, the insecurities, the prejudices.

"I'm not trying to fit in because I don't want to fit in," Carolyn continued. "I'm happy the way I am."

Finch shrugged. "A lot of people view you as an outsider now."

Carolyn could feel her jaw tingling. "I'm not an outsider," she said, trying to remain calm. "I was born here. I went to school here. I grew up here."

"A lot of the townsfolk knew your mother. Saw her deteriorate in those final months."

"My mother was very comfortable in Salt Lake City, being

looked after very well there. I saw her nearly every day when I could until Jodie decided to drag her back here."

"She wanted to die here," Finch countered. "In her hometown. In her own home, her own bed. The place you left. Now you're back, after what, ten years? How do you expect people will react?"

Carolyn gave a mocking laugh and threw her gaze up at the ceiling. "People leave, Finch. That is what they do. You can't stay in one place all your life. I needed a change." Carolyn looked around. "I've changed. I needed to change. I couldn't stay here any longer for the exact same reasons I'm seeing now. The place was slowly killing me."

Finch stared at Carolyn for a moment, not saying anything. He knew she was ambitious. When they first started dating he could tell he couldn't hold on to her forever. Eventually they would go their separate ways. Maybe that's what made her so attractive to him. She was different than all the other hometown girls back then.

Carolyn always seemed to be looking toward a distant shore, her mind elsewhere, telling him about all the plans she had for the future. Plans that didn't seem to involve him.

At first, Finch thought it was just all talk. Just a young woman wishing and dreaming. Even though life was good in Willow Falls and he had no complaints, no regrets, he soon realized she was serious.

Maybe he should have paid more attention to her back then.

And now she was back in his life. He was stupid to think yesterday when he visited that maybe, just maybe, they could pick up from where they left off ten years ago. But looking at her now, ten years later, the young restless teenager was gone, replaced by a young, ambitious, and defiant woman who sat across from him.

Finch knew the void that separated them was now wider than ever.

14

"We found a body," Finch said, finally relenting.

Carolyn sat expressionless. "And?" she said. She could tell Finch was hesitant to tell her. But somehow he looked like he needed to talk to someone else apart from his work colleagues.

Finch looked around making sure they were out of earshot. He tapped his finger on the table. "You can't tell anyone," he stressed.

"Who am I going to tell?" Carolyn countered. "As you said, no one around here trusts me. I'm a stranger in this town so why would I."

"Maybe some of your colleagues back at the bureau. We don't need their help."

Carolyn cocked her head, trying to read Finch's expression. There was something fearful behind his eyes that he was trying to hide. Then it occurred to her. "It's something new," she finally said. "Something you or no one else here has seen before."

"I've seen dead bodies before," Finch scoffed.

Carolyn gave a slight smile. "Yeah. Like old people who have died in their sleep or maybe a hit and run or car crash."

As Carolyn continued to study him, Finch became increasingly uncomfortable. Squirming in his seat, his eyes darting all around the diner, and fidgety with his hands. Finch liked to think of himself as confident, levelheaded, always in control. But something had unhinged him.

"I've seen worse," Finch said, looking away, thinking about the girl in the forest.

Carolyn could see him slowly unraveling in front of her eyes. She shook her head. "But not like this, you haven't."

"How do you know?" he said matter-of-factly.

Carolyn gave a subtle shrug. "I can tell." She leaned forward, her voice low. "By how you're acting. Otherwise you would have told me already. A simple dead body doesn't call for keeping a lid on it, unless, of course, it's politically sensitive or..."

Finch sat back and let out a sigh.

Carolyn kept going. "What did you find?"

Finch's eyes narrowed. "You can't breathe a word of this to anyone. Yet."

"You said that already."

"We found a girl. A young woman, a local, up in the foothills, in the forest."

Carolyn listened intently, coaxing the details out of him.

Finch stared into his coffee cup. "She was dead."

"Bodies usually are."

He looked up. "She was nailed to a tree. With arrows."

Carolyn sat a little straighter. Moved a little closer. Now he had her full attention.

Finch ran his fingers through his hair. He was agitated. Carolyn could tell. He had seen the body, firsthand, she thought. An image branded into his memory forever. Difficult to look at. Impossible to forget.

"Nailed?" Carolyn asked. "Describe it."

Finch did, in intricate detail, expecting Carolyn to show some emotion, the slightest sign of revulsion or reaction. But she didn't. Not a glimmer. She just sat there, poker faced, silent, taking everything in. Cold. Emotionless. The cogs of her objective, analytical mind turning, processing, storing, comparing. She had a certain hardness to her now, something she didn't have when they were younger, no matter how angry she had gotten.

A look around her eyes and jawline, an edginess that Finch couldn't remember seeing on her.

After he was done, Carolyn sat back and looked out the window. Snow-covered trees lined the street. Christmas decorations, red and green garlands ringed the streetlamps. Wreaths made from twisted, fresh, noble fir hung from store doors, bunting and decorations in their windows.

Postcard perfect.

When she finally spoke, her voice was different. Professional, experienced, calm and orderly. "Where is she now?"

"In the morgue at the local hospital."

"And the crime scene? Has that been secured? Processed?"

Finch stared into his hands, knowing that Carolyn was not going to like what he was about to say next. "No."

"Preservation of the scene. Preservation of the evidence. Collecting any evidence *before* you touch or move a body. I'm not about to tell you your job, Finch."

Finch nodded. "I know. I know. But Bates wanted her taken down right away. He said he wasn't going to leave some poor local girl nailed to a tree looking like a butcher's store window."

"So he went up there with you? Saw her?"

Finch nodded again.

Carolyn closed her eyes. As was the case with so many small-town police, the crime scene had been trashed right away, overrun, no consideration given to preserving what little evidence there was around the body. More concern was given to moving the body, making the horrific scene more palatable, making the tragedy seem to go away in order to save face with the locals and project normality in the town.

She opened her eyes again and glared at Finch. It wasn't his fault. There was so much she could have said, but as she looked at Finch, she held her tongue. It was obvious the police up here were out of their depth. Inexperienced in such things. Discretion was her best approach. "So what now?"

"I value your opinion," Finch said.

"Hey, an hour ago you weren't interested in even saying hello to me. Why the sudden change of heart?" Carolyn already knew the answer. It was because Finch had slowly realized that this was something neither he nor his fellow officers could handle.

"Call in more help if you need it. Maybe from Des Moines," Carolyn suggested.

"Bates doesn't want to be seen as weak, that he can't handle the situation," Finch replied. "Wants to keep the investigation local. It's his patch of the woods, so to speak."

"Then let it run its course. But you've destroyed any evidence there was. And with more snow coming, it will definitely be gone."

"What do you think?" Finch asked. He knew if Bates caught him talking to Carolyn about the case he would be reprimanded.

"It's your case. What do you think?" Carolyn deflected. She didn't have enough information to draw any conclusions. She needed a full crime scene report, autopsy report, background checks done on the girl, her family and friends.

Finch explained that the autopsy would be done in the next few days. Then they would know more. They had already contacted the girl's parents, who lived out of town. Bates had driven up to see them last night with the gut-wrenching news that their only daughter was now dead. He didn't go into the hideous details of how they found her.

"Maybe a jealous boyfriend. A hunter. They used a crossbow to kill her. We're looking into that now," Finch said.

Carolyn said nothing. She could tell his mind was in turmoil, not used to seeing death, not like this anyway.

"How could someone do that to another person?" Finch said staring at the tabletop as though the answer lay hidden among the sea of scratches, marks, and grooves in the scuffed surface. "It was like she was on display, a trophy."

"Tell me you got some photos, Finch," Carolyn almost pleaded, "before you took her down?"

Finch just nodded. "All I had on me was my cell phone." He pulled it out of his jacket.

"Not here, Finch," Carolyn cautioned him, touching his hand. This was not the time nor the place.

"I downloaded them to the computer back at the station. Sent them off for the autopsy, but apart from that, Bates wants to keep a low profile on this."

"I agree, until you know more."

"That's the main reason, Carolyn," Finch said. "It's nothing against you." He slid his cell phone back into his pocket. Mitch Bowman, after he had recovered from the initial shock, had been cautioned not to tell anyone, other than his wife. And certainly not to go into graphic detail about the girl's body and how she was found.

Finch looked pale. Sick almost. The horrific images of the dead girl played on his mind ever since he had first set eyes on her. "Bates doesn't want the press nor the news channels getting wind of this. It will ruin the hunting season. The tourists."

"Hunting season?" Carolyn replied. "To hell with that."

"You don't understand. This time of year brings in a lot of money for the town. Hunters flock here for the whitetail deer. Lots of folks around town, small businesses, store owners, restaurants like this, all rely on it. They wait almost all year for the season."

"That just makes it harder to find the killer," Carolyn said. She could tell by the frown that Finch hadn't thought this through. The possibility that the killer wasn't a local. "Maybe they were a visitor, passing through. Could be long gone by now," she added.

He looked seriously at Carolyn. "You think?"

"Could be. Not a local. Could be just a random killing. Might not be random either."

"Why do you say that?" Finch said, confused, but willing to listen, to get any guidance that he could from Carolyn.

Carolyn thought for a moment. She really didn't like to give an opinion on the fly. She had minimal information to work with. "Just seems that if what you say is true, that the girl was on display, pinned to a tree all the way up in the forest, then someone went to a lot of trouble. Seems elaborate. Hunters would have eventually found her. If it was a true crime of passion, like you say, a jealous boyfriend, then it seems like a lot of hard work, if you ask me, to make an example of her. Doesn't seem to fit with the crime of passion motive."

Finch thought about it for a moment. Then he finally spoke. "So what do you think it is?"

"Look, Finch, I don't want to speculate. There's so much here that is missing, evidence, details, I know nothing of the girl, her background."

Alisha returned with the check and placed it on the table. Carolyn thanked her and watched her walk off.

"How well do you know the waitress, then?" Carolyn asked, changing the subject.

"A little." Finch drained his coffee. "I need to get back." He stood and took out his wallet but Carolyn waved him away. "Maybe you should get to know her now that you're back in town," he said.

Carolyn gave him a puzzled look. "Why would I want to do that?"

Finch adjusted his belt and holster. "You know, take the time to get to know the folks around here. Wouldn't do you no harm."

Carolyn rolled her eyes, fearing another lecture from Finch coming on.

"Well, she is your neighbor now, I guess," Finch added.

"What?" Carolyn said, stunned.

"Moved into the house next door to your mom's place, a few years back, Alisha and her girlfriend, that is. Finch zipped up his duty jacket. "Thanks for the coffee, by the way."

And with that, he was gone.

15

Meeting Finch perhaps wasn't such a good idea after all, Carolyn thought to herself as she jogged back home. All the past feelings and bad memories were again bubbling up to the surface in her mind.

Then there was the issue with the body of the girl he had discovered. Carolyn didn't want to get involved. She would offer her advice if asked, but Finch had to deal with it himself. Baptism by fire, that's how she had felt when training those under her. Throw them in the deep end, like how she was treated when she was a green, know-nothing graduate fresh out of the academy. Sink or swim, she was told by her supervisor. And it had worked, Carolyn had learned a lot more by having to work things out on her own, to trust her own judgment, to rely on her own instincts.

The same could be said of Finch. It was his town, his people. He needed to step up now with this new development. Sink or swim.

Crossing the street she couldn't help but think Finch was slightly jealous of her. She could see it in his eyes, how he spoke. He'd been trapped in the town, and now he was too embedded, too well known, too comfortable and complacent to have the courage to leave. To try something different.

That was fine by her. People made their own choices, and she had made hers ten years ago and had no regrets.

She felt some deep-seated bitterness in Finch, she thought when he looked at her at the diner, like she had walked out on him, feelings that Carolyn thought were long gone.

Had she really changed that much? Carolyn found herself dwelling on what he had said as she pounded the sidewalk, navigating around patches of ice.

She felt refreshed. Content. The sun was bright and the sky was blue and the air bracing in her lungs. She felt alive, happy. She did her best thinking when out jogging. She had really missed it.

There was no denying that her last case in Utah had definitely changed her. She knew that. Her leg had fully recovered. She had stayed fit through the recovery but now she wanted to build up her running fitness and endurance again. God, she had missed it, and she felt no ill effects from her injury.

But Utah was a turning point in her life. There was no denying it. She had nearly died, almost bled to death in some dark hole in the side of a cold mountain. She thought she would be fine, would recover. Yet some injuries couldn't be healed by time nor by doctors playing God.

She hadn't told Finch what had happened in Utah. She hadn't even told her sister or mother. The weeks she had spent in hospital she had lied, pretended she was at the office, or working away on a long case and couldn't be contacted. Her work colleagues thought it was strange, her not telling her family. But she insisted with the doctors and her boss not to tell anyone. Wanted to keep it private.

She wasn't looking for pity or sympathy from her family or anyone else. Had shied away from it all her life.

Finch wouldn't understand anyway.

Utah had changed her for the better. That was the truth. It had made her more resilient, stronger, not dispassionate. Maybe a little more selfish with her time. Certainly more impatient, not prone to waiting for others.

It had also given her a new appreciation on life. It was precious. Don't waste it. Do what you want to do and not follow the expectations of others. You only need to please one person and that is yourself.

She increased her speed, pushing herself harder, enjoying the feel of the soles of her sneakers on the solid concrete, the crunching of snow and salt as she ran on.

Then a car eased to the curb a hundred yards in front of her, wisps of white chugging from the tailpipes as it just sat there, the motor idling.

Carolyn slowed.

The car window slid down. Someone called out to her.

Carolyn glanced in and saw Michael Ritter sitting across in the driver's seat.

"Hi, stranger," he said. Warm air flowed out from inside and into her face.

Carolyn rested her arms on the windowsill.

"I would offer you a ride, but you look too determined when you run. Almost like someone is chasing you," he said, a boyish grin on his face.

"It's just a quick run, that's all." Carolyn was a little surprised to see Ritter, but happy that she had. He was a stranger in town, just like her, and because of that she felt a slight connection, like they were allies.

"So what are you doing today?" Ritter asked.

"Nothing really. Just some errands around town and at home," Carolyn said, guessing what he was going to say next. A man doesn't ask a woman if she's doing anything without entertaining the idea of suggesting something.

"Well, how about a bite to eat later? Dinner perhaps?"

Carolyn thought for a moment about the piles of packing boxes, crockery and kitchen items back at the house all waiting for her attention. She had hardly spent any time with Jodie, but she worked shift work, and there was always this afternoon to do something together.

Ritter seemed like a welcome distraction.

"Sure," Carolyn said. It was against her better judgment. She didn't know who he was other than from the brief conversation they'd had in the bakery.

He seemed nice though.

Her old self would have definitely said no, rebuffed his offer. But Carolyn was determined not to fall into a morose, brooding state, locked away in her mother's house surrounded by memories of the past.

The morning run had invigorated her, cleared her mind. She had made a firm resolution to be more open, be a bit friendlier. Not too friendly though.

Only with people she liked.

"Great," Ritter said with a smile. And when he smiled, Carolyn felt a twinge of excitement.

"It's not a date," Carolyn warned him sternly. "Just food."

Ritter raised his hands like he was being arrested. "Hey, I promise. Just food and good company." Ritter held her gaze. Soft dark eyes and a mischievous grin.

"So let's say, I pick you up at around seven tonight?"

"How about we meet at a place instead."

"Sounds good."

Carolyn continued, "How about the diner?"

Ritter gave a drawn out, "OK."

Carolyn could tell from the look on his face, he seemed a little disappointed at her suggestion.

"There's a small Italian restaurant one block back off the main street. I discovered it a few days ago. A hidden gem, really," he said.

"Sounds good. I'll meet you there."

"You need directions?" Ritter asked.

Carolyn smiled. "I'll find it."

Ritter nodded then pulled away from the curb, the tires hissing and crunching.

Carolyn watched him go then set off again, her pace slightly quicker and more urgent than before, not powered by the adrenaline of the run, but by something completely different.

16

The two-story house looked like any other on the street, just a little darker, a little quieter, a little more withdrawn from the world.

Strong, old-fashioned construction, thick edges, steeple roofline, dark slate siding, shuttered windows, all solidly built, and hunkered down for the winter.

The front garden was dead and withered, frosted white, in hibernation like every other garden on the street. Except, unlike most of the other houses, the house next door was bare of any festive decorations. No Christmas lights, no ribbons, no wreath, nothing.

A concrete path led from the sidewalk right up to the front steps and a wide front porch beyond.

Carolyn stood in the front yard of her mother's house, stretching sore and tired limbs, cooling down after her run.

She tilted her head slightly at the adjacent house and let her eyes wander casually over it, taking it all in, the details. Shuttered front windows, the porch, the front door, the side of the house, seeing it all in a different light, paying it more attention now that she knew Alisha lived here, right next door.

Carolyn skipped up the stairs of her mother's house and vanished inside, only to emerge moments later carrying a half-empty trash bag: her cover story, in case someone saw her loitering aimlessly around the side between the two houses.

She walked down the side toward the trash can, her pace slower than normal, her eyes glancing up every so often at the house next door.

More shuttered windows along the side. Still no sign of life.

A simple waist-high wire fence made from galvanized posts and thin diagonal mesh separated the two houses. A gnarly old hedge, brittle and twisted, worked its way along the fence on the other side. Sparse and emaciated, the hedge offered some cover for Carolyn as she continued to walk along the side, observing the house next door.

There was a scatter of fat bushes along the side of the neighbor's house, their tops glistening bright with an icing of snow. More bushes grew next to the ground-floor windows, providing more screening from prying eyes.

Carolyn lifted the lid of the trash can and deposited the bag inside, letting the lid fall with a deliberate loud clunk.

As she turned, she looked directly over the fence and hedge. There was a wedged-shaped set of basement external entry doors, built on this side of the house with heavy hinges that opened outward and thick black handles.

Carolyn hadn't paid much attention to the house next door until now. No need. The place had seemed empty, unoccupied. That was until she saw the car this morning in the driveway, that was now gone. And also from what Finch had told her at the diner.

During the previous day Carolyn had seen no one come or go from there. Mind you, she hadn't spent her day spying on the house, hoping to see someone. During those times when she had been at home, she'd seen or heard nothing, and that now seemed a little strange to her.

While she lay awake in bed last night, after she and Jodie had said goodnight, she thought she had heard something, a machinery sound coming from the garage that was on the other side. Not the garage door going up. It was something else, just a short, high-pitched squeal that only lasted a few seconds. And when she had ventured out at night yesterday in the subzero temperature to put more trash out from the cleanup of her mother's things, and to check on the doors and windows again before bed, she saw no activity at all next door except the faintest glow of yellow light emanating from somewhere deep inside the house.

But there were now subtle things that Carolyn noticed as she watched the house. Like how the heavy window shutters seemed permanently closed, never open. And the steel locking bar and heavy padlock she could clearly see on the external basement doors, securing them tightly in place. Surely they were locked from the inside and didn't need the added precaution of a locking bar and padlock on the outside as well? Seemed like overkill to her.

And how the paths and driveway were clean and free of snow and ice. Yet, Carolyn had not seen anyone actually doing it. It was like someone, under the cover of darkness, had secretly shoveled and cleaned the surface.

Carolyn lingered a little a longer, looking at the side of the house before walking farther along the path toward the backyard.

The rear of the house was layered in dark shapes, shadows, and silhouettes. The backyard bare and desolate, except for an unruly wall of thick, overgrown shrubbery and gnarly bracken that screened the rear of the property from the other neighbors at the back.

There were no recent footprints, no signs of shoveled snow. Everything was untouched, dormant, asleep under a pale blanket of snow. It was like no one ever ventured outside.

Carolyn had learned long ago when on surveillance or watching a crowd of people, that what your eyes didn't see, was just as important as what they did see. Something abnormal and out of place often revealed itself by the absence of what you expected to see.

She walked back to the front and did some more stretches, hoping to see a face at a window or hear a door open, someone coming out to say hello or see what the noise was when Carolyn slammed the lid of the trash can down.

But she saw nothing. The house remained cold and silent. Lifeless.

Maybe it was just her imagination. Perhaps reading too much into the bruises she had seen on Alisha's arm.

She jogged up the steps of her own porch and disappeared inside. There were more important things she needed to do. Like taking a shower and changing out of her damp, sweaty clothes.

Hidden eyes watched the woman from next door. Not real eyes, but digital eyes. Pixels. Clear. No distortion. High definition.

A solitary finger slid effortlessly across a flat glass surface. Not just any glass. Aluminosilicate glass. Manufactured in Kentucky then assembled in China.

Where the finger went, the digital eye would swivel and follow. Silent, unobtrusive, hidden from plain sight.

The solitary finger paused, then was joined by a thumb, and the image expanded. The woman from next door opened the trash can and placed something inside. She was looking at the house. This house. The angle of her head. The direction of her eyes. It was unmistakable.

Nosy bitch.

The woman then moved on along the path toward the rear, where another digital camera hidden high under the roofline picked her up again.

The finger tapped the glass and switched views.

She was now standing at the rear, almost peering over the fence into the backyard.

This backyard.

The woman paused, looking around.

Nothing to see.

Then she turned and walked back to the front where the previous camera picked her up again, totally unaware that she was being watched.

She gave one final look at the house before going inside her own house.

For a full two minutes the front camera stayed activated, its lens fixed and focused on the front porch where the woman had just been.

Then the glass screen faded to black and the silent contemplation began.

Is this the start of a problem? Or is it just a nosy neighbor, some skinny bitch with nothing better to do than poke her head over the fence.

Will this new woman next door be a problem? The other one had been fine, the one who lived there with the mother who had just died.

Maybe she's just a friend or relative of the other one, the one who was quiet. Unassuming. Had kept to herself. Was hardly seen but was known around town, a nurse who worked at the hospital. Worked late, all kinds of hours. But never bothered anyone. Certainly hadn't taken a keen interest in the house next door. This house.

But this new woman seemed different. Too curious for her own good.

Time would tell.

And if, in fact, she became a problem, then she would be dealt with.

17

H e wore bright colors today, deliberately chosen. To stand out, to be conspicuous. Not to hide.

All part of the ploy, the charade.

A bright red jacket and an orange backpack. That should do it, he told himself when he selected what he was going to wear today for a nice, leisurely trek through the forest up in the foothills near the base of the Flint Plains.

How stupid they were, the people in town, he thought as he stepped off the snowmobile that came with the cabin he was renting. He had checked over the machine when he had first arrived, making sure it was well maintained, and it was. No doubt the owner of the cabin was as fastidious as he was. That meant that even though he would clean, scrub, and remove any traces of unauthorized use of the property, the owner would still send in their own cleaning crew at the end of the lease.

He pocketed the snowmobile keys before setting off on foot up the incline. The Flint Plains sat majestically in the distance, his mind thinking about the townsfolk again.

He didn't care for them much. Like all the other places he had been, they tended to be simple folk, clueless as to the wider world and almost bovine in their thinking.

He had walked freely among them. Sat in the cafés and diners. Bought supplies from the stores on Main Street and at the local supermarkets. Filled up his car at the local gas station, in broad daylight, while looking straight at the CCTV cameras. Had even smiled at one that was fixed high on the wall in the corner behind the cashier while he paid for the gas and the take-out coffee he had purchased.

Fools.

His face was everywhere. Seen by everyone. There was no hiding for him. Hiding was for people who had something to hide, and he had nothing to hide.

There were, however, a few among them who did show some promise. Maybe they were outsiders, those not caught up in the daily repetitiveness and the personal stagnation that a small town can instill in you.

Alisha Myers was one of those who had shown promise. She had ambition, wanted to better herself, get off the hamster wheel and shake off the shackles.

And for that reason, he had selected her.

That and the fact of what he had witnessed last night, the kissing, two lovers entwined. It gave him a desperate need to wreck and destroy what they considered to be a beautiful thing.

Taking Alisha should be relatively easy. So would keeping her alive for a few days as he had done with the woman from Indiana, the housewife who had cried and begged for her life. She had also told him something that no one else knew, as though confiding in him would somehow convince him to release her.

At first it amused him, when she had told him.

She was the first person he had imprisoned after snatching them. It was an experiment, something different. But then she droned on and on about her husband, her parents and sister, and how much they loved her and would miss her.

It slowly drove him insane listening to her constant drivel. It gave him no joy.

With Alisha, however, he was conflicted.

He wanted to do something different with her; she showed promise. He hadn't made up his mind what though. A double hunt may prove difficult, impractical.

Perhaps something at night, more of a challenge for him. He wanted the challenge. Not that he was bored. Far from it.

Maybe he would take Alisha Myers right in front of everyone's noses. That would be interesting. One minute she was right there. The next, she was gone, plucked right off the street. He liked vanishing acts. It brought more pain and suffering to the family, creating the unthinkable.

He'd taken a schoolgirl off the street once, virtually in front of her parent's house, just to see if he could do it. It was a spot barely a hundred yards from where the school bus dropped her off, a short walk to the front gate of her home. And yet in those hundred yards, she had vanished.

People on the bus saw her get off, but she never made it to her front door.

Beautiful.

People have been known to drown in six inches of water in their bathtub. He wanted to make Alisha Myers vanish six feet from her front door.

Now that would be something.

After thirty minutes of steep uphill hiking, the ground tapered off, and the edge of a forest came into view across a sparse wide stretch of flat snow. His breath was slow, even, not strained nor labored.

He felt like he could never tire, go on without faltering a step, without the need to pause and rest. The harder he pushed himself, the farther he felt he could go. Exhaustion for him was a thing of the past.

He was on the eastern side of the town. Looking back, he could see the houses, the stores, and streets nestled peacefully below among a blanket of white, surrounded by pockets of woodland on three sides.

Everything looked so crisp, so sharp. The rugged outline of the mountains, the trees, every branch, each individual snowflake, every surface bright and clear, all in exquisite detail.

His skin tingled, and he took another deep breath, savoring the richness of the pure mountain air, untainted by the dirty stain of humanity and machinery that existed in the cities.

All his senses felt alive, every hair follicle, every skin cell, his awareness more attuned, heightened, magnified.

He looked around at the sublime landscape and elegant seclusion. He took a moment to absorb the solitude, the isolation, the huge scale of the vista and the vast emptiness.

He listened intently but only heard the moan of the wind as it curved and swept over the rocky outcrops and across the snow, shaving away wispy layers.

Above him, the ominous shape of the Flint Plains loomed closer now on top of a wide, vaulted ridge of iron-hard granite that stretched for nearly three miles. There were multiple paths that led up through the various fissures and crevices that had been carved into the rock fascia by the wind and the rain.

Beyond that, lay the barren plains of ice and snow, thick wooded forests, frozen streams, and vaulted pinnacle rocks. It was a barren, desolate place abundant in wildlife. It was a place much favored by hunters.

He had been there twice before. It would be the place where he would bring Alisha Myers.

It was special. Just like her.

After another hour of solid hiking, he arrived at the location that he had seen the last time he was here, just a few days ago.

He worked fast, threading his way through the forest. Trees heavy with snow eventually thinned, and a natural clearing appeared, a sparse stretch of ground that was about two hundred yards across at its widest point, a tight oval shape, like part of the forest had been torn out.

He quickly ran the circumference, the only sound coming from the crunch of his boots on the snow and the thud of his backpack between his shoulder blades with the solitude of forest all around him.

He did one entire loop in a matter of minutes.

Perfect.

At the far end, he located the trail he knew was there, a well-trod line through the forest that hunters often used. Where it led, he had no idea. It didn't matter.

He returned to the middle of the clearing before heading into the forest again on the right side. Within a few feet, the ground under him became uneven, brittle with broken rock and shards of splintered stone. Perilous to anyone who came this way, especially if they were running. It would be easy here to twist an ankle, even suffer a fracture.

Perfect.

Satisfied, he turned around and backtracked until he entered the clearing again where he made his way to the opposite side. He vanished into the thick wall of trees. Almost immediately the ground fell away sharply down a steep embankment of scattered rocks and fallen trees. At the last moment he grabbed a thin tree trunk, only just managing to stop himself from tumbling face-first down the treacherous slope.

A thick layer of ghostly mist hid the bottom of the gully, masking what lay at the bottom. Carefully he navigated downward, through the carpet of rocks, fallen logs, and slippery frozen earth.

He paused and looked around.

Perfect.

He scrambled back up the steep slope and returned to the middle of the clearing to the spot where he had started.

Pivoting in place, he took one last look around, then smiled.

He had found the place where Alisha Myers was going to die.

18

Carolyn stood back and regarded the Christmas wreath with a critical eye.

It was late afternoon and the last rays of winter sun bathed the front porch.

Not content, she adjusted the wreath slightly then stepped back again.

Still not satisfied, she fiddled with it some more, rotating it clockwise half an inch on the hook on the front door.

Perfect.

With Christmas only a few days away, and despite Carolyn not being in the festive mood, she felt that her mom's house needed some cheering up, some festive spirit to give it a lift. Just a few simple touches, nothing extravagant.

Carolyn had discovered on the Internet a Christmas tree farm on the outskirts of town that sold fresh fir trees and real Christmas wreaths made from twists of noble fir, not plastic.

Carolyn certainly wasn't going to go overboard and cover the house with lights and ribbons, but Jodie agreed as well that the place just needed something.

They had declared a temporary truce to their bickering, for the sake of their dead mother. So Carolyn dragged Jodie along with her, and they drove out to the tree farm. Together they chose the wreath. Their mother would have liked that, them together in this way.

The wreath they had selected was beautifully decorated with hand-tied red bows, pine cones, shiny red bells, and twists of fresh ivy.

They had then spent the afternoon going through household items, choosing who wanted what and packing up the rest into storage boxes to be donated to a local charity store.

Carolyn couldn't put her finger on it. Maybe it was the act of picking out the wreath together or putting up a few simple decorations around the fireplace that had somehow transformed the air between her and Jodie. She could feel the bonds between them strengthen, a rekindling of sisterly ties that they once had. The backdrop of festive decorations had that effect. Kindness toward one another, not bickering and fighting.

It had been a wonderful afternoon together, first sitting next to the fireplace, reminiscing about their childhood, about their mother, the good times only, seeing and remembering her in her best light, not during those cold, dark days when the disease had taken hold of her.

At times, they laughed. At times, tears filled their eyes as they slowly began to reconnect as sisters, not engage as enemies.

Jodie was starting her shift at the hospital at four, so it gave them enough time to get things done and talk. Carolyn didn't mention about her dinner plans with Ritter, preferring to see how it went first before telling her sister.

They then had moved to the kitchen to tackle the packing of old appliances and dinnerware.

"So tell me about the people next door," Carolyn asked. "Do you know them?" Carolyn was assigned to folding and taping shut the boxes while Jodie was perched on a small stepladder, taking down old appliance boxes for sorting.

"To tell you the truth, I've never really seen them," Jodie said, wrinkling her nose at the layer of dust that had gathered above the cupboards. "Why on earth did our mother need three toasters?" she said, passing down a box for Carolyn to wipe clean and place with the other two toasters.

"Beats me," Carolyn said.

"Two women rent it, I believe," Jodie said, reaching for a large box with faded pictures on the side showing a smiling mother, father, son, and daughter huddled around a cube the size of an old portable television set with big dials and brown-pressed metal top and sides. The writing on the box said that it was some new invention called a "microwave" that GE had just released. She handed the box to Carolyn and said, "I heard around town that they're a couple."

Carolyn took the dusty box. "Each to their own, I guess."

Jodie looked down at Carolyn, hand on her hip, trying to recall. "They moved in a few years back. They keep to themselves, which is fine by me."

"So you've never actually seen them?" Carolyn asked. "In the yard or coming home?"

Jodie shook her head. "One of them works in the diner, and I think the other has a home business."

Coming back to the present, Carolyn gave the wreath one final look then glanced at the house next door thinking about the bruising she had seen on Alisha's arm.

Then she went back inside and started getting ready for tonight.

THEY DIDN'T TALK about Carolyn's past job at the FBI. They didn't talk about his current job as a cardiothoracic surgeon at one of Chicago's preeminent hospitals.

They just sat in a booth in the midst of exposed brick walls, hewn woods, soft lighting, and bright red vinyl, ate Italian food and drank red wine and talked about everything except their own careers.

From the history of the town of Willow Falls, to how come the Falcons lost the Super Bowl in 2016. They talked about politics, religion, terrorism, movies they had seen, books they wish they had time to read, vacations they would like to take, and places they would love to visit.

At first, Carolyn was a little distant, cautious, standing on the sidelines waiting and watching the play unfold. Then slowly she entered the field, enjoying Ritter's company and conversation. Being a doctor, she thought initially, was that she was in for an evening of listening to him brag about the vineyards in the Napa Valley he had been to. Or the French restaurants he had dined at. Or the car that he drove, or the countless lives he had saved or prolonged. She had a preconceived notion that's how most doctors spent their time when not saving lives. Perhaps she was being a little too judgmental.

However, much to her surprise, she heard none of that. And as she sat there, Carolyn got the distinct feeling he was someone different, someone that she would like to get to know a lot more.

He was down to earth, considerate, respectful of her. He gave her the wine list and asked her to choose and admitted that he had no idea about such things. It was both refreshing and intriguing to Carolyn. He had a certain charm, a magnetism about him. He wasn't like past men she had dated, not that there were many. Most of them had an agenda based around getting her into bed as fast as they could, that was often thinly disguised as sincere dinner conversation, or lies about being interested in her career, or feigning interest in her aspirations.

As time whittled away, Carolyn forgot where she was, the people around her. He made her feel like it was just the two of them, in a bubble in the restaurant, as waitstaff hustled past them in a blur. Other patrons faded into the background. He spoke to her, not at her. And listened, really listened to her when she spoke.

Carolyn was a master of studying people, spotting the triggers, the subtle clues of lying, or being disingenuous. She saw nothing like this with him.

And not once did his eyes stray, nor was he distracted by another woman passing by. He gave Carolyn his undivided attention.

When the evening concluded, he walked her to her car. Much to Carolyn's surprise, he didn't ask for her cell phone number or if he could see her again.

He only asked her one question as they stood under a street-lamp next to her car, surrounded by gently falling snow. He asked her if he could kiss her, asked her permission. No one had ever asked Carolyn. Usually men presumed, went in for the kill, all clumsy with groping hands.

Confused and pleasantly surprised, she found herself nodding at the request.

So he kissed her, briefly, just a brushing of their lips, nothing too forward, dipping his toes in the water, not plunging in headfirst. No exploratory root canal work or evasive curbside resuscitation.

It was nice, for a change.

He bid her farewell, said he hoped to see her again around town. Then he walked off along the street, and was swallowed up by the swirling darkness.

19

"Best guess?" Finch asked.

"Based solely on just what you just told me? And don't hold me to this. But I believe it's much more," Carolyn replied.

"Much more?"

Carolyn studied the photos on Finch's cell phone again. They were rough, odd angles, not the most revealing. Nothing close-up. Quick and jumbled, some parts out of frame, not measured or methodical. Unhappy snaps of a horrific montage haphazardly taken while the person holding the cell phone wrestled with keeping down their breakfast.

They were sitting in the living room, the fire slowing dying. It was late, close to midnight, and Carolyn was tired. Finch had texted her earlier, insisting that he come by to show her the photos. He needed her help. Wanted her opinion.

The wrong time but the right place now.

He sat on the sofa opposite her, a coffee cup cradled in his hands, a look of quiet expectation on his face as he watched Carolyn scroll through the photos on the screen one more time.

Hardly forensic quality, Carolyn thought. After a moment, she finally spoke. "Care was taken. Time spent. She was staged, or displayed, as you put it. Whoever did this derived a lot of enjoyment from it. Wanted to savor the moment. Make a statement. That's the real part that worries me, and that should worry you, too."

Carolyn paused then zoomed in on the best image out of a bunch of bad ones. The girl looked like a scarecrow. Arms and drooping head. A body held in place with shafts sticking out of flesh. An unnatural sight.

"'Make a statement'?" Finch said.

Carolyn nodded. "Why not bury her? Why not burn her? Why not hide her so no one will ever find her or by the time they do, nature has played its part?"

Finch said nothing for a moment, absorbing what Carolyn was saying.

Carolyn glanced up from the cell-phone screen and watched him as a slow, horrific realization trickled down his face, top to bottom, from his eyes all the way down to his jaw. Warm to cold. Relaxed to rigid. Curiosity to mortal fear.

"She's the first," Finch finally whispered, disbelief in his voice.

"Maybe not the first," Carolyn corrected him. "And perhaps not the last."

Finch rubbed his eyes. He had a throbbing headache, like all of this was too much, wishing that he could just wake up tomorrow, and it was gone, and the only difficult thing he would have to face was a DUI or a traffic citation. "Nothing like this has ever happened around here."

Carolyn handed back the phone. Her own cell phone pinged next to her on the sofa. She picked it up, checked her messages then placed it back down.

"Who is she?" Carolyn asked.

Finch hesitated, unsure if he should tell Carolyn.

"No one else can know about this, Carolyn. Like we agreed. It stays local." Finch paused, expecting an answer. "OK?"

Carolyn nodded. "I promise." She could see the strain on his face. Washed out, drawn, creased with worry lines. Gone was the sparkle from his eyes, the laid-back confidence, the smile from his face, all replaced with uncertainty, dread, and self-doubt. To Carolyn he looked a whole lot older than he did yesterday.

"Her name is Clarissa Mulligan, twenty-two years old. Lived here with her family all her life."

"You need to get help outside the town." Carolyn felt genuine concern for him. "You only have three police officers here, and you're asking for my help."

Finch gave a thin smile. "I've suggested to Bates to put a call in with Des Moines. We've logged the incident as required, but he's not keen to let it go outside the town. Sees it as a sign of weakness, asking for help."

"Do you think you can handle this kind of thing alone?" Carolyn asked.

"We need to," Finch replied. "Step up, that is. Willow Falls is a close-knit community. Everyone knows everyone. Someone must know something. Must have seen something."

Carolyn wanted to say something, but she thought otherwise. She didn't want to storm in like she was telling Finch what to do, how to conduct the early stages of an investigation. He was competent at doing that, making the initial inquiries, talking to friends and family of the victim, establishing her personality, her habits, routine, where she went, who she hung out with. Once that was established, then the investigation would be expanded from there, like ripples in a pond.

Yet Carolyn couldn't help thinking about the senseless stupidity of moving the body, of contaminating the scene, of not gathering as much forensic evidence first before trashing everything. Some vital clues could have been gathered. Now they were lost forever.

"I'll start with the hunters, the locals first," Finch said. "Ask around who has a crossbow. Maybe check out the gun stores, see if anyone has come in lately, bought supplies. There's a large store on the outskirts of town."

As Carolyn listened to Finch rattling off standard, textbook police procedure, she got the distinct feeling that none of this would matter.

Dark thoughts started to form in her head. The photos, the staging, how the killer had arranged her, pinning her to a tree. It revealed something far more sinister. This was someone who was meticulous, not impulsive. Careful, not sloppy. Not prone to leaving clues behind, no trail to be followed, unless deliberately set for that purpose.

From the cover of the porch, Carolyn watched as Finch drove off. She looked around at the darkened street. Snow was gently falling. Lights glowed deep from within a few of the houses across the street, but apart from that, everything was dark, silent, closed up for the night.

She turned to go back inside then stopped and glanced at the house next door. To her surprise, some of the shutters had been pulled back. A deep warm yellow glow came from somewhere within as it had the night before. She wasn't the only person up at this hour. As she stood watching the house, her mind drifted back to Alisha, wondering if she was home right now. She then thought about the photos that Finch had shown her.

Carolyn looked around at the darkened street, at the houses, thought of the people inside, tucked up warm and safe, oblivious to the shadows encroaching around them and the possibility of a monster lurking there, somewhere, just on the periphery.

Everything looked tranquil, peaceful. Carolyn shivered as she turned and went back inside to the warmth and safety of the house.

In the living room, Carolyn picked up her cell phone again and slumped back down on the sofa. She thumbed the screen to her personal inbox, found the latest arrival, and drafted a forwarding message. Checking that everything was attached, she hit send.

The images of the dead girl took ten seconds to travel the thousand miles east of where she sat by the fireplace in Iowa, before landing in someone else's inbox connected to a computer on a desk in a building in a small town in Prince William County, Virginia. The building sat on the west bank, overlooking the Potomac River, fifty feet away from the invisible watery line that separated Virginia on one side, from Maryland on the opposite bank.

Carolyn checked her watch. Virginia was one hour ahead of Iowa. The person who occupied the desk that the computer sat on was an early riser, had been for as long as Carolyn had known him. No matter what time she called him, day or night, he always seemed to be awake and in the lab working.

Carolyn left the porch light on for Jodie, turned her cell phone notifications to silent and went upstairs to bed. She needed a good night's sleep.

Tomorrow wasn't going to be a typical day in Willow Falls.

20

Cloudland Canyon State Park sits on the western edge of Lookout Mountain, deep in the upper corner of Northwest Georgia.

Rugged and beautiful, it is a pristine landscape of deep water-carved canyons, hidden caves, cascading waterfalls, and dense woodland teeming with wildlife.

The park, with its breathtaking views, is dotted with numerous hiking trails and mountain-bike tracks and is a popular destination during the summer months for backpackers, day hikers, families, and tourists all wanting to experience one of the largest scenic parks in the state.

But in winter, it can be a cold, muddy, desolate place of mist-shrouded escarpments, treacherous rocks, and dark, mysterious caves.

The perfect place to hide a body.

Aaron Wood stood at the entrance of one such cave, at the base of a deep canyon, the ground strewn with misshapen rocks and river pebbles. A ghostly haze of mist ebbed and flowed high above him, long, white bony fingers that caressed the treetops and rocky outcrops. The spray of a nearby waterfall coated everything in a permanent watery sheen, including him.

Despite being tired, hungry, and chilled to the bone, he was utterly focused on the task at hand.

Aaron Wood was in his mid-thirties, with owlish features, long limbs and hands like a world-class pianist, long and delicate, able to forage, poke, and search the narrowest of crevices, thinnest of cracks, and the deepest of spaces in his relentless quest for forensic evidence. His colleagues often said that to watch Wood at his desk on his computer keyboard was to watch Johann Sebastian Bach belt out a feverish rendition of his famous Piano Partita No. 2 in C Minor. At times, Wood appeared to make love to the computer keys. Other times, it was like each individual key was responsible for every childhood failure he had ever suffered.

His usually floppy dark hair, which he constantly had to sweep out of his eyes, was now a sad and soggy pelt plastered to his forehead.

Wood's large peering hazel eyes were magnified by the thick, black-framed spectacles he wore, that made him look like Brains from *Thunderbirds*. He was constantly wiping the thick lenses of his glasses from all the mist and condensation in the canyon. Slightly goofy, plenty smart, truly gifted, and at times, resembling a mad young scientist, Wood, during his short tenure, had tracked down more serial killers than anyone else in the history of the bureau.

Apart from his job, Wood only had two other addictions: Death Wish coffee, the highest caffeine coffee commercially available and caffeine-rich energy drinks that he kept in a fully stocked mini fridge under his desk in his office. It was a dangerous combination and probably the main reason why he slept so little.

He detested social media in all its forms and only had a cell phone at the behest of the bureau, so he could be reached all hours of the day and night.

He hated going into the field, much preferring to remain ensconced in the comfort and familiarity of his office deep within the FBI labs in Virginia. But the discovery of this particular body held a special interest for him.

A brief initial examination of the body in the cold, dark confines of the cave confirmed to Wood that the trek six hundred miles southwest from Virginia was worthwhile. It left him with no doubt that he would be adding another red pin to the large map that occupied nearly an entire wall of his office. There were ten other red pins on the map. The one from Dade County today would be the eleventh. Eleven pins that ran west to east like an ant trail, starting out at Santa Rosa, New Mexico, before weaving its way east across Northern Texas, through Oklahoma, dipping down slightly into Arkansas, then on to Tennessee before heading downward again and entering the northwestern corner of Georgia to the precise location where Wood was now standing.

Evil was heading east, leaving a trail of misery and carnage in its wake.

The question that was on Wood's mind was, will the trail turn north, toward his home state of Virginia? Or would the line of red pins continue south and on through Georgia then deep into Florida?

One thing was for certain: the trail of red pins on his map would not stop unless he stopped it. The small box of red pins that sat in the top drawer of his desk was still half full.

Optimism.

Wood peeled off his gloves, pocketed them, and began rubbing his fingers and hands and stamping his feet, trying to shake off the bone-numbing chill that lingered over him after he had climbed out of the wet, dark hole.

A hundred feet inside the cave entrance, buried in nothing but darkness and frigid still air was the subject of Wood's attention and the attention of law enforcement officials from Trenton City Police Department, Dade County sheriff's office, FBI Atlanta field office, and the Dade County coroner's office.

Occasionally an echo of voices or a shimmer of a flashlight

beam would emit from the yawning dark opening as the team inside huddled, scraped, brushed, measured, and gazed in silent contemplation. For the past hour they had been carefully gathering evidence inside and around the cave entrance.

It would be a few hours more until they would bring her out.

Covered and wrapped protectively for transport, they would treat her with the care, the respect, and dignity that she and her family deserved, before taking her somewhere else. Some place warm, with bright lights and cold stainless steel tables and rows of sharp instruments designed to slice and cut and saw and break open.

But until they carried her gently from the dark, unsavory hole in the side of the canyon, where she had been found, she would remain in situ, to be studied, examined, photographed, her body keenly read like an anatomical storybook of youthful flesh now ripped and torn.

Later, other chapters would be added to her story. Her childhood years. Where she grew up. What she did as a young girl, then her life as a college student. Only at the very end of the story would the final chapters be added. An epilogue of understanding. Of making sense of the senseless. Of how she died and why she died. The latter was incomprehensible. Because no one deserved to die how she had.

To Aaron Wood, everybody he had ever encountered was a mournful story of death. A story that had started out with such joy and hope, only to end abruptly, suddenly, and brutally in a horrific, unexpected, and sad ending.

Premeditated death didn't faze him. It inspired him, drove him to find meaning, to allocate motive, to read the story, albeit backward, a morbid tale told in reverse. And to make it as complete as he could before he read it forward to the courts, to the loved ones, to those left behind, to anyone who wanted to know or listen or understand.

Wood walked away from the cave entrance and checked his cell phone. He had been working inside the cave for almost six hours without a break, and this was the first time he had ventured out today. There was certainly no cell signal inside the cave, and standing outside but still deep in the canyon, the signal was dismal at best. He looked up at the steep, jagged walls around him and the pale sky beyond. The sun was not yet high enough to breach the lip of the canyon and bring some warmth and light down to the cold and dark start to his day.

A few messages landed on his cell, and he thumbed the screen, taking note of one particular message that was sent in the early hours of this morning.

Interesting.

He opened up the attached images as he walked farther away from the mouth of the cave. Pulling back the wet hood of his all-weather jacket, he went off in search of a boulder or comfortable rock to sit on for some privacy. His joints ached from all the kneeling and crouching in the cave.

The images took forever to download on his cell, slowly revealing themselves from top to bottom with excruciating slowness until finally they were all complete.

Wood leaned against a large boulder and studied the images, then read the message from the sender.

He smiled.

Ignoring what time it was, he called the sender's private number, only to discover that there was no cell phone service now. He was too deep, yet the text and images had managed to somehow scrape over the edge of the canyon walls and reach him below.

Pushing off the boulder, Wood panned his cell phone around side to side then up to the sky, pivoting in place, searching the heavens.

Nothing.

"Damn it," he muttered. Wood looked around.

Carefully, he climbed a large boulder the size of a midsize

sedan. The boulder had few footholds, and his feet slipped on the wet, slimy surface despite his thick rubber-soled boots.

He needed to make the call. He needed to tell her.

Wood reached the top of the boulder and held his cell phone up again. Thankfully, a faint signal bar appeared on the screen.

Wood redialed.

This time the call went through, and he waited patiently until it was answered.

A groggy voice came on the line.

"Ryder, it's Aaron Wood." He could hear a sudden commotion on the other end of the line. Sheets and blankets being thrown off. Then a thud of something hard being knocked, maybe a knee or shin. Then someone cursing loudly.

"I'm here," Carolyn replied. "You got my message?" Her voice came down the line garbled in places, echoey, patchy, like she was a million miles away on the surface of the moon and not in Iowa on planet Earth.

"And the images, too," Wood replied. "I'm in Georgia at the moment. Dade County. On scene."

"What the hell is in Dade County?" Carolyn asked.

"Death and mayhem, Ryder. What else."

"Did you get all the images?" Carolyn asked impatiently. "Have you had a chance to take a—" Carolyn's voice cut off before it echoed back in short stutters and broken sentences.

Wood pivoted around on the top of the boulder, hoping to improve the signal.

"Where did you get these?" Wood yelled into the cell phone, not bothering with formalities of how she was and where she'd been.

The line went dead.

"Damn it!" Wood wanted to talk to her and he hated texting.

He dialed the number again, praying it would connect. He needed to let her know.

Carolyn answered on the first ring. "I'm here."

"I'm in a canyon. Crap cell phone signal. Where did you get the photos? Tell me exactly where you are." Wood fired off questions in rapid succession, unsure as to how long the signal would last.

"Willow Falls, Iowa," Carolyn yelled back. "Police found"—her voice cut out again then came back—"body of a girl—the forest."

Wood pressed the cell phone harder to his ear and plugged his other ear with his finger, his face scrunched in concentration. He could call her back in a few hours from now, when he was out of the canyon, back at the police station, or the motel where he was staying.

But the photos Carolyn had sent him begged his immediate attention.

"Ryder!" he yelled into the phone.

"Yes, I'm still here."

"You need to tell me where you found her, the girl in the photos."

Carolyn's voice was too garbled now, a mash of detached words, syllables, and digital squelches.

"I've seen this before—" was all that Wood could get out of his mouth before the call died completely.

21

I've seen this before.

Carolyn stared at the cell phone in her hand, positive that Aaron Wood had uttered those exact words.

I've seen this before.

She quickly hit redial, but got nothing.

She tried again.

Nothing.

I'm in a canyon. Crap cell phone signal.

Carolyn jumped out of bed. Her laptop sat on the small desk charging, its lid closed. She sat down, opened it up, and woke it.

She brought up a search browser then typed in: "woman killed with crossbow." The search brought up an unrelated case in the United Kingdom where a pregnant mother of three was shot with a crossbow by her husband while she was doing the dishes in the kitchen. The unborn child survived but the mother later died.

Unperturbed, Carolyn next searched "Crossbow killer" and came up with a case back in August 2016 where a man in Toronto, after "a heated argument with his mother," strangled her with a piece of nylon rope and then killed his two brothers in their family home using a crossbow. The man was sentenced to life in prison.

Carolyn stared at the laptop screen in frustration. She was accustomed to having at her disposal the full resources of every law enforcement department and agency, across all jurisdictions, local, state and federal, at her fingertips. She once could tap into any crime database, including the foreign crime databases. Now, like everyone else, she had to rely on public search engines and onscreen results clogged with sponsored ads ranging from cheap pizzas to young big-breasted Russian supermodels who were just dying to meet you.

She tried in vain for another thirty minutes until she gave up and went downstairs, feeling alone and a little despondent. You tend not to miss something until it is gone. And her past life was well and truly gone.

Entering the kitchen, she ignored the waiting packing boxes, went straight to the coffeemaker, filled it up, and switched it on. Maybe caffeine would make her feel slightly better. It always did.

On the countertop was a note from Jodie, thanking her for the take-out pasta dish Carolyn had ordered at the restaurant and brought home for her last night that she had left in the fridge. Carolyn smiled at the happy-face doodle Jodie had done. Despite everything that had happened, the arguments, the disagreements, she was still her sister, and Carolyn needed what little family she had left now.

Not waiting for the coffeemaker to finish its cycle, Carolyn grabbed a large, ceramic white coffee mug from the overhead cabinet and poured herself a cup.

Barefoot and wearing just drawstring pajama bottoms and a sweatshirt, she padded to the bay window at the front of the house. It had a cushioned window bench with a mass of throw pillows. It was the perfect spot for Carolyn to curl up and just gaze out the window while she drank her coffee.

As a child she would read for hours in this exact spot, old Trixie Belden "girl detective" mysteries that her mother had once read as a child herself and had kept for her daughters. Despite the books

being aimed at a previous generation of young, impressionable girls
before her own time, Carolyn took to them and read them vora-
ciously. Maybe they were the reason why she joined the FBI. To
solve mysteries. To catch bad people.

Then high school and Carolyn stopped reading altogether.
Reading textbooks, lecture notes, incident reports, and police
records didn't count as reading. Not for pleasure anyway.

Everything seemed much simpler back then, Carolyn thought
as she looked out the window, the view bathed in glorious sunshine
and framed in brilliant white. The trees, the sky, and the snow were
clear, bright, highlighted in infinite detail. Closing her eyes for a
moment, Carolyn basked in the warm rays that slanted through the
window and across her face.

Her brief moment of cozy, warm bliss was interrupted by a ping
from her cell phone.

Carolyn opened her eyes and looked at the screen.

Can't talk now. Skype tonight. 9:00 pm. AW.

Carolyn replied, "OK."

She had so many questions. But she would have to wait until
tonight to get them answered. Wood had never mastered the art of
rapid texting, and she knew reading texts frustrated him. He liked
to hear words, detailed descriptions, not short bursts of abbre-
viations.

Meanwhile, Carolyn needed a plan of attack. She needed to get
organized. She didn't have the resources available to her she once
had, but surely there were things she could do before she spoke to
Aaron Wood later this evening. She was isolated, on her own. Yet
she wasn't the type of person to just sit around. In her head, a
mental checklist was already beginning to form.

Finishing her coffee, Carolyn went upstairs, showered, and
changed into warm outdoor clothing. She checked in on Jodie, who
was buried under a pile of blankets in her bed sound asleep.

By the time she backed out of the driveway and was driving into town, she knew one thing at the top of her list that she had to do immediately.

HE RAN HARD, the pace steady but relentless through ankle-deep snow.

Unsatisfied, he increased his pace and glanced at his fitness tracker again. A little heart symbol flashed steadily on the screen, only registering a slight increase in beats per minute, but his speed had increased by 20 percent.

He was pleased.

He'd been running for five miles now. The screen showed the duration and altitude.

The forest ahead rushed toward him. He vaulted over a fallen log and entered the cool, shadowy interior, following a narrow running trail through the trees.

Nimble and agile, he skirted past tall, thin pine trees, around slippery rocks that poked up through the thin layer of snow. He checked his tracker again then pushed himself a little harder, falling into the steady cadence, enjoying the solitude and stillness of the forest around him.

His eyes scanned ahead, the forest empty. The only sound was his shallow, light breaths and the regular beat of his footfalls on the soft, damp ground.

He ran for another mile through the forest, the trees whipping past.

The ground changed and began to slope upward. He kept going at the same pace, not slowing, testing his resolve, his determination. His strides effortless and unwavering.

After twenty minutes uphill, the ground leveled, and he found himself on a flat grade where the hillside had been cut out, maybe for a road that had never been completed.

He finally eased his pace to a slow jog then stopped completely.

The air was cold and dusty with snow. Flakes settled on his head and shoulders.

He checked his pulse and took a moment to study the digital readouts, watching as the flashing heart symbol began to gradually slow. He was breaking new ground, reaching then smashing his best efforts.

Before, he could run five miles at the same pace before fatigue set in. Now, he was up to eight miles, well above his previous threshold. The results were beyond his wildest expectations. He couldn't believe how well his body had adapted. He knew he was pushing the boundaries, what he was capable of. Everything improved when he pushed himself a little harder, demanded a little more from his muscles, his body accepting the challenge then surpassing it. Human physiology is truly an amazing thing, he thought, as he turned and looked around.

He eased out of the straps of the heavy canvas backpack, and from a side pocket he took out a water bottle and drank.

Securing the water bottle again, he squatted down and unzipped the top of the backpack. Carefully, he took out the rocks, forty pounds deadweight in total, and placed them on the ground, stacking them into a small pyramid, marking that he was here.

He stood up, shrugged the backpack on again, and headed back down the hillside, enjoying the drug-like euphoria he felt surging through his veins.

He was invincible. Untouchable.

And he was just getting started.

22

T he glowing sign loomed up fast. Sharp bright red neon
cutting through a thin haze of white.

Carolyn's brain recognized it immediately, her heart
leapt as only she could understand.

Salvation.

Carolyn hit the brakes, the car skewed to the side, and came to a
tire-grinding halt in a mush of snow and ice, almost missing the
entrance to the parking lot.

She looked up through the windshield again just to confirm
that it wasn't a mirage she had seen. This was certainly a new addition to the town. She smiled and turned into the parking lot.

It had been a slow day for Gus McKenner. Maybe it was the
weather that was keeping people indoors. He had a few regulars in
the new indoor range out the back, die-hard guys that loved to
shoot no matter what time of day or whatever season.

Gus was busying himself stacking shelves behind the counter
with a new delivery of ammunition when a woman walked through
the front door. She wasn't a local; he could tell. Young, late twenties,
nice tight jeans, winter boots, black insulated jacket with a hood

with faux-fur trim and a smile on her face like a kid in a candy store.

Good. That's how he liked them when they came in, all wide eyed and in awe. Despite Willow Falls being a small town, Gus kept enough of a range of guns, ammunition, and various rifles to satisfy everyone from the new gun owner who was looking for something simple to protect their family to the professional hunter.

He also prided himself on having the largest selection of assault rifles on sale in the state, too. They took up almost an entire wall, racked like pool cues, red Christmas tinsel draped over them. A big sign above them read "Ho, Ho, Bang!" with a picture of Santa underneath, climbing through a window, face hood on, empty sack over one shoulder, with the warning, "Stop unwanted home invasions this Christmas. Give someone you love an assault rifle!"

Gus always had a sharp eye and a clear memory of anyone who walked into his store. It was the nature of his business. This woman had a confident aura about her. Her eyes took in everything: him, where he was standing, the long line of glass cabinets at the front counter that held handguns, the racking on the walls behind that held various carbines, the tactical clothing, some special equipment, too.

Gus climbed down off the stepladder as he watched the woman. She moved like she knew what she was looking for. She went straight to the glass cabinets where an impressive array of handguns were displayed on glass shelves, little string labels showing the price. The woman moved with slow contemplation, dragging her fingers across the top of the glass displays as she went.

Gus was tempted to steer her toward the women's section of smaller handguns better suited for her small hands and delicate fingers. Maybe a Luger or Glock 23. They were a good, first-owner choice for women. All reasonably priced. Not a great sale for Gus but a sale nonetheless.

The woman stopped in front of a particular display cabinet,

bent down, then craned her neck sideways at Gus who was hovering to one side. "The Sig Sauer P226. Can I take a look?"

Gus swiftly extracted his key fob in one smooth, practiced motion, unlocked the display, and slid open the back glass.

The woman pointed her finger down through the glass top. "No, not that one. That one there. Yes, that one. The Legion RX."

Gus raised an eyebrow and retrieved the gun. Unrolling a neoprene work mat, he laid the handgun on top on the cabinet. It was an enhanced P226. Night sights, flat trigger for consistent pull, with a short reset.

This was going to be a good day, after all, Gus thought, as the woman lifted the gun. "Just got that beauty in," he lied. Truth was he'd had the gun for nearly six months. Most people around here couldn't afford it because of all the enhancements. It was a lot of money tied up in one handgun.

Gus watched in amazement as the woman broke down the gun into its component pieces in under three seconds. "That's a day-night optic on the slide," Gus pointed out, "for low-light shooting."

"I know," the woman said.

"Flat trigger for smoother pull. Short trigger reset so you can get the next shot off faster."

"I know," the woman repeated as she scrutinized the components, looking for any traces of firing residue. It was clean as a whistle.

Gus was getting the distinct feeling the woman knew more about the gun and how to shoot than he did.

She reassembled the gun like she'd done it a thousand times before. Like all Sigs, it came ready to shoot out of the box, but she still would take it home, break it down again, clean, and lubricate it to her requirements. It was a ritual, stamping her mark of ownership on the new weapon, like a dog marking a tree.

She handed the gun back. "I'll take it."

Gus smiled. He was willing to haggle, offer a discount, but kept his mouth shut.

"And five hundred rounds, 150 grain, if you've got them."

"Oh, I've got them." Gus smiled. "A slightly heavier round, better stopping power."

That's the plan, the woman thought.

Ka-ching! Gus could almost hear the sound of the cash register ringing in his head.

"And a gun-cleaning kit," the woman added. The gun came with two standard ten-round magazines but she also purchased two seventeen-capacity extended mags.

Never to miss an opportunity to upsell, Gus thought he'd push his good fortune with her. "What about a nice holster? Or maybe a proper gun case?"

The woman gazed around the store. She already had a holster. "I'm good." Her reply short and definite. "Can I use the range?"

"Sure," Gus replied eagerly. "No charge." The woman had just dropped close to two grand in five minutes in his store. "I'll give you a free two-day pass."

The woman nodded and handed across her driver's license and a Utah-issued permit to carry.

Gus rang up the sale, placed the gun in its plastic retail case, then filled out the paper work. Moments later, he handed back her credentials. "You're all good to go."

The woman took the gun and two boxes of ammunition. "I'll come back for the rest when I'm done."

"No problem," Gus replied. "Eyes and ears are next to the range door at the rear of the store." And he handed her two paper targets.

Carolyn helped herself to protective glasses and earmuffs before pushing open the door and entering the indoor shooting range. She was so used to having her FBI-issued gun on her at all times that she never saw the need to own another during the last ten years. That was until now.

There were fifteen lanes, and five of them were occupied by other shooters, all men, who all seemed to know each other.

Heads turned, eyes lingered, and expressions changed as

Carolyn walked in. There were a few shrugs, a few snickers, and a few sly smiles.

Carolyn casually walked to an empty stall, distancing herself from the others.

She placed the case and ammunition on the bench in front, popped the latches and took out the Sig Sauer. She carefully loaded up each magazine then set them aside. She dry fired the gun a few times.

She glanced down the line at the other lanes, where the other shooters were. Their targets were positioned mainly at around the twenty-yard mark Carolyn noted: no groupings, just a random scatter of holes punched in paper. More shots rang out, all rapid.

Carolyn smiled.

It was only a matter of time before someone sauntered over to see who Carolyn was.

"Nice gun you got there." The man was tall, lanky. Carolyn glanced over her shoulder at him but said nothing. He was leaning against her cubicle wall, hands tucked under his armpits, cocky smirk on his face, his eyes shifting, not hiding the fact that he seemed to be more interested in her butt than her shooting prowess.

From other lanes, the shooting had stopped, necks craned, heads turned, faces appeared around cubicle walls.

Her unwelcome visitor had an audience. Dogs hunt in packs.

"Seems like a big gun for such a pretty young lady like you."

With her back still turned, Carolyn rolled her eyes and ignored him.

"I've got a smaller gun in my bag that you might be better suited with. I myself have a big gun." The man smirked.

A few chuckles came from the other lanes.

"I'm good," Carolyn replied. She clipped her silhouette target to the overhead hanging mount, pressed the button and sent it out to the fifty-yard marker, more than double the distance the other shooters had set their targets at.

"Hell, lady, you'll never hit—"

"Eyes and ears," Carolyn snapped over her shoulder as she slapped a magazine into the gun, slid smoothly into her stance, not waiting to see if the know-it-all had followed her advice.

Carolyn shut everything else out of her mind. A face appeared in her vision, a mental image she conjured up. She overlaid the face on the target, replacing the blank outline of a head with the detailed face of someone she knew, a face burned forever in her memory: her unforgotten nemesis.

The face of a man called Sam Pritchard.

She peeled off ten rounds in smooth succession, emptying the entire magazine in under five seconds. She did a speed reload, ejecting the empty magazine and slamming in a fresh one before the spent one had even hit the ground.

She did it again.

Then again.

And again, until all four magazines were empty. A collection of spent hot brass casings pooled around her feet, the acrid smell of gun powder thick in the air. She pressed the retrieval button and waited as the target slid back toward her.

The man behind her looked on in disbelief, his eyes wide, his jaw almost touching the floor.

The paper target came to a sudden halt on the rail in front of Carolyn, teetering slightly back and forth.

She took a moment to regard her handiwork. The middle of the head on the target was shredded, tattered, gone, a gaping, fist-sized hole, all shots dead center in the middle of the face.

"Holy cow, lady...where did you learn to shoot like that?" the man behind her stuttered.

Carolyn gave a wry smile, pleased with herself. She hadn't lost her touch. "The FBI," she replied without turning.

The man quickly scuttled back to his own shooting lane, to his friends, his head down, eyes averted.

When she was done, Carolyn stopped by the store counter again on the way out.

A few more customers had come in out of the cold, but Gus instantly floated toward her, smelling another sale.

She pointed to a rack behind the counter. "Have you got a medium in that size? For a woman?"

Gus' face lit up. "Well, let me just see, lady." Quick fingers ran through the sizes on the heavy plastic garment hangers. "Here you go." Gus laid the vest on the counter. "This is all quality. Don't be fooled either. It'll do the job."

Carolyn checked the vest, testing the seams, the compartments, and the stitching. She tried it on. The fit was snug and true. "I'll take this, too."

Gus beamed as he went to the cash register whistling "Jingle Bells."

Christmas had definitely come early for him.

23

After the shooting range Carolyn went on foot, spent a few hours walking around the town and the outskirts, familiarizing herself with the streets, the layout of the place, old memories coming back, and some new ones forming.

She grabbed lunch at a coffee shop before heading home, where she spent a few hours sorting and packing more household items. Jodie had gone out, so Carolyn had the house to herself.

Next, she spent the rest of the afternoon on the internet. She wanted to glean some local knowledge about the hunting season and who the local hunters were. She didn't want to ask Gus McKenner, the gun store owner. It would draw too much attention and she would seem like a cop. So Carolyn opted for a more casual, low-key approach in a more relaxed atmosphere. So what better place to extract this information than at a local bar aptly named Whitetails, that she had found while browsing internet sites about deer hunting in Iowa, and on crossbows.

Apart from the name of the bar being a dead giveaway, Carolyn knew that she had chosen the right place when she slowly drove through the small parking lot that evening. The majority of vehicles were pickups, most of which displayed various tailgate and rear-window decals proclaiming the joys of hunting and undying loyalty to various gun manufacturers.

She couldn't find a spot, so she drove out then parked across the street, down a side street.

"YOU SHOULD TALK TO BEAU HODGES," Laura Bishop replied. As expected, the bar was full. The evening crowd consisted mainly of locals and hunters who drifted in for Happy Hour.

"Who's that?" Carolyn asked. "Who's Beau Hodges?" The air was filled with the sound of grown men drinking and too much testosterone.

Laura Bishop, the owner, was behind the bar. "He's a local hunter. Been here all his life. Longer than me, that's for sure. Big and powerful, a bear of a man. But he has a gentle way about him." Laura wiped the bar surface with a rag as she spoke. "Came in here a few nights ago. They all did, a group of them. Kind of like a ritual they have after they go hunting up in the hills. There's a place called the Flint Plains. Most of the hunters around here reckon it's the best place for deer. Do you hunt?"

Carolyn shook her head. She was tempted to say that if hunting down serial killers, murderers, and terrorists qualified, then yes, she hunted.

"Neither do I." Laura noticed Carolyn's empty bottle and swapped it out for a new, icy-cold one. Laura continued. "Ironic, isn't it? Can't stand the sight of blood. Plus, I don't understand how you can shoot. You know? Sneak up on an animal and pop its brains out. Hardly seems fair. Unsporting like."

Carolyn said nothing. The population of the town had seemed to swell today. A lot of hunters had arrived, and she had to respect their choice. Laura owned the only drinking establishment in Willow Falls that seemed to cater to the hunters during the season so she could say what the hell she liked. During hunting season

Carolyn could see that a place like this would do a roaring trade. So maybe Laura had to bite her tongue, keep her views to herself if she wanted her cash register to keep ringing.

Laura explained that off season, the decor of the bar would revert back to a more family oriented place; the deer heads would come down off the walls, and the menu would change slightly. During the football preseason, helmets and jerseys of the Vikings, the Packers, and the University of Iowa Hawkeyes would adorn the walls as well. She was a shrewd businesswoman who realized early that a drinking establishment should change and adapt to the seasons if it was going to survive and make money for the entire year and not just rely on the hunting season alone.

"Anyway," Laura said, "Beau and his party came in, just a handful of guys, that's all. They sat in their usual booth over there." Laura pointed to an empty booth in the corner. On the brick wall above the booth glowered a Busch Beer neon sign, with the trademark deer head and antlers. How fitting, Carolyn thought.

"They come in after every hunting trip, you know, to celebrate, you know."

It amused Carolyn how Laura kept saying "You know?" as though Carolyn should know, be up to date with the local town knowledge and customs.

However, Carolyn didn't know. These small-town nuances were all foreign to her. "And?" Carolyn said, wishing Laura would get to the point. She liked the woman and could tell Laura was the kind of person who enjoyed dragging out every piece of town gossip. Carolyn had come to the right place.

Laura flipped the rag and kept wiping. "They're usually loud and full of testosterone, you know, plenty of back slapping, toasting each other, comparing the kills they made and the ones they missed. All that big-dick stuff. But not this time."

Carolyn cocked her head, almost willing the answer out of Laura with her facial expression alone.

"This time they were very subdued. Kept to themselves, sat in their booth, hunched down over their beers. No celebrations, all glum-like, as though they were drinking their sorrows away, you know."

"Maybe they had no luck on the hunting trip." Carolyn took a swig of her beer, enjoying the soothing spread of alcohol through her body. It was putting her in a good mood, and she desperately wanted to relax and feel good for a change compared to how she'd felt in the last few days.

She was slowly starting to warm up to the town and its people. "Maybe they came back empty handed. No heads to mount on the walls." Carolyn glanced up at the huge deer head that was mounted on the wall behind the bar. Glassy dead eyes stared down at her, the deer's expression caught in between the split-second thoughts of "what was that noise?" and then "Oh fuck!"

Laura shook her head. "No, that isn't it. They're seasoned hunters. Beau's one of the best. They never come back empty handed."

Carolyn could feel a tingling sensation in her gut and it wasn't from the alcohol now. She placed the beer slowly down on the bar and leaned forward. "So what was it, then?" she asked.

"Billy Dale, one of the group, a really experienced hunter, too, came over to the bar to order another round. I asked him what's up, you know, like you guys look like you're drinking at a funeral, I told him."

Carolyn raised an eyebrow.

"Sorry," Laura said sheepishly. "No offense intended," she said, referring to the recent funeral of Louise Ryder. Carolyn had already explained who she was and why Laura hadn't seen her in the bar before.

"None taken." Carolyn smiled. "Go on."

"Well, Billy wasn't his usual self. For starters, he didn't once stare at my cleavage or ask me out on a date. He does that every time I see him in the bar. It's like a running joke. He's been wanting to get into my pants since the fifth grade."

Carolyn laughed. Laura had ample cleavage. Brighter and more glaring—from the tight, low-cut top she wore—than any of the neon beer signs that covered the walls of the bar.

"Well, Billy just said that for the entire three days they were up there hunting, they didn't see a single deer. Not one. Zip."

"I take it, for this time of year, that's unusual?" Carolyn offered. Not being a hunter she guessed from Laura's tone and the expression on her face that this was a strange event for these parts. Maybe deer migrate like birds do, Carolyn thought. She really had no idea.

"Hold on, hon." Laura lifted a finger toward Carolyn then drifted sideways along the bar to serve another customer.

A few moments later, she sauntered back. "Now what was I saying?" Laura did a show of thinking.

As tempting as it was for Carolyn to give Laura the "wind-up" signal with her hand, she refrained.

"That's right, Billy Dale." Laura shrugged and started polishing a large beer stein she'd grabbed off a rack. "Billy said it had never happened before. Usually they'll hunt deer, maybe turkey if they get lazy. But this time there was nothing," she said thoughtfully, recalling the conversation she'd had with Billy. "He said it was like the forest had completely emptied itself. Like something had spooked all the wildlife away."

Iowa had a rich spread of game to hunt. From turkey to geese, bobcat, rabbit, squirrel, and partridge. The main prize, however, was whitetail deer. A decent-sized buck was what every hunter wanted.

"Could it have been a bear?" Carolyn said. It seemed to make sense. She would certainly run into the next state if she came up close and personal with a bear in the forest.

Laura put down the beer stein and picked up another to polish. "That's what I thought, but that's how ignorant I am." She laughed.

Now Carolyn felt really stupid.

"Billy said there are no bears in Iowa."

"Then what?" Carolyn was growing impatient.

Laura shrugged. "Don't know. But whatever it was, it had gotten them all spooked, if you ask me."

"Really? Grown men spooked?" Carolyn doubted this.

Laura nodded. "And if you've ever seen Beau Hodges, you'd know he isn't the kind of guy who gets spooked. At all."

Sitting back on the stool, Carolyn studied Laura for a moment. Even though the woman was somewhat theatrical in how she spoke, her face had grown deadly serious.

"And let me tell you." Laura leaned forward to Carolyn. "If it was a bear, and a damn big one at that, I'd still put my money on Beau Hodges winning that fight."

OUTSIDE THE BAR it was cold and clear. Carolyn pulled up the hood of her jacket as she walked along the footpath, thinking about what Laura had said. The night sky was a dark blue velvet with a smattering of stars.

She needed to talk to Tyler Finch again. He was doing a good job of suppressing the story, the discovery of the girl in the forest. No one around town seemed to know. Laura Bishop certainly would have mentioned it if she knew. Seemed like her bar was the hub of the town through which local information, truth or fiction, flowed.

Maybe it was small-town pride. Maybe Finch didn't want word getting out that a hunter had killed someone. It would destroy the hunting season this year for sure. But it was a still a killing. Townsfolk had a right to know, to be warned, and take precautions if what Carolyn was thinking was true, that it wasn't some jealous boyfriend or one-off incident.

It was brutal, harsh, and sadistic. It was still possible that it could have been a hunter who'd found out his girlfriend was cheating. He went crazy, killed her for it. But why display the body as it had been? Why go through all the trouble to leave her where she would be found, on display?

The traffic was light, just a few cars crawling down the main street. She crossed the street, then followed the line of streetlamps, passing in and out of pools of light.

She turned the corner then stopped dead in her tracks.

She didn't know why she stopped. She just did.

The side street was deserted, empty parking lots, the stores closed for the evening, bags of trash heaped along the footpath. She could see her car parked fifty yards away in the gloom, the street poorly lit, off the main drag.

Then Carolyn looked up toward the row of buildings on the opposite side, at the roofline. Just instinct. An itching feeling of unease. Something cerebral, perhaps, years of observing, watching, and training that made her look up at that exact moment.

There, against the backdrop of dark sky, she saw a shape, an outline of a person, head and shoulders jutting up above the edge of the roof.

24

C arolyn didn't move, just stared up at the person.

The person didn't move either, just stared down at her. Faceless, just a silhouette.

She could feel eyes on her, boring into her, menacing, unnatural, and horrible.

Then the shape whipped away fast, disappeared below the roofline, and was gone.

Carolyn ran, on compulsion, not toward her car, but the doorway of the building across the street, the same building where the person had been watching her from. Probably watched her arrive, followed her to the bar, then went back and took up position on the rooftop waiting for her to return to her car.

Sweeping aside the edge of her jacket, Carolyn drew her handgun from its holster as she ran, one deft motion, not stopping, a practiced on-the-run move instilled from a career she no longer had. Doing things now she was no longer supposed to be doing.

Maybe it was the reassurance of having her gun on her that made her do what she did next. Maybe it was just blind stupidity, an overreaction. It could have been a homeless person, a vagrant hiding up there, built a home for themselves out of cardboard boxes and whatever else they could forage. A hermit living among rooftop water tanks, exhaust vents, and air-conditioning units.

Yet Carolyn's gut was telling her otherwise.

The exterior door was flimsy, the hinges rusted, cheap plywood installed by a cheap landlord. Prone to breaking under forceful human momentum or unstoppable female determination. Its destruction helped along by a heavy snow boot as well.

The door burst open. Carolyn paused in the doorway, eyes adapting. Search and assess. Gun up, elbows tight, sweeping left, right, up and down, pointing at dark shadows, at lighter shadows, at anything that looked remotely human. Blood and breath surging.

She felt good. Real good. Back in control. Kicking in doors and pulling out her gun. She regretted not buying a gun flashlight when she purchased the handgun. It would have slid nicely under the rail below the barrel. Then again it would have made her an easy target as well.

The space in front was all dark layers, corners, and edges. Her pupils adjusting, the red dot of her night sight buzzing around in front of her like an angry firefly.

A tight corridor peeled off to the right, a narrow steep staircase leading up on her left, the bottom step just three feet in from the entrance doorway. From the outside she guessed the building was three stories, maybe four. Old, run down, uncared for, offices and a warehouse still being used, its heyday long gone.

Above her head she heard the sound of rapid footsteps running across the floor, echoing then fading, left to right on a diagonal, incredibly fast. Either the mother of all rats or the person who was watching her.

Carolyn tore up the staircase, the wooden treads groaned in protest, threatening to collapse inward.

On the first landing she stopped and twisted like a tank turret, arms up, gun in front, straining to listen. The air smelled moldy, musty. Old paper, powdery and inky. There was carpet on the floor, dirty and grimy, compacted from years of heavy foot traffic, worn and torn.

Another sound, above again, far corner, next floor up. She tried to focus where it was coming from in the darkness. Something metallic. A window or steel door sliding.

She tore up the next flight of stairs.

The building was two stories only, not three. It looked taller from the outside.

She paused at the top, could feel the depth of the darkness, wide, cavernous, and empty stretch away in front of her. The floor was wood, rough and splintered, prone to whispers and warnings.

She walked slowly forward, panning the gun left and right, her eyes trying to distinguish the ghostly grays and impenetrable blacks.

Everything on this level had been stripped out leaving behind bare walls with chunks torn out, brick and mortar crumbling. She navigated past large concrete columns, then another metallic sound came from above.

Carolyn looked up at the ceiling.

There were no more levels. She had to get up to the roof. No doubt the person had come down off the roof, was heading down to street level before realizing she was in the building rushing up to meet them. They were back up on the rooftop again.

She searched for an exterior wall, found it with her fingers then traced it back to the rear of the building. Internal stairs and fire escapes typically were located at the rear. She found a narrow concrete stairwell, a fire escape, a tight concrete column. The dusty and gritty stairs went down and up. Angling her gun up she entered the stairwell and began to climb, pivoting her aim upward, twisting her body around the bends as she went. The walls and steps were blanched white, moonlight seeped in through grimy windows. She kept going, slow and steady, gun up, her short, shallow breaths echoed in the tight, hollow space.

She cleared the next corner and saw the set of stairs stretch away in front of her, a shape leaning against the wall up ahead, partially hidden in the gloom, a person looking down at her.

"Stop!" she yelled, her voice bouncing up and back off the walls.

Her trigger finger tightened, then stopped.

Her heart was pounding in her eardrums, blood pulsing in her head and throbbing up her neck.

It was a big old fire extinguisher on a bracket bolted to the wall.

Carolyn settled again, moved around the object, then up to the final landing.

She found herself in a small concrete cube, a steel ladder bolted against the wall led up to a closed hatch.

Holding the gun one handed, Carolyn climbed the first rung, then the second, then the third. Reaching the top she paused, pressed her shoulder against the hatch door, and listened.

No sound.

Five-second window. Do something or do nothing and call it quits.

She counted down then pushed upward slightly. The hatch moved an inch, then another. No lock. No latch.

Cold, crisp air slid into her face.

She pointed the gun through the gap, sideways, ran it along the edge, pointing and peeking at the rooftop through the slit.

Nothing obvious.

Now or never. She'd come too far to hesitate.

She pushed the hatch all the way back until it locked into place and stepped up and out into the open.

Dark sky. Roof ventilators and boxy air-conditioning units. Hissing and grinding. Gas escaping. Vapor spiraling upward into the night.

The rooftop was a slush of dirty snow and ice, slick and wet, over a thick layer of blacktop, and surrounded on each side by similar height rooftops of other buildings.

Carolyn looked around, but it was deserted.

Slowly, she walked around, orienting herself, figuring out north and south, listening for street sounds. She walked to the closest edge and looked down.

Wrong side. An alleyway.

She walked to the opposite side and looked down and saw her car parked on the street.

Out of the corner of her eye, to her right, something grew out of the roof, dark and ominous, then shifted fast, fleeting.

Carolyn took off after it, no words needed. No warning. They were fleeing. She was chasing. No explanation required.

The person was fast, concealed in a hood and jacket, black on black.

The rear edge of the rooftop came into view, a thin line, emptiness and cold air beyond.

Carolyn ran, gun in hand, eyes focused on the bobbing shape in front of her, not gaining, losing ground. She slipped, cursed, regathered, and pummeled onward.

The edge of the roof tilted upward then ended.

The person leapt, arms and legs flailing, arcing out across the void: cold hard concrete far below. She watched stunned as they bridged the gap between the two buildings effortlessly, like it was nothing, before landing softly on the other side, catlike, on the roof of the opposite building.

Reaching the edge, Carolyn skidded and pulled herself back, kicking out a layer of dirty snow and ice over the roof edge and into the gap. It fell, then exploded in a puff of white on the concrete below.

The person turned and walked back to the edge of the other building and looked at Carolyn.

Carolyn stared at them.

The person's face was hidden under the cowl of a hood. They cocked their head expectantly at Carolyn, a hidden smile, as if to say, *Come on! Follow me. Jump across. See if you have the courage to do it.*

It must have been at least eighteen feet across to the other side. Maybe twenty. Below was a wide alleyway and a few dumpsters.

Carolyn brought her gun up, took aim, overlaying the red dot of her night sight over the outline of the person on the other side. Center mass. Can't miss. Flesh and blood, not paper.

The person saw the gun, stepped forward, right up to the edge of the roof, and spread their arms, willing her to take the shot, goading her.

Time stopped. Carolyn tensed. Then she lowered her gun.

The person waited. Waited some more. No shot came.

They dropped their arms, almost disappointed, then turned and walked away.

Not even a backward glance.

25

Carolyn stood her ground, and watched as the person slowly faded into the darkness, the shadows claiming them.

They were out of her reach. She was beaten. Defeated.

And that angered her. She didn't like being beaten, especially when she was giving chase. Then again she wasn't just going to shoot someone for no good reason. They posed no mortal threat to her yet they still ran.

Guilty of something.

They had gotten the better of me. The words twisted and turned in her head.

Not willing to relent, Carolyn spun around and ran back to the access hatch. She needed to get to the ground fast. Preferably not by diving off the side of the building and headfirst into the concrete below.

On the next floor down, she ran to the window, holstered her gun, opened the window, and climbed out onto the metal fire escape platform. Her boots clanged and banged as she hurtled down the rungs, three at a time, the metal handrail cold but offering a rough tactile grip as she spiraled downward.

She emerged into the alleyway she had seen from above, a narrow vertical shaft, tall walls on both sides, a rectangle wedge of sky above. Ignoring caution, she ran across the slick concrete, patchy with slushy snow and sodden trash.

She saw a steel dumpster, a jumble of solid wood crates next to it.

One, two, three jumps up the crates and she was on top of the dumpster, her boots making hollow clangs on the dented lid. She leapt up, caught the bottom rung of a retracted fire ladder bolted to the wall, and landed, pulling it toward her. It unfurled with a grating sound that echoed off the high walls of the alleyway.

"Hey!" Someone shouted at her.

At the end of the alley a man with a flashlight was walking toward her. A security guard or a cop. It didn't matter. She didn't care.

Pissed off and determined, Carolyn began to climb with smooth, fast movements. The steel ladder shook but held. Upward she went, determined to catch the person.

"Hey!" Another shout from below. This time closer, beneath her. A beam of light cut across her legs, up her back then up over her arms, lighting the way. Then more commands from below that Carolyn ignored, her mind focused on getting up fast.

The top of the ladder looped over the lip of the roof, and Carolyn swung, thankfully, between the two grab rails and landed with a thud on the roof.

This building seemed bigger, longer, wider compared to the other. It doglegged around to the right. The rooftop was dotted with squat metal fixtures that sucked fresh air in and spat stale air out. Plenty of hard edges and shadows to hide among.

She drew her gun again.

Pipes hissed, fan blades whirred, white wisps drifted upward from vents and heating stacks. She moved with slow, deliberate steps through a ghostly landscape of walkways, platforms, ladders, guardrails, and boxy condenser units that pumped heated air out into the cold darkness.

Sounds drifted up from the street below. The chatter and laughter of people, car horns, the general murmur of evening shopping.

But up here on the rooftop, it was another world.

Cold. Dark. Isolated.

Something clanged ahead, metal on metal, and Carolyn stopped and aimed into the distance.

The door of an access enclosure was ajar, swinging aimlessly, banging against the jamb. The lock was broken, twisted, and wrenched out together with the door handle itself. Pieces of it lay on the floor. Carolyn nudged the door open farther with the barrel of her gun, a darkened stairwell beyond. Then the sound of another door slamming echoed up from below, far below. Followed by the sound of feet, fading fast.

Carolyn raced down the stairs, one hand on the tubular rail, the other holding her gun aimed downward. With her heart thumping hard, she spun through the turns. There were no other doors until she had gone down two complete flights of stairs. Then the space opened up into another gloomy, cavernous interior with high-vaulted ceilings, ornate moldings and columns, warped and broken floorboards, old heavy drapes. Slits of pale light seeped in from outside through grimy windows.

Glass shattered up ahead, maybe forty feet away.

Carolyn ran on, angling toward the sound that seemed to change direction as she tried to chase it down. It curved left then turned to the right, fading then coming back strong.

Her vision jostled and jerked as she stumbled on, across the wide-open space, past rows of broken chairs and furniture, ripped away from the floor and piled high. An old theater, perhaps, its last performance decades ago.

She reached a narrow corridor and ducked inside, certain the

footsteps had come from this direction. It led to a connecting passageway, an internal juncture that fed into another building. Onward
Carolyn went, totally lost, unsure where she was, a maze of passage-
ways, open spaces, tight corridors. She entered another stairwell
filled with dim light that seeped down from a skylight high above.
She was certain now she was in yet another building, taller, bigger.

Up or down?

She craned her neck down over the rail. The stairs spiraled
downward before fading in a pit of blackness. She glanced up, her
head dizzy with vertigo and saw stairs stretching upward—then a
head, a shape, peeking over the rail back down at her.

The head pulled back and was gone.

Carolyn sprinted up the stairs, two at a time. Around and
around she went, fast feet over creaking old wooden treads, hand
on the rail pulling her up and around. The sound of fleeing footsteps came echoing down to her.

A door slammed, and she ducked through a fire door, following
the sound.

She kept running through a maze of corridors and tight stairs,
up and down, in which direction she had no idea. She just kept
going, chasing the sounds, trying to catch an elusive ghost.

Lurching, stumbling, swaying, cutting corners, more darkened
rooms, empty and musty. Past broken walls, shattered windows,
gaping holes, all melded into one continuous blur as Carolyn
ran on.

Shadows. Silhouettes. Outlines. Dull shapes loomed then
dissolved. Splinters of light. Pools of nothingness. The source
of the sound still in front of her, just out of reach, taunting
her. It was as though the person was deliberately slowing
down if she fell too far behind, then speeding up if she got too
close.

The ground suddenly changed under her feet. The floor
sounded hollow, soft, empty. She slowed but not soon enough.

The floor suddenly opened up, a yawning chasm. Old, rotten

boards collapsed under her, falling away with a thunderous crash, and Carolyn plunged into the abyss.

She reached out, grasped what she could as she fell.

She was dangling from the ceiling of the room below, holding on to part of the floor of the room above, caught between two worlds, an entire section of the floor gone.

Her fingers clung to a wooden floor joist that protruded out of the gaping hole, rotten and splintered.

Carolyn was strong and fit, but she still needed two sets of fingers, hands, and arms to save her. So dropping the gun was a simple automatic reaction just to survive. It tumbled away and landed somewhere far below.

Years of dampness, no sunlight, and poor ventilation in this section of the building had run its course. The section of floor she had stepped on was no longer a floor at all. It had been reduced to a twisted pile of rubble forty feet below her. A long way down.

She could feel wooden fibers coming away from her fingers, separating, fraying, loose, and brittle. She desperately hung on, suspended in the air, legs kicking, lungs and arms straining. She looked down and saw the faint outline of crumbled flooring, like an unlit bonfire, piled up high under her, rising to a deadly pinnacle with her hovering directly over its twisted apex.

Her fingers slipped, particles coming away in a dusty haze, into her face and eyes. She coughed and strained, tears in her eyes.

She could feel the joist move, bend, wood fibers stressing and straining like her own muscles and joints. The rotten joist was going to break any moment. Carolyn could feel it. It bent and shuddered some more.

If she tried to swing her legs up, or pull up with her arms, the joist could break. She needed to reach and grab another piece of the floor, a stronger piece if she could. She looked above her, along the torn edge. There was no girder, nothing metal she could switch her grip to. It was all fragile and decaying lumber.

She could feel her fingers slip again. She had no choice, she couldn't hold on forever. She had to pull herself up and out. She had to try or die trying.

She gritted her teeth and pulled herself slowly up.

The joist moved, bent some more. She screamed and lost her grip with one hand. A lump of ceiling plaster came away, leaving a dusty trail as it tumbled past her shoulder before she heard it smash somewhere below.

She pictured herself falling then hitting the pile of debris below, on its apex. Bones breaking. Splintered lengths of lumber pointing upward from the pile, impaling her.

The wooden joist finally snapped, came away in her bloody hand, and she fell toward the ground below.

Then her body jolted, snapped tight to a sudden stop. Something was clamped on her wrist, vice-like. A hand. Fingers wrapped around her wrist, not big, but powerful. Not crushing but firm. Steadfast.

She began to rise, not fall. Her wrist was tethered to something that was pulling her aloft like a crane: smooth, effortless, certain.

First her head cleared the hole. Then her shoulders, chest, waist, then legs, and finally her feet. She rose, like a dead person from a grave, above the level of the floor then gently to one side.

Her eyes were shut tight with fear, that involuntary reflex we do when certain death rushes toward us. We don't want to see it, so we turn away, close our eyes, and wait for the impact or the strike or the shot.

Carolyn fell back on the floor, onto a solid, firm section not the brittle, rotten area she had fallen through. She rolled onto her side, her gasping breath sending clouds of floor dust billowing.

She felt her wrist release, the pressure come off.

She rolled onto her back, her eyes still closed, praying that it wasn't a dream, not the nightmare where you feel yourself falling only to jolt awake in bed.

But it wasn't a nightmare. It was real.

She waited a full two minutes until her breath settled and her mind cleared before opening her eyes.

She was alone. Just her and the hole in the floor.

No sounds. No footsteps.

She staggered to her feet and looked at her wrist, almost expecting a mark, a bruise, but her skin was intact, unblemished. Her fingers were sticky and wet with blood where cruel splinters and nails had sliced into her as she had tried to hold on for dear life.

She was alive. Should have been dead. Her injuries were superficial, could be patched up with a simple first-aid kit.

She looked around some more, staying well clear of the hole and the broken crust around it.

She was standing on solid ground. Had been lifted up then placed safely there.

By someone.

26

There were twenty-eight high-resolution images in total, together with crime scene reports from several case files and investigation notes.

He was taking a huge risk sending Carolyn the actual photos even if she was a former FBI agent. She was now considered an outsider, no matter how fast she had risen or how bright her star had shone while she worked there.

It was unauthorized and totally off the grid. It was a risk Wood was willing to take. He felt that it was his personal responsibility.

Wood considered her still to be a colleague and would always be willing to help her or offer his advice if required.

He was completely surprised, however, when Carolyn reached out to him, sent him the photos that Tyler Finch had taken.

After she had regained her wits, using her cell phone light, she had retrieved her handgun from the base of the twisted pile of the collapsed floor. The building, an old theater, had been condemned and was waiting for a demolition order. Carolyn then drove home, bleeding fingers bound up, and sat in the shower for thirty minutes, until her aches and pains slowly washed away down the drain.

She then sat in front of the fire, wrapped in a warm blanket, with her laptop and tried to make sense of what had happened. Someone had been watching her, following her. Maybe it was Finch, poking around, keeping tabs on her. So, then, why run?

Her laptop sang a familiar melody, breaking Carolyn from her thoughts.

"I thought you had retired from all this, and were attending your mother's funeral?" Wood started the Skype call saying, along with his condolences once again. Wood was one of just a handful of people who Carolyn had confided in within the FBI. She had explained to him why she was leaving the bureau when she had made the decision.

"I am," she replied. "I didn't go looking for this. It found me."

On her laptop screen was a montage of harsh reds, mayhem, and a blackness where no light could ever reach. Carolyn had all the images he had sent her up at once on the screen, overlaid on each other like a spread deck of cards. In one corner of the screen the face of Aaron Wood stared back at her. He was sitting eight hundred miles away in a small darkened motel room in Trenton, Georgia, just off I-59 and within a ten-minute drive from the entrance of the Cloudland Canyon State Park.

"So tell me, Aaron, what am I looking at," Carolyn asked. In Willow Falls it was just after eight in the evening.

Aaron Wood had worked with Carolyn on several cases in the past. She always could rely on him for succinct, direct, and unbiased analysis of any crime scene. "These are just a sample of the photos taken from the last three cases. All in Indiana last winter." Wood also had multiple windows open on his laptop computer and was filtering through various police reports, images, and his own personal file notes.

Carolyn had gone through all the images. "Three victims, all women, all killed using a crossbow, all of them nailed to a tree with the bolts."

Wood nodded. "Not nailed. They were shot at close range so

that the crossbow bolts pinned them to the tree trunk. He used three to four bolts to hold them in place in most cases."

"At close range?" Carolyn wanted confirmation.

"Each shaft penetrated their body and into the tree trunk beyond, to a depth of nearly a third of the overall length, effectively supporting their weight."

"Were they already dead when they were mounted to the tree?" Carolyn asked. The grisly images reminded Carolyn of the mounted deer heads she had seen in Whitetails.

"As far as we can tell, most of them were still alive. They had other entry wounds on their bodies, different angles, and the bolts for those wounds had been removed. Those wounds were located in the shoulder, leg, or arm regions mainly."

"It would cause a lot of damage I imagine, but I can't see that," Carolyn said. "Hunting arrows are designed to go in one way only. You try and pull one out and you'll pull out a mass of everything else." Looking at the images, Carolyn could not imagine the pain these women suffered, skewered to a tree, slowly dying.

"Correct," Wood said. "All the broadheads he used have snap-open blades. In flight they are retracted. That means they travel faster, more aerodynamic. After they penetrate flesh the blades are designed to spring open, burrowing and slicing into the victim, not dissimilar to the way a hollow-point bullet fragments on entry, doing a massive amount of internal damage as it continues to expand in the body. But..." Wood paused. No one outside of the FBI knew this information. Certain details about how the victims died were kept out of the press. Such key details were then used to vet the hundreds of crank calls that typically came in by any and every one claiming that they were the killer.

"What, Aaron?" Carolyn asked. She knew he was holding back.

"This doesn't go past this conversation," Wood replied.

"You have my word, Aaron."

"He cut out the bolts, removed the first set. Hence, the initial entry wounds in the shoulder, arm, or thigh region."

Carolyn frowned, not understanding what Wood was trying to tell her.

"We found at least one, sometimes two initial entry wounds, where the victims had been initially shot." Wood continued, sensing Carolyn's confusion. "But the bolts had been carefully extracted, cut out cleanly so as to inflict minimal damage."

Shoulder, leg, arms. The words came back to Carolyn, what Wood had said about the other wounds they had found on the bodies. Not superficial wounds but not fatal either. An arrow in the arm, the leg, or shoulder would stop or at least slow down someone as they ran for their life. He didn't want to kill them first. That would come later, in a much slower and horrible way, to be crucified to a tree and left to die.

"Bastard," Carolyn muttered. He was hunting them, like animals. The first shot was designed not to kill them, just to injure, to bring them down like a deer.

"He's mounting them, Carolyn, putting them on display. He doesn't want the first shot to ruin the vision that he has in his mind of what he is trying to do."

Carolyn said, "So he cuts out the first bolt, carefully, so they don't die of shock or bleed out. Then he holds them up against a tree and takes his time to arrange them, then shoots them again, using the crossbow almost like he's stapling a sign to a telegraph pole."

"He's an artist, Carolyn," Wood explained. "He takes the time to hang his work carefully on a gallery wall. He then stands back to admire his work, I imagine, watches them slowly die before his eyes. That's where the real power comes from. Living art where the life is slowly draining out of the subject. He wants to see the gradual transition between life and death, watch their breathing slow then finally stop. Watch them discolor, watch as their life essence literally fades away in front of him."

The photos Finch had taken of the girl he had found were almost identical to the photos of the past cases Wood had sent

Carolyn. These were human beings not animals. Flesh and blood, beating hearts, mothers, daughters, sisters. Carolyn wasn't prone to anger, to let her emotions get the better of her while she was involved in gruesome cases. But she had never seen anything like this before, hunting humans like animals for sport.

"And you have no leads? No suspects, for this...person?"

"We call him Robin Hood," Wood said. "Three years, ten victims, all across the Midwestern states: Wisconsin, Indiana, Minnesota, and maybe now, Iowa."

Robin Hood. Carolyn let the name sink in. The heroic outlaw bandit who robbed from the rich and gave to the poor. But in this case they were dealing with a sadistic serial killer not some good Samaritan. A vicious, evil, and demented person who hunted women.

"He's seasonal," Wood went on to explain. "Usually December to March the bodies were discovered."

A winter serial killer, Carolyn thought. So what does he do during the other months of the year? Why just in winter?

Wood continued, "He is very thorough, careful. No DNA, no trace evidence at all. Nothing left behind at any of the crime scenes."

"He chooses winter because it's cold," Carolyn said. "He can cover up, hide his face under a hood or thick collar and scarf and wouldn't look out of place walking around. Can pose as a hunter in the woods, carrying his crossbow. Nothing out of the ordinary."

"That's what we think," Wood replied.

"What else, Aaron, can you tell me about him?" Carolyn knew that a profile of the killer had been worked up by the FBI. It would have been constantly refined and distilled as new victims were found. But the complete lack of evidence worried her. A killer displaying his victims wants other people to appreciate his work. But he wasn't self-indulgent enough as to leave clues, deliberate or otherwise. Most serial killers enjoy the limelight, the publicity, the notoriety. They seek the recognition, want to outsmart the police, and sometimes at crime scenes they leave clues to taunt and provoke.

"It's all just speculation at the moment, Carolyn," Wood said. He spent the next few minutes describing the profile they had developed so far. Male, highly educated, mid-thirties to late forties. Maybe a hunter, definitely skilled with a crossbow, perhaps other weapons as well. Organized, structured, disciplined. Someone who posed as a hunter, blended in during the season, dressed and looked the part. That made the task of finding him more difficult given the huge number of hunters that descend on the locations he had been during the years.

Carolyn shuffled through the pictures again then suddenly stopped. She noticed something common with them all, how they were posed.

"He lifts them?" Carolyn asked. "Off the ground?"

"You noticed that, too?" Aaron replied.

In every photo the victim was lifted high enough off the ground so that their feet were left dangling. It was just a few inches, but it still required a huge amount of strength.

"I don't know how he does it," Wood explained, "but it would require him to lift them up with one arm, off the ground, hold them in place against the tree trunk, then shoot the first bolt to secure them in place with his other hand. All the shafts were almost perfectly horizontal, no upward angle."

"Is there a second person?" Carolyn said. "An accomplice. Two hunters, perhaps. One lifts them against the tree while the other shoots them with the crossbow?"

"Maybe," Wood replied. "It's not unheard off. But serial killer duos are extremely rare."

There was no other explanation, Carolyn thought. Unless he carried some kind of collapsible ladder or hunting stand with him. It would help support the victim's weight, would make it easier to hold them upright and in place while he shot and pinned them. But why bother? Because it was important to him that he displayed them correctly, using the tree trunk as the wall to hang his macabre piece of artwork.

"So he must be extremely strong, powerful, and tall as well," Carolyn added.

"Correct. We're looking for someone well over six feet, powerfully built," Wood said. "Knows how to hunt."

Carolyn remembered what Laura Bishop has said about Beau Hodges, how she had described him. "Big and powerful, a bear of a man", she had said.

Carolyn decided that she definitely needed to talk to Beau Hodges.

27

Mary Jane Westerman lived in the Benton Township area of Monroe County, Indiana, and worked at Indiana University in Bloomington as a student services assistant.

Married for two years, her husband, Trey Holden, was an EMT specialist at a local hospital.

After working the night shift, Trey Holden came home just after 7:00 a.m. to find their three-bedroom home empty.

Mary Jane was nowhere to be found.

The last known contact Trey Holden had with his wife was at 11:33 p.m. the previous evening when she messaged him on Facebook to say that she was going to bed, that she loved him, and she'd see him when he got home in the morning.

Whenever Trey worked the night shift, Mary Jane always got up early to greet him and prepare breakfast so that they could spend that brief intersection of time together before they both sailed off in alternate directions for the day: Trey to bed and Mary Jane to work.

But standing in the empty kitchen, Trey could feel a slow-building concern in the pit of his stomach as he looked around. The house was silent. The coffeemaker had been filled the night before by Mary Jane as she usually did. She would get up before her husband got home and turn on the machine and greet him with a freshly brewed cup.

But the machine was switched off, the cord still unplugged and wrapped neatly around its base.

The frying pan still hung from the utensil rail over the stove, and the kitchen counter was clean and bare.

As he looked around, Trey thought his wife had slept in.

As a secondary thought, Trey wondered why Zeus, the couple's full-grown, ninety-pound, male German Shepherd hadn't greeted him at the front door, tail wagging with an expectant look on its face. It was a daily ritual where Trey would give Zeus a jerky stick, often behind his wife's back while she busied herself cooking eggs and bacon.

Known for its strong, loyal, and watchful temperament, Trey had deliberately chosen this particular breed of dog for his wife, insisting that she not be alone, especially when he was working the night shift.

But the dog was nowhere to be found either.

Trey looked in the single-car garage and saw Mary Jane's ten-year-old Hyundai sedan still parked there, the hood cold to the touch.

Upstairs Trey found their bedroom door slightly ajar. His wife never shut the bedroom door, preferring the dog to roam around the house at night if needed before returning to the foot of their bed where the dog protectively slept.

The bed appeared to have been slept in. The covers had been pulled back on Mary Jane's side. Trey felt the first stings of alarm when he saw his wife's cell phone, sitting on the nightstand on her side of the bed next to the lamp. His wife never went anywhere, even to the bathroom, without her cell phone. It was her one and only vice.

The mattress was cold.

Trey then checked all the upstairs windows and found them locked securely.

It was only when he went back downstairs that he discovered the patio sliding door had been forced open. The latch was bent back, and the glass door had been slid back in place.

Trey called 911. It was 7:26 a.m.

CAROLYN PAUSED FOR A MOMENT, leaned back from the laptop screen, stretched, then rubbed her eyes before continuing to read the police report Aaron Wood had sent her as part of the bundle.

The first two police officers on the scene failed to locate Mary Jane Westerman after a thorough search of the house. A subsequent door-to-door canvas of the neighborhood revealed nothing as to her whereabouts. Neighbors the previous evening reported hearing nothing unusual, not even the dog barking, which it did from time to time at night. In addition, there were no reported disturbances in the entire neighborhood.

It was typically a quiet street in a small town where nothing usually happened.

The police, and Trey Holden, were baffled. Mary Jane's purse was in a bowl on the kitchen table. Her credit cards and driver's license were still inside.

They checked upstairs again. All her clothes were still in the bedroom drawers and closet, and no suitcases or overnight bags seemed missing.

Then police did locate the couple's dog, however.

The German Shepherd was stuffed into a small closet in the garage. Its neck had been broken and one side of its skull had been smashed in.

The search for Mary Jane Westerman then escalated into a full-scale abduction investigation.

Police evidence technicians soon arrived on scene and combed the entire house, including the front and backyard. They found no DNA or trace evidence other than those of Mary Jane Westerman, Trey Holden, and the dog, Zeus. The house was considered a crime scene given that the patio door had been forced, but there were no fingerprints on the glass.

The Indiana State police laboratory division was called in, and they performed another forensic sweep of the house. But given the total lack of crime scene biology, other than that of the occupants, they could not add anything to the mystery.

Three days later, the police still had no clues or leads as to the whereabouts of Mary Jane Westerman.

In the absence of hard evidence, the speculation began.

It was suggested that perhaps an old boyfriend had contacted her, and she decided to rekindle a past relationship. Perhaps Mary Jane was having an affair? Email records, cell phone records and social media accounts were checked and revealed nothing untoward.

Her work colleagues were interviewed. Her parents, who lived in Illinois, were interviewed by local police, and Trey Holden was interviewed several times by the Bloomington PD.

Mary Jane Westerman was an exemplary staff member, her coworkers would attest. She was a loving, but independent young woman, who adored her husband, loved their dog, dressed conservatively and wore comfortable shoes. She wasn't prone to office gossip and was not regarded as the flirtatious type. In fact, she recently told her family and friends that she and Trey intended to start a family next spring. So excited at the possibility of being a mother, and as a precursor, Mary Jane was watching what she ate, was exercising more, and had given up all alcohol.

Then on the fifth day since her disappearance, they found the body of Mary Jane Westerman, in Yellowwood State Forest, some eleven miles from her home.

An old retired couple were walking the self-guided Jackson

Creek hiking trail in the state forest. It was a cold but clear wintry morning with only a light dusting of snow on the ground.

With a keen interest in local flora and fauna and outdoor hiking, the elderly couple told police that they had walked many of the trails at Yellowwood before. The parking lot was empty when they arrived just after 8:00 a.m., and during the hike they saw no one else on the trail. They said that this wasn't unusual given this time of year and the early morning start. They preferred having the trails to themselves.

The 1.5 mile trail starts out at the Jackson Creek parking lot, a well-trodden path that cuts east over the cold clear waters of the creek itself at the northern tip of Yellowwood Lake. From there it's a gentle meandering loop westward through undulating marsh, pine forest, and central hardwoods.

It was only when they stopped at one of the twenty-three station markers along the trail to read about the deciduous forest that stretched up the hillside in front of them, did they notice something propped up against one of the tree trunks in the distance. At first they thought it was perhaps another hiker, who had come off the trail to relieve themselves and was resting against a tree before starting back down again.

Closer inspection revealed that it was the body of a young woman. She had been skewered to the trunk of a large oak tree and she was quite dead.

After calling 911, the elderly couple hurriedly made their way back to the parking lot where they waited for the police to arrive.

Autopsy tests later would reveal, after taking into account the seasonally low temperatures and other localized weather events, that Mary Jane Westerman had been dead for up to twenty-four hours.

The county coroner would also conclude that there was no singular fatal wound. Pathology would show that she was still alive when she was pinned to the tree. It was estimated that for up to twelve hours she had clung to life during the night when the temperature had plummeted.

The question still remained unanswered. Where was Mary Jane Westerman kept for the four days prior to her death and who had kept her alive?

The autopsy had also revealed that she was six weeks pregnant, a condition that she had kept secret from her husband. Concerned that she may take some time to fall pregnant, Mary Jane Westerman stopped taking her birth control pills in the previous couple of months. She only shared the joyous news with her older sister who lived in Memphis who had three kids of her own.

Trey Holden was devastated, to say the least.

Two people had been murdered.

Carolyn leaned back on her small, uncomfortable swivel chair and closed her eyes, just to escape the horrors for a moment. But all she could see was the young, listless body of Mary Jane Westerman, a carousel of images scrolling left to right across the inside of her closed eyelids.

She looked so peaceful. Almost asleep as she hung from the oak tree, every detail of her face clear and rendered in infinite detail in Carolyn's mind. Her skin, pale and bloodless, almost translucent. Cold blue lips. Drooping head, chin touching her chest, eyes closed, the tips of her eyelashes lightly frosted. Vertical dark icicles of hair jutting down the sides of her face and jaw, a wreath of snow and ice crystals crowning her head.

Carolyn opened her eyes and saw the images of Mary Jane Westerman on her laptop screen. She closed the lid and rubbed her eyes, then pressed the tight and tired muscles at the back of her neck, stretched her limbs, then lifted her butt cheeks one at a time off the chair to relieve the numbness.

She looked at her watch, amazed at the time. She was so immersed in the case of Mary Jane Westerman that midnight had passed. After she had ended her video call with Aaron Wood, Carolyn had moved upstairs to the sanctuary of her bedroom and had shut the door. She wanted to review another of the case files Wood had sent her before calling it a night.

On the small desk, next to her open laptop was the cold, dark shape of her handgun, seventeen-capacity extended magazine in it, a round in the chamber.

She went downstairs and refilled the coffeemaker. While it began brewing a fresh batch, Carolyn went around the entire house again, checking the doors and windows for the third time, her gun in her hand. As she moved about the house, her thoughts went back to Mary Jane Westerman, who had been left to die, pinned to a tree in a cold, dark, and lonely place.

Jodie didn't own a gun despite Carolyn trying to convince her over the years, especially given that she lived alone since her divorce. Maybe Carolyn would get her to look at some of the crime scene photos that were on the screen of her laptop upstairs. That might finally convince her.

No matter what precautions people take in securing their home, anyone evil enough and determined enough can always find a way to get inside.

Mary Jane Westerman didn't own a gun. Instead she had a large, full-grown and loyal German Shepherd.

The veterinary report showed that the dog wasn't baited or poisoned. The killer must have known she had a large, potentially vicious dog. Yet it didn't seem to concern them.

And as Carolyn stood next to the coffeemaker waiting for it to finish, one question played on her thoughts: who in their right mind would enter a house knowing the owners had a huge guard dog?

28

B eau Hodges was a seasoned hunter who lived on acreage on the outskirts of town, up near the foothills and in clear sight of the start of the forest ranges and the majestic view of the Flint Plains beyond.

Carolyn drove, following the directions Laura had given her, lines and scribble hastily written on the back of a beer coaster from the bar, affixed to the sun visor, that she would flip down every so often to check her progress to where "X" marked the spot.

The morning sky, God's heaven, was painted in a pale eggshell blue that stretched all the way to a crescent moon.

In the distance, like an ocean liner on the flat horizon, a big four-wheel-drive tractor crawled along, disking a snow-covered field, gouging furrows in the cold, hard earth, making it ready for spring that was still months away. Even though it was winter, the work never ended.

The surrounding fields were stripped bare, dry and glassy with sheets of ice, bleached yellow scrub, and crop stubble. With the harvest done for the season, silos and barns full, minds were set to other thoughts such as what seed to plant next and what crops to grow when the warmth returned.

Reaching an intersection, Carolyn turned and headed east. Low foothills covered with forest rose in front of her, and beyond that were low jagged peaks, crowned bright with snow.

A mile later, she spotted the entrance to Beau Hodges' property. It wasn't hard to miss with the only structures on a sea of flatness for miles. There was the main house surrounded by a scatter of smaller outbuildings. Away from the main house was a large red shed made from corrugated iron sheeting.

Hodges wasn't a farmer. He was a sheet-metal worker who ran his business from the big shed on his property.

There were two pickup trucks, one next to the main house, the other, a much larger one, parked next to the red shed. The larger pickup was painted olive drab, with a huge front bull bar and a row of large spotlights. It had jacked-up suspension, big thick tread tires, and looked like it would do well in any zombie apocalypse.

Carolyn eased her car next to the smaller pickup in front of the house. Even though it was the smaller of the two, the pickup still dwarfed her car as she climbed out.

Then the barking started, loud, deep, and guttural.

Large outdoor cages made of tubular steel and thick gauge mesh sat toward the rear of the house. Dark shapes roamed inside the dog cages. Fur, froth, and sharp flesh-tearing teeth boiled, bellowed, clawed at the mesh as Carolyn stood next to her car.

The house was large and well maintained, built from a mix of brick, stone, wood, and steel sheeting, fashioned by someone who had an eye for practical design, measured angles, and quality workmanship.

The air was crisp and heart-stopping cold.

Hopeful, Carolyn spotted a twist of woodsmoke rising from a large stone chimney that was built into one side of the main house.

The front door of the house opened, a command given, followed by ensuing silence with the occasional whimper from the cages. The dark shapes continued to pace back and forth, fierce eyes focused on the unfamiliar visitor.

Carolyn turned back to the house and let out a muffled gasp at what stood there.

It was true. Beau Hodges was a bear of a man who had to stoop his head in order to get through the front door.

"Don't worry about the dogs," he called out to Carolyn.

It's not the dogs I'm worried about, Carolyn thought as she approached the bottom of a wide set of stairs that led up to a big front porch. "Mr. Hodges, my name is Carolyn Ryder. I'd just like to speak to you if you don't mind."

Hodges came down the stairs and seemed to grow bigger with each step until he stood like a giant in front of her.

The words came out before she realized it. "You're black."

"You're white," Hodges replied.

"I just—" Carolyn stammered.

"You just assumed what?" he asked.

"You're a hunter. You hunt."

Hodges nodded. "So you assumed I'd look like a typical hunter. White, with a beard, scruffy-looking, maybe a redneck?" Hodges pulled at his shirt. "I guess I've got the right shirt on?"

Carolyn cast a critical eye over the towering man in front of her. He wore a thick plaid-red shirt, drill pants smudged with metal grime and grease, and heavy work boots. She guessed he was about six foot six, maybe a pinch over, and at least three hundred pounds of solid muscle and restrained menace, with broad shoulders, tapered waist, calm but piercing eyes.

Carolyn categorized him as quiet, unassuming, a thinker. Not a shy person, but someone who pondered, not prone to rash actions, someone who preferred to think things through, a patient man. Traits that many people might misinterpret as being slow or simple. He was neither.

He had working hands that shaped, cut, and bent metal, big and powerful, like he could plow a frozen field with just his fingers.

"You remind me of The Rock, you know, Dwayne Johnson." Carolyn threw the compliment out there, thinking it would ease the awkwardness she felt, hoping it would break the ice with Hodges. That, and the fact that Hodges did look like The Rock.

Hodges stared at her, pondering what to make of this...rude white woman.

"But more handsome," she quickly added.

The awkward silence was suddenly broken. Hodges grinned.

That did the trick.

"You're Louise Ryder's daughter," he said. "The other one."

Carolyn didn't know how to respond. She had never been labeled "the other daughter" before. She felt a pang of guilt.

"I'm sorry to hear about your mother," Hodges added. "She was a good woman."

Carolyn smiled.

"Come on inside." He beckoned to Carolyn.

The inside of the house was all heads and eyes. They stared down at Carolyn from the walls. Vacant and wide eyed, faces frozen in that final moment just before a 150-grain bullet traveling at over two thousand feet per second, hit them unawares.

The living room was orderly, comfortable, and rustic. It had a hunting-lodge feel to it with a beautiful open fireplace of hand-built stone with an industrial steel hood.

Carolyn didn't feel uneasy, just conscious that numerous dead eyes were looking down at her. Hodges indicated for her to sit next to the fire and lifted with one hand a large log, like it was just a twig and placed it on the embers. The log caught immediately as flames licked and caressed it. Without asking, he went to a large open kitchen and returned with a coffee mug the size of a German beer stein and placed it on a table next to Carolyn.

He sat down across from her on a beautiful leather sofa, chocolate brown, the hide supple and smooth.

"So how can I help you, miss?" he asked, his voice not gruff, just deep with a rich smooth gravel timbre to it.

"Please call me Carolyn. I heard around town that you're a

hunter." It was a pointless statement given the other company in the room.

Hodges nodded slowly. "Do you hunt?"

Carolyn shook her head. "No, but I'm interested in the hunting around here. I don't mean to pry, but I was speaking to some of the people in town, and they said that you're the best hunter to talk to."

"A group of us go out when we can, when we have the time." Hodges spoke slowly, his eyes never leaving Carolyn's. "You're with the feds, aren't you?"

For a small town, news certainly travels fast, even to the outskirts. Now her label around town had expanded to, "the other daughter, the fed."

"I don't mean that disrespectfully," Hodges added. "I'd just like to know why you're here."

"I have no official capacity anymore, Mr. Hodges."

"Call me Beau."

"Beau. I used to work for the FBI, but don't now."

"But that doesn't stop you from being a little curious, asking questions."

Carolyn shrugged. "Can't help it. It's in my blood. I can't sit by when I hear or see something that I want to know more about."

Hodges took a deep breath, his chest expanding to the size of a locomotive under his shirt before letting it out slowly. "You've been talking to Billy Dale or some of the other hunters around town?"

"No. But I just heard that your last hunting trip was..." Carolyn didn't know what word to use, then said, "uneventful?"

Hodges said nothing for a moment, just gazed into the flames, the only sound in the room coming from the crackling and hissing of the logs in the fireplace. When he finally spoke, his expression had changed. His voice was low, and Carolyn thought she could detect something. Fear. She could be wrong. It seemed so out of place for a man of Hodges' size and presence. It seemed like nothing would scare him. She dismissed the notion as just her imagination.

"A group of us were up on the Flint Plains a few days ago. It's a cold flat stretch of woodland high up in the hills. Usually it's a good spot to hunt deer, whitetail, if you're patient and willing to stay out in the wilderness for a few days. But this time it was different." His voice trailed off, and he frowned, like something didn't make sense to him. "It was like there was someone else there, up on the plains as well."

"Another hunter, perhaps?" Carolyn suggested. "Someone you know?"

Hodges shook his head slowly.

"Were you being followed? Did you see anyone?"

Hodges gazed into his hands, looking for answers among the numerous cuts, nicks, and old scars. "We weren't being followed. There's a difference," he said, looking at Carolyn.

Despite sitting next to the fireplace, Carolyn suddenly felt bone-cold as she watched Hodges. "How so?" she asked.

"Call it hunter's instinct," Hodges said slowly. Firelight danced off his face, his eyes cold and lifeless. "We weren't being followed," he said again. "We were being tracked."

Carolyn gave a quizzical look. She felt a little confused, but Hodges cleared up any confusion she had by what he said next.

"It felt like we were being hunted." He stared Carolyn right in the eyes. "By someone else."

29

Beau Hodges placed another log on the fire before settling back on the sofa to tell his story to Carolyn.

It was unsettling, and she felt more than a little unhinged as she listened to what he had to say about the hunting trip up to the Flint Plains two days ago.

Hodges stared into the flames. "I've been hunting up in those hills since I was ten years old. My father bought me a .22 single-shot rifle. Remember it like it was yesterday. He taught me how to shoot, how to track deer, hunt them, gut them, too."

Carolyn sat intently watching Hodges. His eyes seemed to glaze over as he spoke, recalling his childhood, fond memories of a boy spending time with his father, life skills being passed from one generation to the next.

The passing of time in the living room was measured by the shrinking of the logs in the fire. From smoldering wood down to blackened husks before breaking apart into a jumble of hot, glowing embers.

"We were up on the plains before then, not more than two weeks ago," Hodges continued. "Saw plenty of turkey, and then deer started coming out around dusk. We camped up there for three nights, moving a few miles farther in each day. Good hunting on that trip. We tracked a few big young bucks, whitetails. Got them, too."

"So what happened on the last hunt?" Carolyn asked. It was obvious something had changed since Hodges and his friends were up there two weeks ago.

Hodges looked directly at Carolyn. "When you're hunting an animal, tracking it, you may not see it for days. But you know it's there, somewhere ahead in the forest or in the tall scrub. You can feel it, judge the distance it has on you up ahead."

Carolyn had no clue on hunting for anything other than criminals. Animals left clues just like humans did, she imagined. Her clues were fingerprints, foot marks, trace DNA. Whereas for Hodges, a professional hunter, it was about animal tracks, disturbed foliage, animal feces, smell, and gut feel.

Hodges explained that there was a group of them, four hunters in total. They'd driven up in two pickups, left them at the base of the hills, then made their way on foot like how they had done a thousand times before. They carried rifles, hunting backpacks, tents, and a few provisions. They intended to camp out in the wild. "But this time it was different," he said. "There was nothing up ahead, no feeling that anything was there, just dead empty air."

"Like nothing? No animals?"

Hodges shook his head in disbelief. Even now as he described it, it still seemed absurd. "We used one of our best kill plots—"

"Sorry," Carolyn interrupted. "You used a what?"

"A kill plot," Hodges explained. "It's just a small tract of open ground, heavy cover around it, adjacent to a large feeding plot. Deer come out at dusk and mingle and feed a little there. They feel secure."

An ambush more like it, Carolyn thought. "OK. So what happened?"

"Nothing. Not a single deer. We hunted that particular plot last season and two weeks ago as well. So we trekked farther into the forest. Saw plenty of tracks, but no deer, no nothing. Then on the second day, things changed dramatically," Hodges went on to explain. They went deeper in the Flint Plains, and still nothing. "About midmorning on the second day, we were out hunting again. I could feel something behind us, at our backs. The others could feel it, too."

"Hunter's instinct?" Carolyn said.

Hodges gave a slight nod. "And that's where it stayed, at our back, like something was behind us, moving as we moved, mimicking our movements."

"Another animal? Deer?"

"No. It was like in reverse," Hodges said. "Something was tracking us, like a predator. Deer don't do that."

"Mountain cat?" Carolyn offered, feeling really out of her depth now.

"Didn't feel like it," Hodges replied. "The air had a certain feel to it, a certain menace. Can't explain it. Been hunting near on forty years up there in those hills and up on the plains and ain't felt anything like it. The animals must have felt it, too. As I said, we saw plenty of tracks but no actual animals. Not even a single rabbit. Something was pushing them away. It was like the forest had emptied. All that was left was us and the birds."

"And you felt this always at your backs, from behind?" Carolyn felt her skin turn cold as she listened.

Hodges nodded.

"And you saw no one?"

"Saw no one, heard no one. We switched up trails, changed direction, followed different tracks. But it was still there, that feeling constantly behind us. Real strong at times, then it would fade off, back away a little, but it never really went away."

Carolyn understood what that meant. Something was stalking them.

"Hell, we even tried to double back, catch them unawares, come around and up behind them, Billy on one side of the arc, me on the other while the other two stood their ground in the middle. But we saw nothing. Not a damn thing."

Carolyn could feel Hodges getting angry, his face all furrows and frowns, trying to make sense of something that didn't. These were seasoned hunters, maybe the best in Iowa. Maybe the best in the entire Midwest for all Carolyn knew. They knew the terrain, the ground, the lay of the land, hunted on it. Had done so for many years. Four experienced hunters, with guns, and Beau Hodges leading them—a man as big and as menacing as you can get. Yet Carolyn got the distinct feeling even he was spooked by what had happened.

Hodges caught Carolyn's expression. "I know, I know," he said. "It sounds insane. It felt insane, believe me."

"So what did you do next?"

"Snow came in pretty heavy, late in the afternoon. So we set up camp. In a clearing in the forest. Built a sheltered fire, ate, then slept with our rifles by our sides."

Hodges said nothing for a moment, his face twisted, like he was going slowly mad.

"Beau?" Carolyn said gently. "What's wrong?"

Hodges looked up, suddenly broken from the spell of confusion. "Bastard walked right into our camp, at night, while we were all asleep."

The fire raged but the living room felt icy cold.

Carolyn cocked her head questioningly.

"The next morning we found footprints in the snow. The bastard came out of the forest, right up to our tents."

Outside the dogs started howling.

30

I
t was midmorning when the weather changed, and snow had
started to fall again by the time Carolyn left Beau Hodges and
headed back into town. The heating in the car turned up to
full, and her gun sat on the seat next to her.

The wiper blades slugged back and forth pushing the snow and
ice to the sides. Carolyn's mind was also going back and forth as she
thought about what Hodges had said.

She was a little more than creeped out by the entire story he
had shared with her. But it *wasn't* a story. That was the disturbing
thing about it. It was true. She had no reason to think Hodges was
not telling the truth or exaggerating either.

At first, it sounded like some old hunter's tale, a piece of folklore
or urban myth meant to frighten fellow hunters as they sat around
the campfire at night drinking and swapping tall tales to scare each
other.

If that was its intended purpose, it had certainly worked.

She needed to talk to Finch again about Clarissa Mulligan, see
if the autopsy had come back, and find out exactly where the body
had been found. She hadn't mentioned it to Hodges, and he had

said nothing either, which meant the police were doing a good job keeping the story suppressed.

As she reached the town limits, Carolyn wasn't expecting Finch to tell her much or anything at all. Either way she was still going to try, use a more subtle approach, get him to offer up the information without directly asking him for it.

Carolyn slowed and turned into the parking lot of Olsen's Coffee & Bakery to grab something to eat. She'd skipped breakfast and now was starving. Much as she would have liked to have believed, she couldn't function properly on coffee alone.

She drove past a few cars in the lot then slowed. In a parking space toward the end of the lot was Ritter's Jeep parked by itself, no other cars around it. She pulled up next to it and climbed out, checked the license plate, and noted the rental company stickers. It was definitely his car.

She took a few moments to make sure no one was around before she casually glanced through the driver's side window. With the glare and the window tint she had to cup her hands to the glass to peer inside.

Everything seemed clean and neat. No discarded take-out wrappers. Not even an old coffee take-out cup.

Glancing back over her shoulder, she saw no one approaching from the bakery.

Moving to the rear of the vehicle, she cupped her hands again to the glass next to where the spare tire was mounted.

She could make out a thick rubber floor mat, and sitting to one side looked like a large plastic hard case, a storage box with steel latches. She angled her hands, craned her neck to get a better look.

Her heart skipped a beat. There was something hidden under a tarp. A curved limb jutted out, a pulley wheel at one end, with cables.

It was a crossbow.

"Can I help you?"

Carolyn whirled around.

Michael Ritter was standing behind her, a take-out coffee in his hand.

"Christ!" Carolyn said. "You scared the hell out of me." She backed away from the rear of his car.

Ritter smiled and nodded toward the bakery. "Sorry. Didn't mean to. I just stopped by to grab some coffee."

There was an awkward silence for a moment, Carolyn trying to think up an excuse as to why she was looking into the back of his vehicle. Ritter just stood smiling, knowing full well what she was doing.

"I didn't hear you come up behind me," was all she could say. "I saw your car, so I parked next to it, thinking you were inside."

Ritter smiled. "Well, I'm glad you did." He took out his car keys and opened the door, placed his coffee in the center cup holder then turned and looked back at Carolyn. "Look, I had a great time the other night." He came around and faced her.

"I had a great time, too," she replied sheepishly.

"I'd like to do it again," he said. He grabbed the handle of the rear door and swung it back.

The crossbow sat there, clear as day, in plain sight now, an old tarp covering only part of it. Ritter seemed to ignore it as he grabbed an old cloth from a side pocket.

Then he noticed Carolyn's gaze and smiled at her. "Would you like to take a look at it?" he asked.

"It's a crossbow," she said, stating the obvious.

Ritter pulled the tarp away. "I know." He retrieved the crossbow and held it toward her. "Here, take a look."

Carolyn looked at it hesitantly before taking it from him.

It felt light in her hands. Machined aluminum frame, short limbs, telescopic scope, lethal, extremely modern looking, almost like a compact assault rifle. "Didn't expect it to look or feel like this," Carolyn admitted, handing the weapon back to Ritter.

He placed it back into the rear and covered it fully with the tarp.

"They've come a long way with technology and lightweight materials."

"I thought you didn't hunt."

Ritter closed the rear door and turned back to her. "I don't. I just like to go up into the woods when I can. Take some paper targets and just practice. I like the solitude. It's much nicer up in the woods than going to an indoor range. I find it a great stress reliever."

Carolyn regarded him with skepticism.

Ritter held up his hands in protest. "Hey, let me assure you Bambi is quite safe around me."

Carolyn nodded.

"So what about dinner again?" Ritter said. "I insist I cook for you."

Carolyn was more than a little curious. Ritter had a certain way with words, a trusting aura that made you believe everything he said. Not question him. Just believing. And yet Carolyn was used to seeing past that façade with people, breaking them down, and getting past the lies and to the truth.

Before she could answer, he ducked back inside the front seat and was scribbling down directions. He tore off the sheet of paper and handed it to her. "Here, I'm renting a cabin just out of town, up in the hills."

Carolyn stared at the piece of paper, undecided. Seeing the crossbow had intrigued her, and she wanted to know more.

Ritter glanced at his watch. "Look, I've got a few more errands to run. But I'll pick up some wine and some groceries."

Ritter wasn't taking no for an answer, Carolyn thought, and he could be very persuasive. "OK," she answered. "What's on the menu?"

Ritter's face went blank. "Venison."

Carolyn glared at him for a moment until a genuine smile burst across his face. He touched her arm playfully. "Just kidding," he said. "What about some nice steaks, some red wine, and a tossed salad?"

Carolyn breathed a sigh of relief. "Sounds good. What time?"

"Say around seven?"

Carolyn nodded. "What can I bring?"

Ritter climbed inside, lowered the window, started the engine, and leaned out. "Just a sense of humor, Carolyn. Lighten up, it'll be fun."

Carolyn gave an awkward smile, her mind torn. She watched him back out of the parking space and wave to her as he drove off.

She looked at the piece of paper in her hand again.

It was an invitation her curiosity could not refuse.

31

"Have you spoken to a Dr. Michael Ritter?" Carolyn asked.

They were sitting in the one and only interview room of the Willow Falls Police Department. It was simple, small, with a laminate table, and two plastic chairs that seemed rarely used.

"Who is he?" Finch asked.

Carolyn shrugged. "Maybe a person of interest."

Finch looked thoughtfully at Carolyn. "Is that so?"

She gave a slight nod, not wanting to go too far or reveal too much. She was testing the waters, but in reality she was telling Finch his job. She would if she had to. She just couldn't help herself.

"A person of *your* interest?" Finch asked.

"Perhaps you should take a look at him," Carolyn offered casually.

"Now, why would I want to do that?"

"He owns a crossbow."

Finch gave a puzzled look. "So do probably hundreds of people in town. Thousands of people own crossbows in the entire county, I imagine."

Carolyn began rubbing her wrists under the table, out of sight from Finch. He would remember. He used to frustrate her a lot. "Look, all I'm saying is that maybe you should look into him."

Finch gave a sigh of exasperation and reluctantly took out his notebook and pen.

That was a good sign. He was taking her suggestion seriously.

"Why him, Carolyn? Why this person in particular?"

"He lied to me," she said. "He told me he didn't hunt. Then I found out he owns a crossbow."

The notebook still remained shut. "And that's cause for suspicion?"

The wrist rubbing went up a notch under the table. "Why would he lie?" she said.

"Maybe he doesn't like to admit that he is a hunter. It can turn people off, you know. Also not everyone who owns a crossbow uses it to hunt."

The comments were aimed at her, she could tell. They'd hit a cat once with Finch's car when they were dating. Finch was happy to just leave it on the side of the road, but Carolyn insisted they cancel their dinner reservation and take it to a vet because it was still alive.

Carolyn brought her hands up from under the table and began ticking off points on her fingers. "He's not a local. He's passing through, just a visitor. He's a surgeon. He owns a crossbow. Clarissa Mulligan was killed with a crossbow—"

"Whoa, back up," Finch said. "What's he being a surgeon got to do with anything?"

Carolyn paused. Crap. It had just come out before she could think.

She couldn't tell Finch about what Aaron Wood had said, that the killer had removed the initial crossbow bolts from his victims, carefully and skillfully, so he could then take his time to pin them to the tree and watch them slowly die.

Finch looked at Carolyn suspiciously. "What's the surgeon angle?" Finch had just read the autopsy report this morning. He knew about the initial wounds. The coroner had said it was likely that Clarissa Mulligan had been shot in the shoulder first and that the bolt had been cleanly and expertly cut out using most likely a scalpel. Then the wound was patched up.

The coroner had also found traces of QuikClot in the wound to stop the bleeding. Someone wanted to injure her only, so that she was still alive when she was mounted to the tree.

"Do you know something that maybe I should?" Finch leaned forward and pressed his hands on the table.

"No, not really," Carolyn lied. "I just think you should take a look at him." She could tell from the look in Finch's eyes that the autopsy had come back. His ears had pricked up a little too fast when she mentioned that Ritter was a surgeon. Finch now knew about the initial wounds to the victim, to bring them down first. It would be detailed in the autopsy report.

"This is not your case, Ryder," Finch said firmly. He always switched to calling her "Ryder" instead of Carolyn when he was angry. Some things never change, she thought.

"Hey, you came to *me!*" Carolyn spat back.

"Just to take a look at some photos and to get your take on them. Not for you to go around town like some half-assed vigilante and start accusing people."

"I haven't accused anyone of anything!" Carolyn snapped. "Just you for acting like a stubborn prick!"

And with that, the floodgates opened. Ten years of angst, pent-up frustration, vindictiveness, regret, jealously, and bitterness came pouring out into a small room that was hardly big enough to hold two grown adults who were now acting like two spiteful children.

"Fuck you, Ryder!" Finch snapped.

"No, surely you mean fuck my older sister!" Carolyn snarled.

"Because you did, you bastard!" This was a long time coming, and she wasn't holding back.

The insults came thick and fast.

Apparently, Finch had a little dick, and Carolyn had to fake orgasms in bed so he wouldn't develop an inadequacy complex.

Apparently, Carolyn actually had grown a dick that she used to fit in like "one of the boys" back at the FBI, and that's how she got the job.

Finch had no balls.

Carolyn had three balls, along with too much male testosterone.

Finch was weak and spineless.

She was aggressive and only thought of herself and her career.

Carolyn insisted she'd only slept with Finch because he had pestered her so much and she had finally relented just to shut him up. It was either that or pretend she was a lesbian.

Finch said Jodie, her sister, was a far better lay than Carolyn ever was.

Carolyn told Finch he would fuck a drunk-and-unconscious woman if he found one on the side of the road.

On and on it went.

"So it's not ancient history like you said the other day!" Finch yelled.

"It was until you decided to dig it all up again!" Carolyn yelled back.

Then the flood of insults subsided, both realizing they were acting like a pair of fifth graders.

The silence ran on for a few minutes. Finch sat staring at the table, a scowl on his face. Carolyn, arms folded, her face pinched, took a sudden fascination in the perforated ceiling tiles.

Finch was the first to break the silence. "There's no need to look into Dr. Michael Ritter," he said gruffly.

Carolyn continued to stare at the ceiling. She finally relented and focused her eyes of fury on Finch. "You know, I don't care anymore. It was a mistake coming here."

She went to get up but Finch held up his hand.

Exasperated and angry more at himself for allowing the conversation to deteriorate into a slinging match, Finch gave a smug look at Carolyn, then flipped open his police notebook, and began to read his neat handwritten notes, one-inch margin on the left, today's date at the top.

"Dr. Michael Philip Ritter, MD. Age 46. Lives in Chicago. Highly regarded and respected physician at Northwestern Memorial Hospital. Board Certified in Thoracic and Cardiac Surgery. Earned his degree from Yale University School of Medicine. Undertook a Fellowship at Middlesex Hospital in the United Kingdom. Not married. White male—"

"Stop!" Carolyn held up her hand.

"You see, Carolyn," Finch said. "Dr. Ritter came in this morning, just before you did, in fact. Heard the news about the girl we found, Clarissa Mulligan."

Carolyn stared at Finch in disbelief. After Ritter had driven off, Carolyn had gotten takeout from Olsen's then spent the next half hour sitting in her car eating breakfast and drinking coffee and strategizing how to best broach the subject with Finch of Michael Ritter and the crossbow she had seen.

But it was all academic now. Ritter had driven straight to the police station and spoken to Finch already.

"How did he know?" Carolyn said. "About Clarissa Mulligan. I thought you were keeping a lid on it?"

"We were until her parents decided to talk and tell everyone."

"I can hardly blame them," Carolyn said. "Their daughter was brutally murdered. Of course, they're going to talk."

"Well, it has spread like wildfire around town," Finch replied. "I'm surprised you hadn't heard."

Carolyn hadn't been in town all morning until now. She got up early this morning to drive up to see Beau Hodges.

Finch continued, anger building in his voice. "The details of how Clarissa Mulligan was murdered were somehow leaked to the local newspaper last night. It's probably gone statewide by now. We think it was someone at the morgue who opened their mouth. Probably on a retainer with a local journalist, you know, to keep an eye out for anything juicy that might come in, something newsworthy." Finch waved his hand dismissively. "Doesn't matter now anyway." He went back to his notebook. "Anyhow, Ritter came in, asked if he could help with the case given that he is a surgeon. He was very helpful, understood that we are just a small police department up here, and maybe we could use his medical opinion on the body. I thanked him but said that we had it under control."

Carolyn just looked at Finch. They had nothing under control.

"But wait, there's more," Finch went on.

She could tell he was enjoying going one up on her, like it was a competition, small-town cop showing up a big-city federal agent. Ex-federal agent, that is.

"The good doctor actually brought in his crossbow this morning."

Carolyn let out a slow breath.

"I've got the crossbow in the evidence locker out the back. I refused, but he insisted that we check it forensically. Said that it would be fine by him. Can you believe that?" Finch said.

Carolyn said nothing. There was nothing to say. Finch was already having a bad day before she walked in, and now she'd made it worse by making accusations about Ritter.

Finch leaned forward. "The guy volunteered to help. Then volunteered up his crossbow for us to take a look at. He was very gracious about it. He said he uses it just for sport, a hobby, to shoot at paper targets. He brings it on vacation with him. Rents a cabin up in the woods and likes to go on hikes, takes the crossbow with him. He admitted that he's not a hunter, but likes to spend time outdoors hiking and just shooting at shit in the forest. Not at deer and certainly not at people."

Carolyn could tell Finch was quietly fuming at what had happened. The code of silence about the case was quickly collapsing around him, and he was snarly. Their little spat was just the trigger that set him off.

Finch closed his notebook. He had a few more pages he could have gone on about. Judging from the sullen look on Carolyn's face, there was no need.

It all seemed a little too convenient for Carolyn. No sooner had Ritter shown her his crossbow, did he walk straight into the police station and volunteer his medical expertise and his crossbow to be checked.

Finch's gaze softened. "Look, Carolyn, we're making inquiries; we have a few leads. It looks like Clarissa Mulligan did break up with some guy a few months back. We're looking into it. And I'm sorry about your mother dying."

Carolyn's eyes flashed. "Don't patronize me," she whispered. She still felt the churn in her stomach and the heat in her face from the outburst they had just had. "This has nothing to do with my mother or how I feel right now." The plastic chair grated noisily across the floor as she suddenly stood. "When I'm done here, with my mother's house, I'll be gone, out of your hair. Then everyone will be happy. You won't need to worry about me. I won't be back."

At the door she paused, turned back to Finch, her face defiant. "But you'll still have some crazy sicko running around killing women in this town, and you won't have a clue as to who they are. This isn't some one-off domestic incident. I know. I've seen this before. You haven't."

Finch sat in silence for a moment, pondering on her words after she had gone.

For the sake of everyone, he hoped Carolyn was wrong.

Outside in the parking lot, Carolyn unlocked her car and climbed in, still furious at Finch. She sat for a while, heater turned up, the engine running, but not moving, enjoying the warm air that came through the vents.

On the seat next to her sat her bag; inside was a folder with all the photos Aaron Wood had sent her, printed out in full graphic color from Jodie's printer that Carolyn had borrowed to run them off on.

She hadn't shown them to Hodges this morning. Didn't want to until she had the measure of the man. But now she felt she needed to trust him, show him the photos, and get his opinion as a hunter.

The more Carolyn thought about it, trying to reconcile the other cases with the discovery of Clarissa Mulligan's body, the more she felt Robin Hood had come to Willow Falls. He was here, right now. The similarities were too close.

If Tyler Finch persisted on going down the path that Clarissa Mulligan had died at the hands of a jealous boyfriend who killed her in a fit of rage, then she would take matters into her own hands, make her own inquiries.

To hell with Finch.

Carolyn put the car in gear and headed back out of town to see Beau Hodges again.

She wasn't prepared to just sit by and wait for another woman to be abducted, butchered, then put on display.

32

Carolyn opened her folder and spread out the pictures and said nothing, just watched as Hodges studied each one. Some pictures he dwelled on a little longer, others he passed over after a cursory glance.

Carolyn offered no words or explanation. Just stony silence, allowing the hunter to formulate his own opinion through eyes that Carolyn would never understand. The only commonality they shared was an appreciation of hunting. Carolyn the human kind. Hodges the animal kind.

The silence dragged out as his eyes moved back and forth trying to formulate a three-dimensional rendition of a two-dimensional snapshot of human death. Pixels on paper, laid down on Jodie's old inkjet printer, one excruciating dot at a time.

"Someone killed these women. The same person, I believe. Now I think they're here in Willow Falls."

Hodges said nothing, just gave a nod, his attention absorbing the death and carnage in front of him.

She could almost see it in his eyes. He was no longer in the room, had been teleported to the crime scene, trying to imagine the smells, the noises, the feel of the atmosphere, the texture of the ground, the leaves, the earth between his fingers, the rot, the stink of death, blood, and cooling flesh mixed with everything else. Trying to imagine what was just out of frame, not in the photos, farther to the left, a little to the right, off the border, what may have been there, what it could have looked like if he was standing alone in some desolate wooded forest in the middle of nowhere.

Five more minutes of excruciating silence passed, Hodges staring at the photos, Carolyn staring at him, studying his expression, his eye movement, his wrinkles, the edges of his mouth, the flare of his nostrils, all the time her mind wondering if it was him. Was he Robin Hood? Was he the killer? Was he, in fact, appraising his own handiwork? Picking it apart. Could it have been better? What would I do differently next time? No room for improvisation. Just careful, meticulous planning.

Finally Hodges sat back and uttered two words. "Kill plot."

Carolyn sat a little straighter. "Kill plot?" Then she recalled he had briefly mentioned it before, for animals not for humans.

Hodges looked at her, his face more of an apology than a smile. "You're not going to like what I'm going to say. The whole hunting thing goes against your grain."

"Try me."

"You're not a hunter. People get funny, take offense, can't imagine or understand why hunters do what they do. The time taken, the effort, the detail, it can be a little obsessive."

"My only obsession is finding him." Carolyn pointed at the spread of photos. "Tell me what you see. As a hunter."

"He's using a kill plot in some of these situations. I can tell from the terrain, the land, how things have been set up, arranged." Hodges pointed to the aerial photos that had been taken by a police drone that Carolyn had printed off.

"What is a kill plot?" she asked again. "Explain it to me, in detail this time. I need to understand how he is using it on people, not animals."

"It's what hunters use to lure their prey, deer mostly."

"Tell me everything; explain everything; leave nothing out at all," Carolyn insisted. She wanted desperately to understand everything about the killer, how he thought, what and why he did what he did. She wanted to get inside his head, no matter how dark and sinister and disturbing a place it would be. It was the only way she was going to catch him. She just prayed that when it was all over, all done, the damage to her own state of mind would be minimal.

"I can see definite similarities," Hodges said. "But I can only explain how it's done for deer, for animals."

Carolyn nodded. "We're all animals in one form or another."

"First you find a narrow stretch of open land, a clearing, close to where deer bed down, and sleep. You then clear it, usually with a backhoe, smooth it out and remove all debris and trees. Then you seed it with grasses that deer like to eat."

"Like a mousetrap?" Carolyn asked. "Cheese is the bait."

"I guess that's one way of looking at it. Except deer are much more attuned to the environment, what's around them. They want to feel safe and secure, no imminent threats of danger, otherwise they won't wander into your kill plot."

"So you entice them with food," Carolyn said. It seemed pretty simple to her.

"But food alone won't do it. They must feel safe, protected. That takes time. So you sit in a hide or on a tree platform and wait. Often for hours. Sometimes for days."

"Days?" Carolyn was astonished. "You sit in a tree for days?"

Hodges gave a slight smile. "Like I said, it can be an obsession. Especially if you're after a certain deer, a large buck. Maybe one you missed last season." Hodges turned and pointed up at a deer's head on the wall. "That big one there. I sat in a tree for four days to get him. Had ropes and a hammock rigged up, food and water as well up in the tree. But I finally got him."

It hardly seemed fair, Carolyn thought. It was the worst kind of predatory stalking she could imagine. She could see how easily, though, it transferred to the human kind of hunting. She had never really thought about it, but serial killers and stalkers had adopted the same methodology that animal hunters had used for centuries. They spotted their prey, watched where they lived, followed their daily routine, their patterns, their commute to work, what route they followed, where they parked their car, their daily habits. "So you make the deer feel safe by concealing yourself really well and waiting it out. Like you're not there."

"Almost invisible, camouflaged, even use special sprays to neutralize body scent."

"And sitting still for long periods of time," Carolyn nodded, taking in the bizarre ritual.

"Motionless," Hodges replied.

"So how does this translate to hunting humans?" Carolyn said. More of a question to herself than to Hodges. "Jesus..." Carolyn finally said.

Hodges nodded. He could now see the transference of similarities as well.

"I guess you could use a disguise," Hodges added. "Dress up like a person of trust, a cop, a doctor, someone they would never suspect."

Carolyn's mind was racing. This tactic had been done thousands of times before, killers posing as phone company workers and the like, knocking on doors. Even fake cops pulling their victims over on the side of the road. Ted Bundy had used an arm in a sling, pretending it was broken, to coax sympathy from his female victims into helping him load up his VW Beetle with furniture. It was a despicable act of evil, a mousetrap for humans.

"A familiar face, maybe," Hodges said, looking at the photos again. "Friend, family member. Someone they know."

"He would have been caught by now if that was the case," Carolyn replied. "The victims are all unrelated." The victim's family, friends, coworkers, neighbors would have been heavily investigated. It was the first step in the process, and the most common way to catch the perp.

"What about the bait?" Carolyn asked. "You said you use a food source, feed pellets, plantings to lure the unsuspecting deer."

"The food, the bait, is an offer, a promise, perhaps," Hodges said, his perspective slowly changing to Carolyn's point of view of hunting humans not deer.

"Something that they want, something enticing maybe?"

"Or the opportunity to help," Hodges offered. "Humans naturally want to help if we see someone who needs help. It's in our nature, I guess. Most people, that is."

"Someone broken down on the side of the road. Someone injured. Someone in trouble." Carolyn smiled. More thoughts of Ted Bundy in her mind again. "That would work around here, in a small town, good old-fashioned hospitality. But in the cities, bigger towns, everyone is more suspicious. Fat chance of anyone stopping on the side of the road to help you."

Carolyn pondered the small towns' angle for a moment. Maybe that's why he preferred them to the big cities. People in small towns tend to be more hospitable, more likely to offer help: community spirit and all.

Hodges picked up the series of aerial shots of the various crime scenes, mainly woodland and forests, plenty of snow. A red cross on each photo marked where the body had been found. "These locations"—he pointed at the red cross—"he sets up his kill plots in the forests where he hunted them."

Carolyn bent close. "What do you mean?"

"The terrain," Hodges replied. "He's using it to his advantage. It's exactly how I would set up the area." He slid his finger along the photos, pointing at invisible lines and hidden areas, only he could see.

Carolyn could vaguely understand what Hodges was saying.

Seeing doubt still in her face, Hodges stood, went to a side table and came back with a thick red pen. He gestured at the aerial photos.

"Sure," Carolyn said.

He began drawing thick lines, boxing off parts of the terrain on the paper. "You can see them here. Small, narrow clearings, where the bodies were found or close by. He drove them into these locations, and they had no idea it was a trap." He held up one photo. Then another. Then another.

Carolyn looked at the aerial photos, the lines, the rectangles Hodges had drawn, outlining a clearing in the forest, no trees or just a few, little or no foliage, a narrow corridor, a path to be followed that led to where death awaited.

"Follow the yellow brick road..." Carolyn whispered.

"They entered at one end and made their way toward this location here." He spun all the photos around and indicated on each one. "I'd stage myself here, and here. Easy line of sight and just enough heavy cover on the edges to be invisible."

It was not obvious at first, but suddenly the photos had taken on a whole new meaning. Like there was another photo hidden underneath the original, something no one would have seen or expected unless they had brought in a hunter to study the scenes. The FBI hadn't.

"But if you're running for your life, wouldn't you want to stay in the cover, not be out in the open?" Carolyn countered.

Hodges smiled, anticipating the question. "How do you force someone to do or go where they don't want to go?" Hodges paused, not wanting to spoon-feed the answer. He wanted Carolyn to learn, to start thinking like him...and like the killer they were going to track.

Carolyn stared at the series of photos. Then she saw it. The terrain changed in front of her eyes, like one of those 3D pictures you need to look at differently until the real image hidden underneath reveals itself. Carolyn ran her finger along the photos. "Thick forest along here, on the right side. A wall of rock, too, a natural boundary."

Hodges nodded, pleased that Carolyn was finally stepping into his world, seeing things how he did. "Would slow you down, correct?"

"Correct. Or a dead end."

"Especially if you're running, fleeing for your life," Hodges added. "What else?"

"This looks like a ridge, on the left, the edge of a drop-off. Nowhere to go except down. Looks too steep to traverse safely to the bottom."

"Exactly," Hodges said. "So there's a natural tendency to take the risk, to break cover and run across the clearing. Nowhere else to go. Maybe the cover looks thicker on the other side. Maybe he places something there, something you can see in the distance. That's the enticement."

"Damn." Carolyn let the word out slowly. She grabbed another aerial photo from her folder. Another forest. Another red cross. Another victim. This time it took her just seconds to see the kill plot, didn't need to mark it out with a pen. Again, it was a seemingly narrow corridor of clear forest, bordered on one side by a wide wild river and on the other side by a steep wooded area. The clearing acted as a funnel, a natural path to where the killer would have been waiting at the other end or near the sides.

"They unknowingly came to him," Hodges said. "He didn't have to track or chase them. Easier that way."

"They didn't have a clue," Carolyn said, bitterness in her voice, feeling sick at the revelation Hodges had pointed out. "They thought they were running away from him. They were actually running *toward* him."

Hodges stood, picked up their coffee cups to refill. "A true hunter lies in wait. Lets the prey come to them. Economy of effort."

Carolyn looked up at Hodges. "Or a true predator does."

33

Madeline Bennett paused in the forest, dark brooding pine trees all around her. A vertical wall of thin trunks that seemed to replicate itself in all directions no matter where she looked.

She had to stop, take a breath, force herself to calm down and think. It was the only way she was going to live through this.

Her own body heat, tinged with fear vented up through the collar of her torn jacket. Yet her skin felt icy cold. Layers of her clothing were clammy and wet and clung to her skin.

Darkness was coming, and with it came the evilness that she was certain was out there, somewhere, chasing her.

He was there, just beyond the edge of the frozen white, lurking in the periphery, pulling at the limits of her sanity. Madeline couldn't see him; she just knew he was there. His eyes were everywhere. In the trees, among the black gnarly branches, even staring up at her through the snow at her feet.

She had to decide, but decisiveness had never been her strongpoint. One thing she was certain of was that she wasn't going to die here, today, in this wretched place.

No. She had plans. Marriage, children, and a long, contented life ahead of her with her soul mate and family. And to think she had told him all this! She hardly knew him. He was a stranger, not a familiar face in town, yet he had this aura, this way about him, a reassuring presence that had eased her initial fears, softened the usually cautious exterior she had whenever she met strangers. He was alluring, charming, nice. There seemed to be no ulterior motives to his friendliness, his carefully chosen words and indifferent smile.

Or so it seemed.

He was so helpful without the usual pretense. And she had needed his help at that brief moment when their paths crossed on the side of the road. It was a shortcut, along a back road she had taken a million times after work, to get home quicker. It typically saved her a full ten minutes in travel time.

She wasn't mechanically minded either. Left all that to her boyfriend and the tools he habitually left scattered all around her garage.

The stranger seemed to know his way around under the hood when he pulled up alongside her and offered to take a look at what the problem was.

Her car had started up perfectly fine when she had left the parking lot. Then after a few miles it began to make a sort of groaning sound, forcing her to pull over to the side of the road. She turned off the ignition then the car refused to start again.

To top it all off, her cell phone was dead. It was working perfectly fine, too, when she was texting and driving a few moments before the engine started to groan.

Madeline knew she shouldn't be using her cell phone while driving. A friend of hers had died a few years back, texting her boyfriend while driving down the highway. It was just a moment of distraction but enough for her friend to slam into the back of the truck that had slowed down in front of her.

It was getting colder. Madeline had to move. Every second she stood still catching her breath, the forest around her was turning a darker shade. Night was seeping down through the branches above, making the task of finding a way out of the forest and back to civilization infinitely more difficult.

She set off again, a steady pace, her boots crunching on the ground, a mix of icy churn speckled with rotten leaves, twigs, and forest debris.

It is natural human tendency to follow a straight line, especially if lost in unfamiliar terrain. A few times Madeline felt herself drifting off the invisible line she had set in her head. She corrected her direction as best she could, but there were no distinct landmarks, nothing she could use as a point of reference, just an endless wall of trees, a hall of mirrors.

The terrain began to slope downward. Again, there was a natural tendency to believe that downward meant the bottom of something. The bottom of a hill. The base of a cliff. The bottom of a high-rise apartment block. So it was a good sign in Madeline's mind. Maybe a way out.

She carefully traversed the slippery slope, using small trees and thin saplings to steady herself as she continued downward, her pace quickening. Roads usually were at the bottom of hills, weren't they?

The ground flattened and the faint outline of a path opened up in front of her.

Yes. A trail, she was certain. Ferns that usually drooped over had been cleared back, stems broken, some cut away. The ground looked well-trod or raked by the boots of other hikers.

Her spirits lifted.

The trail would lead somewhere. They always did. Maybe it looped back to the start, to a parking lot, or a road with signs and cars.

Spurred on by the discovery, Madeline increased her pace following the narrow path as it wound its way around rocks and through low bracken.

The trees thinned, and she emerged into a long narrow clearing.

She stopped and took it in.

Dying light bathed the clearing in watery, insipid dullness.

Then she saw it. Her heart leapt.

A tent, bright blue was pitched at the far end of the clearing. Another person, a hiker setting up camp for the evening.

Then she heard laughter. A woman's laugh, light and merry. It came from the tent at the opposite end of the clearing.

The laugh came again. No, Madeline hadn't imagined it.

Madeline began to run, toward the tent, across the clearing. The ground was firm, frozen mud with a light covering of snow. The tent glowed in the middle, a warm hazy ball of light that filtered through its nylon walls. A beacon, calling her toward it, a moth to the flame.

A lantern. Someone was inside the tent.

The woman inside the tent laughed again. Louder. Clearer.

Madeline ran faster, ignoring the burning coldness in the back of her throat, her face streaked with frozen tears.

She was safe. People were here. They would help her.

She gave a weak cry, "Help me, please!"

She came to a halt at the front of the tent. The tent door was open, a triangle wedge of material, unzipped and tied back. The opening beckoned her inside.

The woman inside the tent said something to another person. Then she giggled.

Madeline crouched down and peered inside.

Her heart stopped. Her mind stopped. Her breathing stopped.

Relief melted into confusion for Madeline.

The tent was empty, bare, just thick, black plastic flooring and translucent nylon walls.

A small digital voice recorder lay on the floor. Amazon's Choice. Forty bucks plus postage and handling delivered right to your door. Free if you had Prime Membership.

Madeline knelt in and picked up the device.

She saw digits counting backward on a tiny blue screen, playing back a track from a sound file that had been downloaded for free off the internet, from a website that offered everything from the sound of waves crashing on a beach in Fiji, to a married couple talking casually at the dinner table. Ten minutes of a woman's voice and laughter played in a continuous loop, the volume turned up just enough to sound realistic through the walls of the tent and to anyone who was outside in the clearing.

Confusion faded into fear as Madeline slowly turned the device over in her hand, trying to comprehend the incomprehensible.

The woman laughed again, but this time the sound came from Madeline's hand. The woman was talking, making light playful dinner conversation with another equally nonexistent person. Her voice was crystal clear, coming from the built-in speaker on the side of the device.

Madeline dropped the digital voice recorder like it was a scorpion in her hand.

She backed out of the tent fast, stumbling backward as she went.

The woman inside the tent laughed again. The same tone of merriment. But this time it sounded like she was mocking Madeline. *You fool!*

Breathless with fear, Madeline turned to run. She took three steps before her left thigh exploded in pain.

Throwing her head skyward she let out a muffled scream and collapsed sideways, her hand instantly groping at her thigh where the excruciating pain was coming from.

Her fingers found something warm, sticky and wet buried in her thigh. Madeline looked down in horror and saw a foreign object that shouldn't have been there: a thin black shaft with colorful fins at its tip was protruding out of her leg. Warm blood seeped through her pants where the bolt had entered her thigh, missing the femur but shredding through skin, muscle, and fat as it sliced inward before finally stopping deep in her thigh.

Madeline gritted her teeth, placed all her weight on her other leg and limped forward, almost dragging her dead leg, leaving a bloody trail in her wake.

He came out of the tree line behind her with the haunting slowness of a ghost, a reaper, the bringer of death. Silently, stealthily, deadly. Pausing at the tent, he reached in, picked up the voice recorder and hit the off button.

He turned and slowly pocketed the device.

He watched her for a moment, hobbling away from him at a snail's pace.

There was no rush. She wasn't going anywhere.

He took a moment to admire the natural beauty of everything around him. Tall dark pines, their limbs caked in pure white. The watery haze of the dying sun behind the shimmering clouds above. The crisp, cold air, the smell of pine needles and spruce, tainted now with a slight coppery scent.

But it was nothing compared to the natural beauty he was about to create, to fashion with his own hands, adding his own artistic flair.

He began to walk toward the hunkered, stumbling, whimpering shape of Madeline Bennett.

Hearing that someone was behind her, Madeline turned her head and looked over her shoulder then let out a scream and willed her crippled leg to drag faster.

Visions of marriage, children, and a long, contented life spent with her soul mate and family was slowly fading from her view.

34

H odges returned with the coffee and sat back down again. "Hunt, capture, release, then hunt again."

"Where he finally kills them," Carolyn added.

Hodges said nothing. Just agreed with his eyes.

"Each location, each kill plot, is carefully chosen," she said, thinking out aloud. "In advance. Some place desolate enough that he can hunt in private without the risk of anyone seeing him or stumbling across his little game."

"Probably would just kill them, too, if he was discovered. But that doesn't fit with what you've said: his pattern."

"No," Carolyn said. "He's too meticulous, doesn't want the interruption. He wants to take his time with who he has chosen. Doesn't want to just randomly kill someone. So there is no chance of him picking a place too obvious."

Carolyn thought back to the case of Mary Jane Westerman. Her body was found just a few hundred yards off a hiking trail. More risky. More chance of being seen, close to park facilities. Maybe he wanted more of a challenge. Maybe he hunted her in the dark, when the park was closed, with night vision. It was vile and inhuman. Carolyn could feel her skin crawl thinking about it.

He had injured her, Mary Jane Westerman. She had almost made it to the hiking trail. Maybe that was the incentive, the thinnest sliver of hope that if she made it to the hiking trail she could find her way out of the forest, get help. Carolyn had a sickening thought. Maybe he had given her a flashlight as well, a map too, marking where the trail was. Another kill plot carefully selected then staged.

Carolyn tried to imagine the nightmare she must have gone through, the mother-to-be, running in the dark, carrying her unborn, turning her head to look back in pure fear at the slightest sound, unaware that evil was slowly reeling her in. Trying to save her child's life more than her own.

In the darkness, too, he would have easily seen the flashlight wobble and shake as she ran and stumbled through the trees. The mother of all nightmares that we only see in horror movies but never really imagine happening in real life.

But monsters do exist in real life. They aren't imaginary. Carolyn had seen them. And now she wanted to find this particular monster really badly.

Carolyn sat back and contemplated everything she knew so far, what she had learned from both Aaron Wood and Beau Hodges. As she sat in silence, there was only one question she had wanted to know.

Carolyn opened her mouth and was about to ask, "How do we—"

"Do you know where they found her?" Hodges interrupted. "The girl from here, Willow Falls."

Carolyn shook her head. "They won't tell me. Up in some forest, by the look of the photos. I can't imagine they can keep it a secret for too long. Parents will talk; word will get around."

"Then how did you get the photos?"

"I took them, copied them." No point in hiding the fact now.

Hodges was quiet for a moment.

"Would it be easier if we knew the exact location?" Carolyn asked.

Hodges shook his head. "I imagine he wouldn't return there. He'll move on to another place. I know that's what I would do. Not hunt the same patch twice so soon."

Carolyn had to coax more out of Finch. She wanted to know exactly where the girl was found, maybe even go up there with Hodges and take a look at the terrain. See if they can find the kill plot. She really needed Hodges' expertise as well.

Carolyn took a deep breath then asked flatly, "Can you find him?"

Hodges narrowed his eyes at Carolyn. The thought had occurred to him, but he had never tracked another human being. And this was no ordinary human being. Hodges and his group had tried to find out who was following them but to no avail. The person was too clever. Too cunning.

Animals, to a certain extent, were docile, easily led, and malleable. But humans, the most intelligent of the species on the planet, were something entirely different. And this person was a cut above that as well.

"It's not like we didn't try," Hodges said, referring to the last hunting trip up on the Flint Plains. "There were four of us."

"I know. But..." Carolyn said.

"But what?"

Carolyn had to choose her next words carefully. "How would you lay a kill plot to catch him?" She pointed at one of the more graphic photos. "The man who did this."

Suddenly it felt colder in the room. The only sound came from the logs crackling then breaking apart in the fireplace.

Hodges sat back and rubbed his beard, a habit Carolyn believed he did when contemplating a difficult problem.

"Why not leave it to the police?" Hodges asked. "They have dogs, men, weapons. They are trained for this kind of thing."

"What?" Carolyn raised her voice. "The police around here?"

she scoffed. Then she realized how arrogant she sounded and had to check herself.

"Look," she said, her tone more reasonable now. "They're out of their depth. They think they can handle this themselves. Truth is they can't. I know, I've seen it before."

Hodges said nothing, just listened.

"If we can just find out who this person is, maybe catch them before another woman turns up dead and nailed to a tree like the others."

"How do you know it's the same person?" Hodges asked. It wasn't a pointless question.

Carolyn started rubbing her wrists, a nervous habit she displayed when she was getting frustrated.

"Take a look at the photos," Carolyn exclaimed. "They are almost identical. It's the same person."

"I mean the guy who was following us up on the Flint Plains. How can you be sure it's the same person who also did these?" Hodges pointed at the photos that were spread out in front of him. "How can you be certain? It could have been just another hunter fooling around with us up there."

It was true, and Carolyn knew it in her heart. There was no link yet. She had no real proof, no real evidence, and here she was asking Beau Hodges to chase and catch some ghost, some enigma in the forest.

"Look"—Carolyn leaned forward, her eyes on the photos—"I don't really know for sure." She picked up the photo of Clarissa Mulligan, held it up in front of Hodges' eyes. "But I am certain that whoever did this to her, this woman from Willow Falls, is the same person who killed all of these women, too." She pointed at the other photos, a morbid gallery of pain, suffering, and brutal death.

Hodges took the photo from Carolyn's hand and stared at the image some more. Nothing would give him more pleasure than to confront whoever had done this, and then do the same to them. Hodges was old school. Wasn't interested in letting it go through the courts and leaving it to smart-assed lawyers with their silver tongues and fancy suits. Even though he didn't watch the news much, basically it was just a lot of fake crap and hogwash anyway; he'd seen enough and heard enough to know that plenty of people, some of them killers, too, walked free because of the law.

He looked up at Carolyn again. He understood her plight, he truly did. He wanted to exact his own form of justice on the person who did this to these women. But he needed more to go on. What she was asking him to do could land him in prison with a life sentence if they got it wrong.

Hunters are a very defensive breed. They like guns. They like to hunt, and most of them have the Second Amendment framed on the wall at home. If you corner another hunter, in the wild, and start making all kinds of accusations, then it could get ugly real quick. Especially with everyone holding a gun.

"Suppose we find this person," Hodges said, still holding the photo of Clarissa Mulligan. "Are you just going to go up to them, show them this picture, and ask them, 'Did you do this?' and see what they say?"

Carolyn let out a sigh of exasperation, not aimed at Hodges, more aimed at herself. She didn't want to hear what he was saying. Maybe she needed to. She knew she was impatient. Her colleagues and boss back in Salt Lake City never got tired of telling her that fact.

However, she could feel the rekindling of her spirit, the ambition that drove her. The same ambition and drive that she had lost while bedridden in a hospital recovering after being shot.

Now she felt she had purpose, something to drive her again. These women had given her this. Carolyn thought she had lost the spark, the drive she had felt catching bad people. And she knew that the person who had done this to these poor, helpless women was one of the worst kinds of monsters imaginable. She desperately wanted to catch him.

There was some selfishness in her motives as well. But it had only been exacerbated by Tyler Finch refusing to accept her help. If the local police were too stubborn or too proud, then she would go it alone. Trust her instincts. Trust her gut.

"I don't know what I'll do," Carolyn admitted. "I'll cross that bridge when I see them face-to-face."

35

E very town has it, a decaying part, an ugly part, an embarrassing part where the bright lights and charm of the town run up hard against the raw blunt edge of desolate emptiness and unsightliness.

It may be as simple as crossing the street or turning a corner. Then the atmosphere changes. Cross that divide and you will see boarded-up buildings, cracked footpaths, and faded hope. Hidden among the unkempt scrub and unruly weeds, you will see the hollow remnants of ambition gone broke, moved on, or closed down.

Willow Falls was no different.

It was near dusk when Tyler Finch parked his police cruiser in an empty lot at the side of a building that had once been the warehouse for an irrigation parts manufacturing company. Now it was just a sagging hunk of bricks and steel, rust and ruin, dead dreams and abundant despair.

Apparently, there was a disturbance, a complaint from an unknown caller. Probably kids fooling around. Old abandoned buildings like these were a haven for bored teenagers and enterprising couples.

However, it was a short detour for Finch. He was heading home after his shift. It would be nothing major, he imagined, a quick search, in and out in a few minutes with nothing to report.

The ground was cold and hard, strewn with layers of the building that had peeled away like skin over the years, countless summers, endless cold winters. All the windows of the building had been broken years ago. So not much more damage could be inflicted by bored kids or the homeless who had been drinking and busting stuff up.

Around the side, Finch found a boarded-up doorway where a few wooden boards had been pulled away, just enough space to squeeze through.

The cavernous innards of the building were a cold damp void of tumbled-down decay. Piles of trash, twisted iron, spindles of wire, broken glass, dead birds. Shards of dying light, dusty and pale, filtered down from the ceiling where sections of the tin roof had rusted through or had peeled completely away, the wooden joists rotted and broken.

Finch carried a flashlight on his duty belt. He left it in its pouch though, preferring not to startle anyone—if anyone was here. There was enough light; however, it would soon be dark.

The floor was a crumbled layer of rubble, concrete, dust, and industrial debris, blotchy in some places with animal feces and human stain.

The back of the warehouse yawned wide and black, a train tunnel of darkness where the outside twilight couldn't reach. Somewhere in the darkness above, feathered wings fluttered.

To one side he saw torn walls, the skeletal remains of workshop bays with cement columns, chipped and rust stained. A framework of steel gantries hugged one wall leading to somewhere overhead.

Weeds grew through cracks in the floor, pushing upward, trying to reach the ceiling and the sky beyond, while parts of the ceiling had fallen to the ground below, an opposing cycle of growth and decay.

Finch worked his way forward, careful where he stepped, boots crunching on the uneven surface, following a rough channel through the debris field.

The place was empty, soundless, and soulless. No one was here, or if they had been, they were long gone now.

Finch wondered who had made the call, complained about the disturbance. The nearest house was maybe half a mile away.

He stepped around puddles of frozen water where snow and sleet had come through from the holes in the roof and melted then hardened again.

Reaching the middle of the building, Finch paused, did a complete turn, looking floor to ceiling all around. The place was deserted, empty, a shell.

Pockets of shadows grew and expanded. The tiny bit of natural light that seeped in was almost gone, the sun outside finally sliding from the day.

A thin funnel of snowflakes started to drift down from above, settling in a growing pile of white on the cold floor.

There was nothing here. A waste of time.

Finch decided to take a quick walk to the rear, just to make sure, then he would leave. He was looking forward to putting his feet up, grabbing a beer, and maybe grilling a steak and catching the start of the basketball game. All of which were a much better alternative than poking around an old, cold, empty factory in the dark.

Slipping out his flashlight, he moved on again. It was like the building had become the dumping ground for other people's trash. The farther in he went, the more rubbish and debris seemed to accumulate around him. Some of it had been pushed aside, and it made it easier for him to walk.

Then a sound from above.

Finch paused and panned his flashlight upward, playing the beam over dark rafters and joists, some warped, others rotted completely through. He saw the faint outline of a bird, nesting somewhere in the crux of the beams.

He moved on, quickening his pace. He wanted to get it done and get out.

Up ahead, part of an interior wall had collapsed forming a pile of bricks and old mortar. There was a row of old offices to his right, gutted, windows smashed, Sheetrock walls punched and torn open.

The beam of his flashlight fell onto an object twenty yards directly in front of him. The object looked out of place, order where there was disorder. Placement where there was displacement.

A wooden chair, sat upright ahead. It stood in a small clearing, rubbish and debris pushed back and away from it. Alone, by itself.

Something glinted, caught in the beam of his flashlight.

Something on the chair, on the seat.

Finch walked up to the chair, his eyes, his entire focus on the chair, on the object that had been placed in the middle of the seat.

Finch stared at the object. It was shiny, small, and delicate. A pendant on a silver chain, with a name engraved on it.

Clarissa.

Finch's jaw tingled, and his skin rippled with a sudden unease.

Then he realized among the disarray was some order, subtle, but there. Things had been shifted, swept back, a path through the chaos and decay, a path to be followed without thinking. Without realizing that you were following a path at all.

Something moved in front of him, beyond the chair, in the background.

Instinct screamed at Finch to tear his eyes away from the object on the chair, to look up.

He did.

His flashlight following where his eyes went, but lagging in precious seconds.

A thin shaft of black carbon, impossibly fast, impossible to see, sliced through the air then sunk deep into Finch's right shoulder.

He felt a sharp sting of searing pain. Nerves and tendons spasmed then released. The flashlight fell instantly from his grip. It bounced once, throwing a scatter of light before rolling then settling, a cone of light pointing ahead along the ground.

His brain told him to go for his gun, the holster on his right hip, right there, within reach. But his arm wouldn't move. His entire arm felt gone, amputated, not there, disconnected from the fingertips all the way up to the shoulder socket.

Looking down he saw that his arm was intact, still there. So was something else, a foreign object, buried deep in his shoulder with part of it sticking out at a right angle to his arm.

He tried again, going for his gun. Still his arm lay dead.

The wall of darkness in front of Finch rippled, distorted, then parted. A shape separated itself from the blackness around it and slowly moved toward him.

Finch brought up his left arm this time, reaching across. It was awkward, unnatural, taking one's gun out of its holster using your least favored hand, but still possible, if your life depended on it.

Finch's move had been anticipated, like everything else.

Pain, sharp and raw thudded into his left shoulder this time. His left arm went limp and fell back. It hung by his side, just like his right arm, a useless piece of dead meat.

A third bolt thudded into his thigh just below the hip and Finch sunk to his knees. Blood trickled down both his arms, dripping from his fingertips, watering the cold, dusty floor. All he could do was look up as the figure approached then stopped in front of him, the face hidden by a hideous mask.

The person looked down at Finch. No pity. No empathy. Cold, calculating eyes scrutinized the placement of each shot in Finch's limbs. Satisfied, the person walked to the wooden chair, reached down, and gathered up the small silver necklace they had placed there. Pocketing the necklace, the person returned to where Finch knelt.

Finch was sweating, his teeth clenched, his face twisted in pain. He stared defiantly at the person who stood before him.

The mask came away.

Finch gasped.

It was a face he recognized.

36

As she pulled up at Ritter's cabin, Carolyn was greeted by the warm glow of light pouring from the windows and the smell of woodsmoke that spiraled lazily into the air from a stone chimney.

Everything was crusted with a thick layer of white. Like snow foam, it covered the roof, clung to the trees and bushes, and painted the surrounding ground. Icicles dripped along the edge of the roof, and the sky was a darkening shade of indigo that glistened with the first evening stars.

Ritter's Jeep was parked under a carport away from the cabin, and a path had been cleared through the snow that beckoned Carolyn to the front steps and up onto a wide porch built from hewn logs and wide, rustic wooden floorboards.

The front door opened before Carolyn had a chance to dust off her boots and knock.

Ritter stood there, a smile on his face as he greeted her.

Inside, he took her jacket and hung it next to his. "No problem finding the place?" Ritter asked as Carolyn followed him down a hallway toward the rear of the cabin where the kitchen was.

"No, not at all," she said, looking around. A set of stairs near the entrance led up to the second story. There was an open living room with comfortable sofas, rugs on the wooden floors, bookcases crammed with leather-bound books, and a beautiful stone fireplace as the centerpiece where logs crackled and flames danced. In the kitchen Carolyn was hit by the wonderful smell of herbs, onions, and garlic that came from a saucepan simmering on the stove.

Ritter opened a bottle and poured Carolyn a glass of red wine. "You must forgive me for my attire," Ritter said, pointing down at his clothing. "I got in half an hour ago, and I haven't had a chance to shower and change. Just been running around getting everything ready."

Ritter wore a fleece vest over a plaid flannel shirt and trail pants. He looked like he'd been hiking outdoors all day.

He looked perfectly fine to Carolyn. "Look, I'm sorry about today," she said. "I shouldn't have been looking in your car."

Ritter waved her off. "Nothing to apologize for." He opened the refrigerator and took out a heavy casserole dish and placed it on the countertop. "I hope you're hungry." The dish was covered with cling wrap, and inside were two massive steaks marinating in red wine, crushed garlic, and fresh oregano. "Picked up these after I saw you this morning."

Carolyn took a sip of the wine and began to relax for the first time today. She was glad she was here but disappointed in herself for jumping to conclusions about Ritter. Maybe some of the things Finch had said about her were true. Maybe she needed to take a breath, slow down, and not steamroll in and treat everyone as a suspect.

"Look, I'm going to take a shower, get out of these grubby clothes," Ritter said. He turned down the flame of the pan simmering on the stove top. "Can you just keep an eye on things?"

"Sure, no problem," Carolyn said, studying Ritter's face.

"What?" he said expectantly, noting her look.

Carolyn shook her head. "Nothing." Carolyn could feel that tingling in her gut. She could tell from the way he looked at her that the evening could lead to other things. He didn't need a shower; he smelled good enough now. That musky, earthy scent of sweat, woodsmoke tinged with traces of garlic and crushed herbs still on his fingers.

Ritter gave her a beguiling grin and playfully warned her, "Watch the stove; it's my trademark steak sauce that I've got reducing."

As she watched him walk back down the passageway, Carolyn could feel her face flush with heat. Maybe it was the wine. Maybe it was something else. What the hell was a guy this handsome, this considerate, and this alluring, doing vacationing in a place like Willow Falls?

Something just niggled at her.

Looking around, she spied a wooden spoon on a small dish next to a large knife block on the counter. A wonderful rich aroma laced with red wine and ripe tomatoes wafted into her face as she gave the smooth velvety mixture in the saucepan a gentle stir.

"Help yourself to some more wine." Ritter's distant voice echoed down the passageway toward her from somewhere out of sight.

Carolyn wandered around the kitchen, opening then closing doors and cupboards, seeing what was inside.

The refrigerator was well stocked. No junk food in sight.

She bent down and opened the cabinet under the sink. Inside, bottles of cleaning products were neatly lined up. Then she noticed a small steel can. It was pushed to the back, almost hidden.

She withdrew the can and read the label, big red letters at the top, and a sea of fine print underneath. Strange, maybe it had been left by the owner, she thought to herself. She placed the can back, closed the cupboard, and wandered toward the pantry.

There was a door next to it. She tried the handle but it was locked. She looked around for a key and saw a bunch of them hanging on the wall next to the back door.

Carolyn looked over her shoulder, back down the hallway. She heard the shower running somewhere upstairs, the sound of water running through pipes in the ceiling above her head.

She tried all the keys on the bunch but none of them fit.

The running water stopped, and she quickly returned the keys to the wall hook.

Moments later, Ritter came back downstairs. His hair was still wet, but he had changed into a crewneck sweater and jeans. As he walked past Carolyn, she caught the woodsy scent of sandalwood and spice.

"That's better," he said as he refilled her wineglass.

She held up her hand in protest. "Careful, I have to drive back."

Ritter took a wineglass from a cabinet and filled it. "You can always stay the night," he said with an inviting grin. He watched her over the rim of the wineglass as he took a sip, his eyes enticing.

Carolyn raised her eyebrows. "We'll see."

They sat in the open living room, at a small table he had set up next to the crackling fire. Flickers of orange and yellow danced off the stone walls as they ate, drank, and laughed together. The wine was doing its trick, and Carolyn could feel the tension, aches, and pains of the day seep out of her.

Ritter had grilled the steaks to perfection, and the tossed salad was a marvel of color and textures. His special steak sauce was like drinking liquid gold.

"Where did you learn to cook like this?" Carolyn asked as she ate. The food was wonderful, and the wine was perfectly matched to the steak and the meatiness of the sauce.

Ritter shrugged. "I hardly get the time but when I do, I like to cook." He raised his wineglass to Carolyn. "But very rarely do I get the opportunity to cook for such a beautiful woman like you."

Carolyn looked into his eyes, at the pools of dark chocolate she could happily drown in. He was over fifteen years older than her, but he played it to his advantage. Experience, confidence, certainty, assertiveness, stability. They were all traits that women wanted when they were ready to settle down and find a provider. Ritter had them all, yet he wasn't married.

"I bet you say that to all the young women in the hospital," Carolyn said. "Make them all swoon, I bet."

"Hardly," Ritter scoffed. "Most of them are skittish, boring, self-obsessed, can't hold a decent conversation, and wish that life in a major hospital was like *Grey's Anatomy*."

Carolyn had to confess, Ritter did look a little like Patrick Dempsey with a touch of Dr. Ross thrown in for good measure.

"I heard today that the police found the body of a girl in the forest," Carolyn said as casually as possible, fixing her gaze on Ritter to see his reaction.

Ritter gave a look of empathy. "I know, it sounds awful, if you ask me. I heard it around town this morning. I believe it made it into the local newspaper, too."

"Apparently, someone killed her with a crossbow," Carolyn said, her eyes still fixed on Ritter. "Pinned her to a tree with arrows."

Ritter held her gaze. "Bolts," he corrected her. "They're called bolts not arrows. Arrows are for bows not crossbows."

"Whatever," Carolyn said with a wave of her wineglass as she took another mouthful.

"I can't begin to imagine what it's like to be hunted like an animal. The initial shock, then the horror and fear you feel when you realize that someone is hiding in the trees, or in the scrub, or in the darkness, waiting for that right moment just to kill you." Ritter held her gaze, his words haunting, firelight flicking off his eyes.

Carolyn cocked her head at him. "Well, imagine what it's like for a fucking deer, then, and you'll have a pretty good idea."

"Must we talk about all this?" Ritter gave Carolyn an appealing look. "I see enough death in my profession every day."

Carolyn relented. "Sorry, I just find it so appalling."

Carolyn remained at the table while Ritter cleared away the plates. She stared deep into the fire, thinking about nothing in particular.

She heard Ritter return from the kitchen, come up slowly behind her, felt his hands on her shoulders as they began to knead tired and knotted muscles.

She didn't pull away. Instead, she leaned back into him, closed her eyes in ecstasy as he slowly and gently caressed her shoulders and neck. He was good with his hands, knew exactly which muscles, tendons, and nerve endings to massage.

His hands drifted down the front of her chest, soft and delicate fingertips lightly moving across the tops of her breasts.

She arched her back in response, like a cat, her breasts lifting and swelling, tight and restrained. She felt a simmering heat building inside her.

Gentle hands pulled her up off the chair, and she opened her eyes as she faced him.

She wanted this. Needed this. She was ripe to burst and longed for that sweet release.

Fingers glided over her chest, just the slightest touch, following the curve of her breasts, the heat beneath her shirt burning her skin, the flames in the fireplace stone-cold compared to the furnace that raged inside her now.

She stared at his lips, warm and inviting.

Then he kissed her, his mouth over hers, measured but sensual. Calm, masterful, his exploration guided by her responsiveness.

She felt his powerful arms wrap around her waist, drawing her in. Her breasts melded into his torso, a natural fit, two solids melded together as one, his body hard, rigid with muscle, hers brittle with heat.

Hands expertly tracked down the small of her back, flowing over the curve of her buttocks, pausing, feeling, touching, searching before moving around to the inside of her thighs, and slowly working their way up to the cleft of her groin where the furnace raged the hottest.

37

The sensation she felt changed in a heartbeat.

What had started as a gentle caress changed into something that screamed alarm in Carolyn's mind. His fingers now were searching, feeling, probing, not simply touching.

Carolyn's eyelids burst open, and she pulled away violently. Fear and revulsion boiled up in her throat. She felt physically sick as she stared, bewildered at Ritter.

"Did you just try and frisk me?" Carolyn asked, her voice low, almost a growl. She couldn't believe it. She felt confusion, then coldness, then anger, tumble through her head.

Ritter smiled, withdrew a few feet, then sat down on the sofa. He crossed his legs casually and regarded Carolyn as she stood there.

She had never felt so violated in all her life.

"Killing, it's the sweetest thing you will ever taste," Ritter said, his voice calm, almost dreamlike. Arrogance and evilness began to seep around edges of the carefully constructed picture he had painted of himself.

It was a masterpiece of illusion and deceit.

Carolyn stood still. She had no gun. No cell phone. Both were back in her car. The last thing she wanted was for Ritter, after he took her jacket, to see that she was armed. And the handgun she had chosen wasn't exactly something that could be easily concealed under her shirt at the dinner table.

She had no ability to just kill him here and now. Except perhaps with her bare hands, a table lamp, or a piece of furniture. Then the images of his victims, lifted powerfully with just one hand before being pinned to a tree came flooding back to her.

But Ritter didn't look physically imposing, powerful. Sure, he was tall, lean, broad broad shouldered. And yet Carolyn couldn't imagine him as the killer.

She still needed a weapon. He had subtly and skillfully checked her body for one. And her cell phone, too. Suddenly she understood he had no intention of the evening ever going down the path she had been anticipating. He had led her here, to his cabin, lured her like he had his other victims.

"Fear," Ritter said mildly, his voice polite, self-assured, "it's what makes ordinary people do extraordinary things."

Carolyn looked at him as he slowly morphed into his true self right before her eyes. His real self. The clever façade was gone. It had been a construct. A fabrication. He didn't look any different to Carolyn, but in her mind, her interpretation of him had changed completely. But there were subtle changes. The corners of his mouth, the edges of his eyes. His stare, his voice, how his eyes watched Carolyn.

"Trust your instincts, Carolyn. You know in your heart it is true."

"Don't use my name," Carolyn hissed. She wiped her lips, her mouth, vigorously on the back of her hand. No matter how hard she tried, she could still taste him. Something so sweet just seconds ago now tasted bitter, dead, and rancid.

Ritter continued smiling, amused.

Carolyn looked around the room.

The small table where they had eaten dinner had been cleared of any cutlery, deliberately. Oddly, there was no poker next to the fireplace. It had been strategically removed, too.

The nearest implement was a heavy lamp on a side table, maybe six feet to her right. She imagined smashing its heavy metal base into Ritter's skull. Over and over and over again. In her mind she saw blood and brain matter splash against the fabric of the sofa.

She looked back at him. "Why did you do it, kill them?"

Ritter tilted his head and let out a bored sigh. "I can't explain it to you. To anyone. I just enjoy it. Taking a life. I find it as normal and as natural as breathing."

Carolyn's eyes darted back to the heavy lamp. To go for it meant crossing where Ritter now sat. He would cut her off in a second. "Why tell me?" she asked. "You know I'll go to the police. You've just confessed." Carolyn knew the answer was simple. He didn't intend her to leave his cabin alive.

Ritter slowly shook his head like a disappointed parent scolding a child. "It's one thing to know. It's another thing to be able to prove it. You, of all people, should understand that."

"Your car. This place." Carolyn waved her hand around the room. "We'll pull it apart. Everything. Your home in Chicago, too. Your office. Everything. We'll find the evidence."

"Please," Ritter replied. "Don't treat me as the fool you now look. You, or anyone else, will not find a thing."

Carolyn replayed in her head everything Aaron Wood had described to her about him. She compressed it, ran it at three times the speed. Powerful, extremely intelligent, vain, egotistical, meticulous, obsessive, always chose the most difficult path to test himself. Ritter had left no tracks, no evidence, and no clues. Everything was carefully planned to the nth degree. He would have thought everything through, approached it not like a hobby or a sport, but like a profession. His killing was his chosen vocation, and he pursued it with the same attention to detail, vigor, and compulsion as everything else he did in his life. That is what Aaron Wood had said.

In his eyes, Ritter wasn't insane. He wasn't mad. He wasn't a sociopath. He was a brilliant surgeon, saved countless lives. He had mastered that aspect of his profession, the act of saving lives, to be godlike. But like God, Ritter wanted to experience the full spectrum: to take life as well. He wasn't content with just excelling on one side of the mortal equation. To cut, to remove, to suture, to clamp, to beat death also meant he wanted to beat life, to take it away so suddenly, so unexpectedly, and so brutally from others.

Then to her surprise, Ritter said something. "I'm not going to kill you," he stated. "I'm not even going to harm you."

"You're lying," Carolyn retorted. Yet somehow, even though she had uttered the words, she didn't believe them. It was something Aaron Wood had said, about Ritter being different, wanting to be different, not like the others. To do the most difficult of things. It would be too easy for him to kill her, bury her so no one would find her. But easy wasn't what Ritter wanted. He wanted things to be deliberately hard, Wood had said. To challenge himself. Then it dawned on Carolyn.

"How?" she said.

The smile vanished from Ritter's face. She understood. "That is for you to decide," he said.

He was going to hunt her. He wanted the challenge.

"You're free to go," Ritter said.

"What if I run, leave town, disappear?"

Ritter's eyes narrowed. "Then I'll hunt your sister instead. I know where you two live in town. I've been there, walked up the path at night. Stood on your porch. Looked inside, been inside, too. You can't keep me out. No one can."

Carolyn felt mortified. Ritter had been watching her. He was the man on the rooftop she had chased two nights ago. He had been inside her mother's house. Touched things. Seen things.

"Why did you save me the other night, in the building, when the floor had collapsed?"

"It wasn't the right time," Ritter replied, sounding aloof. "That was unexpected, the floor giving way."

"What do you want from me?"

"To take the chance I'm offering you, Carolyn. The chance that I offer all of them, the opportunity to escape, to beat me. If you go to the police, they'll think you're a fool, making accusations that you can't support. I will invite them up here, tell them they can turn this place upside down if they wish. They will find nothing of value. They'll just put it down to a woman's scorn. I'll say that I rejected your advances, and you got angry, wanted retribution. So you're now making wild claims about me." Ritter leaned forward. "Who's going to believe you?"

"I'll make them believe me," Carolyn snarled, balling her fists and taking a step toward Ritter, angling toward the heavy lamp.

The move wasn't lost on Ritter. He glanced at the lamp then back at Carolyn, a smug look on his face. He gestured at the lamp. "Be my guest. Go for it. Make the evening interesting."

Carolyn didn't move. Just stood weighing up her options, then deciding she wasn't going to try for the lamp. It would be futile. This was a man who had lifted her, one-handed, out of a hole in the floor, away from certain death.

After a moment of inaction, Ritter spoke. "Good choice," he said. "You're not that stupid. That's why I'm giving you the choice: you or your sister. Which is it to be?"

Ritter was going to hunt her, Carolyn knew it. Jodie wouldn't stand a chance. How and when she was unsure. But it was a chance she was willing to take. She glanced at the front door.

"I won't stop you leaving right now," Ritter reassured her. "But like I said, if you leave town, run, I will hunt down your sister in your place."

38

S he could tell right away that something was wrong.

A certain kind of sadness reached out toward her, across the desolate open ground, from where Hodges stood alone, a solitary shape on a flat horizon, under the early morning sun.

Carolyn felt a cold shiver ripple across her skin then a knot of dread tighten in the pit of her stomach as she drove her car toward him.

Hodges was digging with the rhythmic rise and fall motion of an oil drilling pump. Strong and methodical, a heavy mattock in his hands, the forged steel head making slow work of the hard, frozen earth.

The landscape was empty, except for Hodges and the three mounds of earth, aligned in a neat row next to him. He was working on the last gaping hole in the ground, making it deeper, making it wider, like the others.

Carolyn slowed her car then stopped. She hadn't slept since leaving Ritter's cabin last night. She'd spent the dark hours before dawn sitting at home, next to the fire, gun in hand, her mind turning over the sudden revelations of the previous evening.

Hodges paused for a moment, glanced up. His face blank, expressionless. Then he returned to his sorrowful task. Up and down the mattock went.

Carolyn got out of her car. The air was cold and hard, leached of all warmth from the lingering night.

The dog cages were empty. The holes in the ground he had dug weren't.

The dogs were dead—all of them. Four graves, four loyal friends—more than friends. Lifelong companions. Family. His family. He was burying his loved ones.

When she stood beside him, Carolyn couldn't find the words, so Hodges found some for her. He stopped his digging and looked at her, his face wet with perspiration. "We're going to kill him, aren't we." It wasn't a question. More of an affirmation. This is what is going to happen. Certain. Absolutely. No question.

She saw sorrow in his eyes and something else, too. A cold malice. An iron-hard resolve and an almost manic need for retribution that Hodges was struggling to contain. Up close, he looked like he had grown even bigger, more formidable; such was the hatred that now filled him.

Looking away, he held back tears, only just, and resumed digging, deep earthy thuds that Carolyn could feel through the soles of her boots. A giant trying to split the planet, venting what he felt inside.

Carolyn had seen it before, plenty of times. The fine, thin line that any normal, sane person usually walks. A line that is only one violent step away from them serving ten years to life in a federal prison.

Hodges stopped.

The last hole was done.

He stepped toward Carolyn, his face streaked with dirt, the mattock held in one massive hand. He felt no anger toward her. It was directed at someone else. He spoke again. "We're not going to just find him, are we?" Deliberate, even words. "We're not going to bring him back so he can be studied, put in one of your institutions." His voice like gravel. "We're going to find him and kill him. Destroy him. Yes?"

Carolyn looked at the three mounds of dirt. The fourth hole was deep enough now. Next to it sat a wrapped bundle, a single honey-brown paw poking out between the folds of an old blanket.

Her eyes returned to Hodges. She nodded just once. Now it was Carolyn's turn to step forward, closer to where Hodges stood, just inches from his face. He towered over her, blocking out the fading stars and the brightening dawn sky. She looked up into his eyes. "I want you to hunt him, turn the tables on him. Can you do that for me?" As she said the words, Carolyn knew there was a chance Ritter wouldn't be in his cabin waiting for them. The hunt had already begun as soon as she had left his cabin last night. Killing the dogs was just a precursor of what was to come.

Hodges offered no smile. He'd lost the compulsion to ever smile again. His answer instead burned in his eyes.

Carolyn continued. "You'll get your chance to kill him, just between you and me. No one else needs to know."

They said nothing for a while, just a look of understanding between them.

The earth slowly rotated, the light of a new day crept inch by inch toward where they stood on the flatness.

Carolyn nodded, and stood back.

With uncharacteristic gentleness, Hodges picked up the last wrapped bundle. He used a thick blanket on all of his dogs. The earth was cold, and he wanted them to be warm wherever dogs go to when they die.

It was gut-wrenching to watch.

Hodges knelt down and placed the bundle into the hole. He mumbled something, a promise. Reaching into the hole, he stroked the wrapped bundle one last time, and began pushing the mound of dirt near the edge, filling the hole in, while still on his knees, using just his bare hands.

Carolyn turned and started walking toward the house, tears at the corners of her own eyes, leaving Hodges to grieve and to be alone with his dogs.

It was better that way.

She pointed to the four bloodied crossbow bolts that lay on the ground nearby. Hodges had cut them out of each dog before he had carefully wrapped their bodies. It wasn't right leaving them in.

"Bring those with you when you come inside," she said over her shoulder. She walked on, purposeful, deliberate steps while inside her head, her mind was racked with fear and uncertainty.

THERE WOULD BE no prints on the bolts. That was too much to expect. That and the fact that Hodges would have almost certainly ruined any residual evidence there was when he removed them from the dogs. Yet Carolyn wanted to look at every piece of evidence, to understand every detail of what they were dealing with, the kind of man they were going up against. And she needed every advantage she could find, no matter how small or insignificant it seemed.

Hodges took a shower and cleaned up before he started a fresh pot of coffee brewing, while Carolyn sat by the fire, staring at the flames, alone with her thoughts, her mind consumed with the task at hand and the self-doubt that she felt inside. It was just going to be her, Hodges as well. But there was no backup as there had been in the past. No army of agents to follow her into battle. No special tactical team to kick in doors and breach buildings for her to follow safely in their wake. She had no choice as Ritter had said. Either it's her or her sister.

Carolyn intended to go nowhere else today other than here. She wanted Hodges' opinion, and she wanted to formulate a very clear plan as to when and how they were going to stop him.

Hodges had wrapped the crossbow bolts in an old towel and had placed them on a table.

He built up the logs on the fire, and they sat on the sofas and said nothing for a while as they drank coffee and watched the room brighten through the windows.

Finally Hodges spoke, his eyes gazing into the fire. It was like he was talking to no one in particular, just saying his thoughts out loud. "I didn't hear a thing. Not a sound all evening. Then I woke at around 4:00 a.m., which is unusual because I normally sleep through and wake up like clockwork at around five. But not this morning."

"Did you hear anything at all?" Carolyn asked. "A car? The dogs?"

Hodges continued to stare into the fire. He shook his head slowly. "Nothing. Not a sound. Not a bark or a whimper. But something didn't feel right," he said.

Carolyn frowned but said nothing.

"I could tell as soon as I opened my eyes that something was wrong; I guess that's what woke me up. Like a kind of sixth sense. I could feel it. It was the same feeling I had when we were up in the hills last time hunting."

"So what happened next?"

Hodges took a deep breath. "Dogs usually are quiet in the morning until I go outside and feed them, and that's when they see me and start making a racket. So I got dressed, pulled on my boots, and went outside."

Hodges' jaw worked back and forth slowly; he was grinding his teeth in anger. "Nothing. I heard nothing from them," he said. "I thought they were just lying down, you know, like, still sleeping. They would have heard me shut the front door, but they just lay there. I called out to a few of them, whistled, and they didn't move.

It was only when I got a few feet away that I noticed the crossbow bolts sticking out of their bodies."

He turned his head toward Carolyn. "It's the same person, the one who was tracking us up in the hills. I'm certain it's him." Hodges balled his fists, thinking about his dogs. "He'd shot them. Snuck in during the night or early morning. Went right up to the cages and killed them all," he said, his teeth gritted, trying to swallow his anger.

"How can that be?" Carolyn asked. "They would have heard him, smelled him coming. Gone berserk as soon as they laid eyes on him."

Hodges stared into the flames of the fire. "I don't know. I can't explain it. He may have baited them. But that would still mean he would have had to have gotten close enough to throw something in the cages. And still they didn't raise the alarm. It was almost as if they knew him, trusted him."

"There's a bigger issue at stake here," Carolyn said. It was the first glaring thought that had entered her mind as soon as she'd seen the dead dogs.

"He knows where I live," Hodges answered. "So why didn't he just come right up into the house? Kill me?"

"Because he's taunting you, destroying the things around you that you care about, your dogs. He's evil. He enjoys it."

"I'm not scared of him." Since the discovery of the dead dogs, Hodges's had armed himself. A handgun was concealed under his shirt, and he'd set up several hunting rifles scattered around the house, fully loaded.

"I know," Carolyn said. "He understands that. He wants you to do exactly what you're going to do. He wants you to come after him, so he can lure you into his domain, into his territory. He knows you'll want revenge. He knows you'll come after him."

"You sound like you know who it is?" Hodges asked. "Not just a theory you had."

Carolyn hesitated for a moment. "There's a man," Carolyn said slowly. "His name is Michael Ritter. He's not a local. He's vacationing here."

Hodges looked at Carolyn. "And you think it's him?"

"I know it's him."

"How?"

Carolyn had to say it even if it sounded foolish. "Because he told me."

39

Hodges rose to his full height and faced Carolyn. He bunched his fingers into balls of hard knuckle and iron bone, the sinew and muscles of his forearms tightening, veins bulging under the skin. "He admitted to killing my dogs? To killing these women you told me about? The ones in the photos you showed me?"

Carolyn had to think for a moment. Ritter hadn't exactly confessed to anything specific, who he had killed. He was far too clever for that. He would have covered his tracks, destroyed all evidence that would implicate him. If challenged, Carolyn knew he would deny it all, that he had admitted nothing to her. Say she was making things up because he had rejected her advances. Ritter's words came back to Carolyn. *It's one thing to know. It's another thing to be able to prove it.*

"Not exactly—"

Before Carolyn could finish, Hodges got up, disappeared for a few minutes, then returned carrying a large rolled-up map. He motioned Carolyn toward a large high table under a window and unfurled the map then pinned down the corners. "Where does he live?" Hodges asked impatiently.

Carolyn hesitated. The last thing she wanted was Hodges tearing up to Ritter's cabin full of rage and revenge. Plus there was no chain of evidence. She had nothing incriminating, just a loose admission by him that wouldn't stand up in any court in the land. Ritter was playing with her, toying with her mind.

She could call Aaron Wood. Get his team here, tear Ritter's cabin apart, see what they might find. Yet somehow, deep in her gut, Carolyn knew they would find nothing. For three years Ritter had gotten away with it. There was a reason for that. Carolyn needed to gather the evidence first, otherwise she'd look like a fool. That's what Ritter wanted, to professionally shame her.

"Let's watch him for a while," Carolyn finally said. "Observe him and see what he does."

"So you're not entirely convinced that it's him?" Hodges asked skeptically.

Carolyn knew it was Ritter. But the "shoot now, worry about the evidence later" approach didn't sit well with her. She couldn't ignore the years of training she had and the principles that she had instilled in the other junior agents who she had supervised. She didn't want to see Ritter walk out of court due to a lack of evidence or on a technicality.

Carolyn leaned over the map. "Here," she said, her finger resting on a spot high up in the foothills.

Hodges looked at the spot where she was pointing.

"He's renting a log cabin here. I've been there. There's only one road in, a dirt road, and the same road leads out."

Hodges' eyes narrowed as he studied the map. He knew the place. It was a log cabin that used to be owned by Ben Hogan, a local who had died a few years back. Left the place to his son who must have now rented it out.

Hodges traced his finger south along the map. "We're here." His finger stopped then tapped the map. "Five miles south of the cabin."

"In a straight line," Carolyn said, her mind already formulating the beginnings of a strategy, a plan as to how they would reach the cabin without being seen.

"There's an access road here," Hodges said, "that you would have driven along. Cuts off the main road. There is no other way in."

"If we use the road," Carolyn said as she followed the squiggles on the map. There were blocks shaded in green indicating forest. Blue lines, like cracks in glass indicated a few creeks. The location of the cabin was surrounded by blocks of green on three sides.

"Between my property and his cabin is open ground," Hodges said. "Until we reach the start of the forest. Then we have ample cover for the next few miles. We can use that. He won't see us coming."

"Unless he's already in the forest," Carolyn said. "Maybe that's the part of the forest where they found the girl?"

They weren't placing their bets on Ritter being inside his cabin when they came. He could be in the forest, scouting out his next kill plot. Or he could be in town looking for his next victim. Or he could be outside right now staring at them through the window.

Carolyn jerked her head up instinctively. But the window was bare. There was no face, no killer's eyes watching them.

As if reading her mind, Hodges looked around. "Don't worry, if he comes so much as a mile of this place, I'll put a bullet in his skull."

Carolyn could see a rifle propped up next to the front door with another next to a table under the window.

But he had, Carolyn thought. Ritter had come right into Hodges' property, right up to the dog cages. And Hodges had no idea that he was right here until it was too late.

Carolyn just nodded.

As she returned her attention to the map, she couldn't help but feel a little tense. She wasn't afraid of anyone. However, Ritter wasn't just anyone. She had seen the case files, the pictures of his victims, how Aaron Wood had described the killer. He was like nothing she had ever seen or ever dealt with before.

"We'll take my snowmobile," Hodges said, pointing at the map again. "Make our way across the fields then into the forest."

"Won't he hear us coming?"

Hodges shook his head. "Plenty of snowmobile riders use these trails this time of year. It's a wide-open ground, and it's fairly flat until we reach the foothills. It's all forest after that, all the way to the cabin."

"And then?" Carolyn asked.

Hodges looked at the map, trying to calculate scale and distance. "Maybe a mile or so on foot. There should be enough trees and forest."

Carolyn stared at the map, thinking about the plan.

"When do we leave?" Carolyn asked.

"Today," Hodges said. "We'll leave late afternoon, at dusk."

Carolyn's mind swirled. The sudden decision to take immediate action had taken her off guard. She usually had backup, an army of agents around her, tactical support, air support as well, if needed. Now, it was just her as a civilian and a local hunter, who she didn't know all that well.

"OK," she stated slowly as the realization hit that this was really happening. She felt fear and excitement all at once. She wanted Ritter, but she needed proof, solid evidence and for her self-defense that would stand up in court. If he walked free because of her care-lessness or eagerness, he would vanish completely.

Carolyn looked down at what she was wearing. She had on her waterproof snow boots, jeans, and a few base layers of clothing and a light jacket. She'd left her heavy snow jacket back at the house. Doing outdoor surveillance in the snow, and at night, wasn't what she had in mind when she drove here this morning. Thankfully, she had kept a few other things in the trunk of her car. "I'm not dressed for this," Carolyn said.

Hodges stepped back and looked Carolyn up and down. "What

you are wearing is fine," he said. "Maybe a better jacket. I've got everything here we're going to need," Hodges added.

The mudroom was near the kitchen at the rear of the house. A wooden bench seat ran the length of one wall, an assortment of boots tucked underneath.

There was a large cupboard, with wooden shelves and cubbyholes filled with gloves, scarfs, and wool hats. The floor was a layer of cutout thick rubber matting used for stamping feet, dislodging mud and snow that could be easily pulled up and hosed into a drain grate underneath.

Bulky winter wear hung from old railway spikes that had been driven into a length of recycled railroad tie. Hodges had fashioned it together from pieces he had foraged from a disused rail line on the outskirts of town.

He took an insulated winter jacket off a spike and handed it to Carolyn. "My sister, she lives in New Orleans, came up a few seasons ago. She left this behind. You look about the same size."

Carolyn shrugged into the jacket. It fit, just was a little short around the sleeves. But she had on thermals that covered down to her wrists. Hodges selected a thicker pair of gloves for her and a better woolen hat than what Carolyn had with her.

Off the mudroom they came to a solid door made from heavy rustic lumber with hand-forged iron hinges and decorated with large iron nail heads. It was beautifully made and had a formidable lock casement. Carolyn looked at the heavy door. Something like this would cost a fortune in some trendy custom furniture store in the city. But like most things in the house, Hodges had made it with his own hands from discarded materials he had found.

Taking out a thick key, Hodges unlocked then opened the door, flipped on a light switch that was on the inside and pushed the door wide open for Carolyn to go first.

Carolyn paused on the threshold.

"Gun room," he said.

Carolyn stepped inside and found herself in a true hunter's den.

There were several locked glass front gun cabinets and workbenches fashioned, again, from heavy recycled wood, and shelves filled with gun-cleaning tools and supplies. It was like a small armory, probably more firepower here than what the police had back in town. One gun cabinet held several assault rifles. They sat snugly in foam mounts and sported military-style modifications including hi-tech optics. Another cabinet held an array of beautiful hunting rifles, polished walnut stocks, match grade stainless-steel barrels, expensive scopes, all lovingly oiled, cleaned, polished, and stored.

"Take your pick." Hodges indicated with a sweep of his hand.

Carolyn turned, pulled aside her jacket and lifted the side of her shirt that was loose and not tucked in. She drew out her Sig Sauer handgun from its holster and placed it on the bench with a heavy thud. "Don't need to."

Hodges picked up the gun, noted the day-night sights. "Nice," he said, appraising the weapon like it was a lover's thigh. "But good for only up close." He handed the gun back to Carolyn, who slid it back into the waistband holster. "I intend to get up close and personal," she replied. She was carrying two full magazines on her hip, hidden under the shirt as well.

Hodges unlocked the gun cabinet that held the hunting rifles. He selected his go-to rifle then filled a large military-style backpack with ammunition, binoculars, and other equipment. When he was done, he stood in front of Carolyn, the rifle nestled under his arm, the full backpack slung over his shoulder.

Carolyn eyed the amount of ammunition and supplies questioningly.

"Just in case," he said.

Carolyn nodded.

40

The last rays of light were beginning to fade.

Carolyn clung to Hodges like a baby koala to its mother's back as they hurtled along, the track of the snowmobile churning up the snow, the engine growling underneath. There was no regular drip of highway lines to measure distance or progress, just a featureless landscape of opaque whiteness. Unmoving. Unchanging.

Cold air whipped past Carolyn's face, snow and ice stung her cheeks, the goggles and face scarf she wore offering some protection.

The snowmobile rocked and bounced, and she dug in a little deeper behind the huge frame of Hodges, the warmth of the engine seeping up through her thighs. Their equipment was stowed in a compartment under the padded seat, Hodge's rifle sat snug on a scabbard attached to the side.

Every so often, Carolyn would peek out from behind the bulk of Hodges, but there was nothing to see except the cold, lonely emptiness.

Hodges wanted to reach the cabin before dark, preferring not to have to use the headlights on the snowmobile for the final leg.

As soon as he had straddled the snowmobile and turned the engine, his demeanor changed. Conversation was curtailed to either a simple nod or one-word answers. His face firmed, his eyes opened wider, taking in everything. Whatever humor or softness there was, had fallen away, replaced with a determined hardness. Carolyn knew that he had dropped into a hunter's mode, focusing purely on the task at hand.

The machine surged onward through the snow. They saw no one else. Any sense of civilization soon fell away. A barn in the distance, the thread of a fence line, all vanished into the cold white.

Ahead, the edge of the forest finally loomed into view. The wide, tall wall of trees seemed to spread farther sideways to the edges of Carolyn's vision with each passing second. She clung on tight and tried to plot their position in her mind from the map they had pored over that afternoon as they prepared for the trip. The snowmobile jerked and swerved over a patch of lumpy ground, and Hodges eased off the throttle.

He glanced over his shoulder, making sure she was all right.

She nodded, and he opened up the throttle again. The snowmobile accelerated and they continued their relentless churn through the snow toward the forest.

The wall of trees in front soon blocked out everything. The sky vanished as a massive glacier of greens and browns dominated the foreground.

Carolyn felt infinitely small, dwarfed by the massiveness of nature. The snow ahead turned a shade of dark gray as they entered the edge of the shadow cast by the tall trees, the temperature dropping instantly. They breached the tree line, and the dark forest swallowed them completely.

Hodges slowed and expertly threaded the machine through the labyrinth. Shadows pressed in all around them in the gloom, the drone of the engine cutting the silence.

Carolyn looked left and right, but all she could see was an infinite camouflage of bark patterns that stretched away in all directions. She had no idea how Hodges was navigating his way through the forest.

The going was a lot slower, and the deeper they went, the darker it became.

Finally Hodges eased off the throttle, and they coasted to a gentle stop next to a huge fallen log. He switched off the engine and they dismounted.

Carolyn peeled off her snow-crusted scarf, raised her goggles. It took a few moments for her eyes to adjust, for the constant throb of the engine roar in her ears to finally subside.

She looked around, orienting herself.

It was cold and silent. The air smelled of pine needles and a dank earthiness.

The only sound came from the cooling engine of the snowmobile as it crackled and ticked. Darkness seeped slowly toward them from above. They had about an hour of daylight left, at the most.

Ritter could be here, now, watching them. Hidden among the vertical camouflage of muted grays and pale whites.

Hodges took out his backpack, slid out his rifle, then held his arm up, pointing in front of them. "It's about two miles that way."

They were going the rest of the way on foot, deeper into the hall of mirrors.

Hodges led the way, Carolyn keeping pace just off his left shoulder.

The ground was hard with a thin layer of mush and brittle sheets of ice that crunched under their boots as they trekked. The snow never really made it down this far to the forest floor. The thick canopy of branches above caught most of it leaving only a light dusting on the ground.

Hodges focused intently ahead, his eyes sweeping left and right, taking everything in, looking, watching, sensing.

Carolyn, on the other hand, kept looking back over her shoulder, back to where the dwindling shape of the snowmobile sat. She felt tethered to it, like a ball of string, her only link back to the outside world. When it finally vanished from view, she felt unease grip her, hoping they could find it again in the dark, so they could leave this haunting place.

They trudged on for half a mile until Hodges held up his hand to stop.

Carolyn stood still, watching the back of Hodges. She could see his head turn to the right, imagined his gaze staring off into the distance, his rifle still slung over his shoulder. He seemed to be sniffing the air.

She squinted into the gloom, the light all but gone. She saw nothing.

They had brought flashlights. But Hodges wanted to squeeze every drop of daylight out of the forest before using them.

Carolyn shuffled up next to him, said nothing. A second later she smelled it. A faint meaty tinge that rode the coldness.

Now she knew why he had stopped.

Hodges crept forward: soft, deliberate steps, avoiding twigs and branches.

Carolyn followed.

He angled to his right. Still the rifle remained on his shoulder.

A hundred yards farther forward Hodges stopped again. He crouched down, removed a glove, then touched the cold earth and snow with his fingers, a groove, an indent.

Carolyn stood behind him, peering forward into the gloom, seeing nothing, but smelling something. "What is it?" she whispered, her heart thumping in her chest. The scariest things are those things you can't see, but you know they are there, just out of sight.

From his crouching position Hodges looked ahead. "There's something in front of us," he whispered out of the side of his mouth. "Something dead."

Carolyn could feel her jaw tingle, her throat tighten.

She crouched down next to Hodges and immediately saw the

stain at his feet. His hand came away from the snow. His fingertips glistened with velvety red crystals.

Frozen blood.

Carolyn's eyes tracked forward, away from her, across the ground, across the snow and ice. A thin trail of red snaked away from where they were crouching.

Hodges brought his bloody fingers to his nose and sniffed. His eyes narrowed.

He stood up. Without turning he reached behind him and drew his rifle off his shoulder.

Carolyn tensed, felt a cold rush and stood up.

Her mind raced. *Ritter.* Robin Hood. He was here, in the forest, with them. He is just a man. But his evilness seemed to permeate everything.

She had never felt fear until now.

Slowly she unzipped her jacket, peeled back the flap, the webbing of her hand found the contoured beavertail of her handgun. The reassuring feel of a protective dome descended over her as it always did whenever her gun was in her hand. She was confident in her skills. Confident she could stop any threat. Even Ritter.

He is just a man, she kept telling herself.

They edged forward some more. The frozen blood trail grew darker, heavier.

Hodges raised his rifle slightly, aiming forward.

Carolyn slid her handgun out, gripped it two-handed, barrel low, shoulders relaxed. She stepped farther around to her left, opening up the angle in front of her, away from behind Hodges. Covering him if needed, a wider arc of destruction.

Something came into view. A shape separated itself from the repetitive background.

It was a person, standing a hundred yards in front of them, staring back at them.

Hodges snapped his rifle up, scope to his eye and took aim.

A millisecond later Carolyn had the person in her sights as well.

Carolyn and Hodges stood perfectly still, both aiming at the same person.

"Jesus," Hodges whispered into the rifle stock, his eyes peering through the scope, the crosshairs centered over the magnified face in the aperture.

Through the scope Hodges clearly saw the person in infinite detail, enlarged, like the rifle barrel was pressed up against their chest, a few feet from where he stood.

Carolyn just saw a blurred shape, unmagnified. However, at this distance, she knew she could easily send several bullets into it.

Hodges lowered his rifle. His eyes refocused.

Carolyn looked at him sideways, still holding her aim on the person ahead, unconvinced there was no threat.

They got within fifty feet, and Carolyn finally lowered her weapon.

Her stomach churned at the sight.

She had seen death plenty of times. But not like this. Her mind tilted sideways as a mix of pure anger and gut-wrenching disgust boiled up inside her.

Carolyn had spent hours studying the crime scene photos of Robin Hood, trying to imagine the reality from just colored pixels on paper, nothing more.

Now it was right in front of her.

As horrifying and repulsive as it was, it held a certain macabre beauty to it.

Two crossbow bolts had pinned the woman to a tree trunk, either side of the sternum, burrowed deep in her chest. Her head hung limp, a young fragile face, dead eyes staring at the ground, mouth wide open, a last frozen gasp like she was coughing something up. Her hair, spun with ice crystals, glistened and shimmered, picking up what faint light was left from above.

Her eyelashes, her cheeks, the tip of her nose were frosted with ice. Lips of pale blue, a thread of frozen blood dribbled down her chin, her young, innocent face etched in shock.

The blood trail through the snow led right to the base of the tree where she hovered, doll-like, an ice angel with her tiny feet just inches off the ground, an unearthly sight.

Hodges glanced at Carolyn and nodded.

This was her domain.

Carolyn holstered her gun and stepped forward while Hodges backed away and stood guard, his eyes scanning the forest around them.

Hodges knew the ice angel was there, somewhere lurking at the blurred edges of his vision, but he kept his eyes averted. He had seen enough. He knew the more he looked at her, the more his insides would tear with rage.

He was going to kill Ritter. Or die trying.

Either way, only one of them would see the end of this day.

41

I
f Alisha Myers had been more observant as she drove down the street, looking for her driveway, then she would have noticed that not all the cars looked the same as they had every other evening when she had driven home after her shift at the diner.

Olivia, as she often did, had let Alisha use her car to go to work this morning because Olivia was working on a long online project all day that she was already behind on. That and the fact that it was cold and dreary outside, and she much preferred to stay indoors, warm and snug in front of her computer.

It was nearly seven o'clock, and Alisha knew that Olivia would be counting down the exact minutes from the time her shift ended to when she would pull up in the driveway.

Dark shapes, hunkered down for the evening, lined both sides of the street. Cold engines with roofs and hoods dusted with snow.

All but one.

Alisha turned in and parked in the driveway, the required distance from the garage door. Olivia would know otherwise.

No sensor lights came on. There were none. There was no need.

Deep inside the house, a square tile appeared in the upper left corner of one of Olivia's computer screens. She zoomed in with her mouse and smiled as she saw Alisha sitting behind the wheel.

She closed the CCTV window and went back to the lines of code she was editing on a massive vertical screen. Another few hours and she would upload it and get paid the balance of what she was owed.

Outside on the dark street, death appeared. A car door opened silently, hinges well lubed, the interior cabin light bulb deliberately removed, and a monster quietly slid out from within. The door was left slightly ajar.

The monster moved soundlessly up the driveway. Its face was long and drawn, hideous to look at. Gaping slits, arched black eyebrows, sunken cheekbones and a mouth of bared teeth, frozen in a terrifying, heinous grin.

Alisha Myers exited the car and shut the door behind her, unaware that death was within reach.

Something swarmed toward her, behind and to her right. A shadow, a slight ripple in the darkness.

She turned and saw its face. It filled her vision, and she filled her lungs to scream. The darkness enveloped her, took her in its embrace. She felt a sharp sting in the side of her neck that smothered the scream, stopping it dead before it could leave her throat and mouth.

Then last thing she saw was its eyes.

There were none. Just hollow empty slits, pitiless windows in to the chasm of hell.

DEEP INSIDE THE HOUSE, Olivia paused mid-keystroke, her fingers suspended over her keyboard. She glanced at the clock in the upper corner of the computer screen.

Strange.

With a click of her mouse, she activated the porch CCTV camera. A window popped up on her screen, a dark still image of her car parked in the driveway. No sound. No movement. No Alisha.

She glanced over her shoulder and listened to the sounds within the house.

Silence. No familiar footsteps from below on the polished floorboards. No echoing of the staircase as someone climbed it. No hiss of old copper pipes in the walls below as someone turned on the shower.

Olivia clicked another icon, and another window opened on the screen, another camera angle. She leaned forward, like she was going to ram the screen with her head.

"Bitch!" she hissed. Two shapes, huddled like lovers on a cold winter's night were hurriedly moving along the driveway—away from the house.

She leapt up, grabbed her spare set of car keys and her cell phone off the desk and ran downstairs, trembling with rage.

In the kitchen pantry she unlocked a cupboard, punched numbers into a keypad that was on the safe inside and pulled out a compact handgun. She ejected the magazine, checked it, then slammed it back into the gun. "Little dirty whore," she said. "After all I've done for you."

Next to the front door she threw on a snow jacket and a pair of winter boots.

Locking the front door, she turned and just caught a glimpse of an SUV as it turned out sharply between two parked cars before rapidly accelerating up the street. Olivia hustled down the porch steps cursing under her breath, thinking up all sorts of unimaginable horrors she was going to bestow on Alisha when she caught her.

Her own car lights blinked once and Olivia jumped in. She placed her cell phone in the dash cradle then inserted the car key.

The engine roared to life, headlights blaring, and she thrust the shift into reverse and skidded backward out of the driveway, barely missing a car that was parked on the corner.

"Fucking bitch!" she screamed as she kicked the gear into drive and floored the gas pedal. The wheels spun and skidded on the icy street as Olivia wrestled with the wheel to straighten the vehicle.

She sped off into the darkness.

42

Maybe she had a boyfriend? A secret lover that Olivia was unaware of. *Maybe I'll beat the living daylights out of them both when I catch them.*

Olivia hunched over the wheel and glared through the windshield, the wiper blades pushing a constant sludge of snow and ice back and forth, the landscape ahead dark and empty, the beams of the headlights caught in a snowy haze. She could see no other cars, no red taillights in front of her, nothing to follow.

Her eyes glanced at her cell phone that sat in a cradle mounted to the dash, the red blinking arrowhead of her car weaving its way across a digital landscape of roads, highways, and empty fields. Little symbols appeared while others slipped from view—gas stations, restaurants, ATM points, and a host of others. Olivia didn't need gas. She didn't want a food stop or a motel for the night. What she wanted, what she craved, what was eating her up inside with every mile she drove was the desire to find Alisha. To find out who she was with, and to kill them both.

No one had run from her—ever. It had taken two years of hard work, of infinite patience, coercing, and training, to get Alisha to where Olivia could trust her, could believe that she was committed to her, that she would never leave.

And now this.

But why did she drive home first? To drop the car off? Surely she could have just run from the diner? Maybe there was something more to it. Olivia tried to convince herself that Alisha wouldn't be that foolish.

Was she kidnapped? Right out in front of her own home? Who would be so stupid to try that?

No. She was definitely running.

It was beyond betrayal. Beyond dishonesty. Alisha had conspired behind Olivia's back, lying, waiting, biding her time, until she was ready to run, to escape from her. Someone was helping her. Someone had poisoned Alisha's mind with dirty ideas. Someone she met at the diner perhaps. That was really the only place she was allowed to travel to on her own.

Olivia cast her mind back to the other night, when she had picked Alisha up, on one of those rare occasions. The kiss had lingered in Olivia's mind. It was so convincing, so sweet, so genuine. Now it just left a bitter taste on her lips, the taste of betrayal. It was all an act, to get Olivia to relax her guard. To make her believe Alisha was fully committed to her.

As she drove on into the darkness, Olivia thought about the last girl, the one before Alisha. Three months into that relationship, Olivia knew it wasn't going to work. The girl was too rebellious, couldn't be controlled, still talked about her parents and the unfaithful boyfriend.

Olivia liked them young, found that they were more malleable in her hands; she could mold and shape them into what she wanted. The key was finding an "in." A crack where Olivia could slip through, comfort them, tell them she had a genuine concern for them. Being older meant Olivia could automatically position herself as a motherly figure, a surrogate for what was lacking in their lives. They all had something missing in their lives, a void, a hole left by a drunken mother or an overbearing father or an unfaithful boyfriend. Everyone had cracks in their lives: some large, some small. And Olivia was a master at finding then widening such cracks before asserting herself as the surrogate paternal figure.

Putty in her hands they were.

Domesticating the candidates was just the first step. Sexual domination was where the real control was, where the real power lay. And Alisha was nearly there, Olivia had thought from the previous evening. Alisha was right on the cusp, ready to take that next step.

Now she was running.

Olivia glanced at her cell phone again. Half a mile later she turned off the highway, slowed, and took a left turn onto a smaller road.

"Run, Alisha, run," she whispered as she accelerated again. "But Mama is going to find you."

THE SIGNAL WAS WEAK, barely there, but a signal none the less. Carolyn stood some distance away from the girl, cell phone in her hand, Aaron Wood's number up on the screen. Her thumb was poised over the call button. Carolyn was having second thoughts; maybe she couldn't do this alone.

She hesitated and looked at the girl again. They couldn't touch her, even just to close her fearful, staring eyes. The scene needed to be processed, and this time, Carolyn wasn't going to leave it to the local police.

She looked at the number on the screen again, thinking.

Ritter was close. This was his handiwork. Carolyn wanted him, wanted him bad. He was within reach. Calling Aaron Wood could set in motion a chain of events that she would have no control over. She would be pushed aside, just a civilian now, yet in her mind, right now, as she stood in the dark forest staring at the latest victim of a monster, she felt the need to avenge those women, all of them.

If she placed the call, the FBI would descend on Willow Falls like a tidal wave. Men and women, guns, big black SUVs, maybe air support, too. Anything but subtle.

But that wasn't always the best option, especially for someone like Ritter. He could easily get spooked. Flee. Slip through the road-blocks set up by the army of field agents and the incompetent local police.

There was a reason why Ritter hadn't been caught so far. He was nimble, cunning, smart. Maybe smarter than all of them.

But not smarter than her.

The cavalry swooping into town hadn't worked in Utah, and Carolyn was acutely aware of that failure. Agents had died. Some-times the size and complexity of the FBI machinery was its own downfall at times.

Carolyn believed what was needed to catch Ritter, a sole opera-tor, was discretion, a small ripple, not the crashing wave that the FBI tended to make when they arrived in force. Statewide and nationwide manhunts often failed, especially in the wide-open spaces where Ritter roamed, where he hunted.

She was here, on the ground, with Hodges right now. They were more nimble, more subtle, and more discreet. In her mind, she knew they had a better chance of catching Ritter without the some-times clumsy sledgehammer tactics of the larger agencies.

Carolyn canceled the number and pocketed her cell phone.

A sense of remorse settled on her as she glanced at the dead girl again. She felt no remorse for herself, but for the girl who they couldn't touch. They were going to have to leave her, alone, in the forest, in the dark, suspended in limbo, between the harsh rawness of death and the respect she and her family deserved of being taken down, taken away from this horrible place and rightfully cared for.

Carolyn turned her back on the girl and walked slowly toward where Hodges was standing.

"We're going to leave her."

Hodges glanced past Carolyn, toward where the girl floated, rage simmering inside him.

Carolyn could sense his anger, his willingness to take care of matters, just the two of them as they had agreed.

Hodges gave a slight nod, and they moved on through the forest.

Night had fallen, and Carolyn could feel the evilness that was in front of them, in the distance, hiding, drawing them both toward it. Like that moment just before a tidal wave hits, the water being drawn out from the shore, nature in reverse, pulling everything toward it. The birds and wildlife running, fleeing in wild panic as Hodges had described before.

A stillness had settled over the forest.

Carolyn felt it with each step she took. So did Hodges.

No sounds. No nocturnal creatures. Nothing. Like all the life had been sucked out of the forest, leaving just the two of them alone.

43

Olivia killed the headlights and coasted slowly to the side of the dirt road.

The edge of the forest, dark and menacing, was on the right. There were no other lights, just the warm yellow glow that came from the cabin in the distance nestled under the velvety midnight-blue backdrop of the clear night sky.

She checked her cell phone again to make certain.

She turned off the engine, took her foot off the brake, turned the wheel and gently came off the shoulder where there was no snow, letting the car amble quietly down the slight incline in neutral. Tires crunched on the frozen scrub, and she pulled up next to the tree line.

It would be impossible for anyone to see her car from the road now, and no one from the cabin would see her approach in the smothering darkness.

She flipped the interior light off, grabbed her gun and cell phone, and exited her car.

Staying off the dirt road, and using the edge of the forest as cover, it took Olivia just a few minutes to cover the cold ground toward the log cabin. Mist swirled and clung around her ankles, the ground mushy in places.

A Jeep Wrangler was parked near the front of the cabin, its boxy, dark shape was hunkered down under the frame of a steel carport.

Olivia paused and looked at her cell phone again.

Satisfied, she thumbed her phone to silent, slid it into a pocket and pulled out her handgun. She quietly racked the slide, making sure a round was in the chamber before cutting a direct line closer to the cabin, using the silhouette shape of the Jeep as cover.

Reaching the rear of the Jeep, she crouched down. She could feel heat rippling off the tailpipes, and the crack and pop of steel cooling came from under the chassis.

The front porch of the cabin was perhaps thirty feet away, across a stretch of open ground, no cover, nowhere to hide. The carport had thin metal sides with open ends. There were shelves, a few boxes stacked inside. Backing out, Olivia made her way around and outside. She crouched down against the metal side of the carport, hidden from view.

The exterior lights of the log cabin threw off wedges of light across the ground. Beyond the edge of the light was pure darkness. One side, the side closest to her, wasn't illuminated. There were no exterior lights on that side, just windows with a faint glow from within.

She decided to circle around to the rear of the cabin, approach it from behind, and use the darkness on that side as cover. She wanted to find a window or a door where she could take a look in, undiscovered, find out who else was inside. Then she would confront them.

She pushed off and faded into the shadows. Following a wide arc she began to circle around to the rear, looking forward to surprising the hell out of Alisha and her accomplice inside.

THE TREES THINNED as Carolyn and Hodges reached the edge of the forest. The moon in the clear night sky provided enough light for them to navigate.

Through the trees, Carolyn could see the faint glow of the log cabin. It was set back in a field of nothingness as she had remembered.

They had only gone another fifty feet toward the last row of trees, when Hodges held up his hand to halt them. Following his gesture, Carolyn looked to her left. A squarish dull shape sat in the gloom, back off the dirt road and on the edge of the forest. Someone had parked a small SUV there.

Moonlight glinted off the windshield of the empty SUV as Hodges and Carolyn approached it. Carolyn gently felt the hood. It was still warm.

Hodges looked at Carolyn.

She shrugged as if to say "I don't know."

Hodges lifted his rifle and panned across the clearing until the scope found the log cabin. There was no sign of movement in the windows and the front door was closed. All the exterior lights were on, pools of yellow ringed the snow but the right side of the cabin was in darkness. He could see Ritter's Jeep parked under a steel carport in front. They could reach the carport first then decide how best to approach the cabin itself without being seen.

As he panned to the right, something caught his eye beyond the light, a ripple of movement in the gloom. A shape, slow and stealthy. "Someone's out there, on the right, in the dark, making their way around to the back of the place."

Ritter? It was the first person who came to mind for Carolyn.

Hodges adjusted the magnification and squinted through the lens harder. "Can't really tell, but I think it's a woman."

Carolyn glanced at the SUV behind them. She was tempted to try the doors but the vehicle could have one of those alarms that went off as soon anyone touched it. That was the last thing they needed, the piercing shriek of a car alarm going off in the middle of the night.

"What's the play?" Hodges asked, his eye still focused through the scope. He then lowered the rifle. "Whoever it was, they're gone. But it was definitely a woman, hanging back in the dark, watching the cabin. Moving slowly toward the rear, away from us."

Carolyn had to think. Maybe it was another one of Ritter's victims, stumbling around in the dark. Maybe he was outside, with them, stalking the woman with his crossbow. She trusted Hodges' hunting instincts and his eyesight better than her own. "Keep an eye on the cabin, and see if you can pick up the woman again," she said. "If you see a man outside, and if it looks like he's after the woman, shoot him."

Hodges gave a slight nod, no smile, no warmth in him.

They moved forward and settled in behind a log. Hodges rested his rifle on the rough bark and nuzzled in behind the scope, the stock burrowing into one bristly cheek. The weapon was absorbed seamlessly and naturally into his body like it was flesh and bone, not steel and wood. He moved with a cold, detached efficiency, a killer, a hunter becoming one with the environment and his weapon.

Carolyn squatted next to him, her eyes focused on the house, wondering where this night would lead.

A LINE of footprints led up to the door at the side of the cabin. Someone had been here, walked to this side of the cabin recently. Only one set of footprints. Deep, wide impressions in the snow. Olivia wondered why there weren't two sets of footprints, or maybe more.

She quickly dismissed it from her mind and came out of the edge of the shadows.

A single bulb hung above the side door. It was switched off.

The main living areas were obviously around the front and on the other side.

The side door had a small glass window, dull light shone from deep within.

Olivia trudged carefully through the snow toward the door, placing her feet exactly into the existing footprints. She passed a small woodpile that was covered and tied down with old green canvas, and a chopping block with deep clefts hacked into its surface. No ax.

Pressing herself next to the door, she quickly glanced in. The room beyond was small and narrow, rows of cabinets, overhead cupboards, heavy outdoor clothing hung from hooks, thick rubber matting on the floor. Dim light shone through from a passageway beyond. Olivia could see the outline of an arch deeper inside and warm light bouncing off an internal wall.

She placed her finger on the handle and pulled it down gently and pushed.

Nothing.

She pushed some more. The door opened inward, with a sticky hiss from the rubber weather strip that ran around the inside of the doorjamb.

Olivia listened. There was no sound. She stepped in and gently pushed the door shut behind her.

She paused again to listen.

Still nothing.

Muted light framed the opposite end of the narrow room. Olivia stepped forward, her feet silent on the rubber matting. She entered a small passageway, dark slate floor, pale rustic walls. Ahead she could see the edge of the wall on her left where it opened up into another room, bright light coming from there.

She leveled her gun, aiming at the edge of the wall, ready to shoot anyone who came into view. Reaching the edge of the wall she paused, took a breath, then pivoted around the corner.

44

I t took a few moments for Olivia's brain to register what she was seeing, to comprehend the scene in front of her.

Alisha wasn't standing. She wasn't laughing, not celebrating having escaped from her life of imprisonment.

Instead she lay slumped, unconscious. A man, a stranger Olivia had never seen before, was holding her. Alisha's limbs hung vertical, listless, all jelly and no bones.

Olivia leveled the gun at the man's head, her finger tightening on the trigger. She stepped out from the shadows and into the living room. Olivia said nothing, no need, a pointed gun said it all, she just waited for her presence to be felt.

Ritter looked up, shocked, and he was a man who was never shocked.

Olivia's eyes narrowed. The man was older than Alisha, maybe the same age as Olivia, a fact that surprised her. She was expecting someone younger, closer to Alisha's own age, a young dumb millennial full of hormones and self-righteousness, who had somehow convinced Alisha to leave, to run.

The man was tall, with short, dark, wavy hair, dark eyes, maybe mid-forties. He had a vain, arrogant air about him, a glare of superiority in his eyes, after the initial surprise of seeing Olivia had faded.

Then it dawned on Olivia as she studied him. She was looking at herself, only the male version this time, a surrogate, but a father surrogate, the other parental figure who had also been missing from Alisha's fractured, pathetic childhood.

Olivia's eyes shifted from Ritter to the lifeless body of Alisha in his arms, then back to Ritter. "What have you done to her?" she hissed.

Ritter regained his composure. Outwardly he remained calm, in control. On the inside, however, his mind had gone into overdrive, racing at a million miles per hour, trying to comprehend how the woman had found him. He wasn't followed when he snatched Alisha. He was certain of it.

Yet here she was, standing in his cabin, Alisha's partner, pointing a gun at his head.

Olivia took another step forward, brandishing the gun as though Ritter hadn't seen it. "I said what have you done to her?" Her voice now a deep snarl, teeth exposed like a rabid dog.

For a moment they just stood facing each other. Two predators, one sadistic and cruel, the other infinitely worse.

One held a gun, pointed at the other. The other held the property of the one holding the gun.

"Put her down." Olivia gripped the gun tighter. She was going to kill him, shoot him here and now. She didn't care who he was or what he was. He had kidnapped Alisha. Taken what was rightfully hers. Drugged her somehow then had thrown her into his car and drove here to some isolated log cabin in the middle of nowhere.

God knows what he intended to do with Alisha.

In the blink of an eye, all was forgiven. All thoughts of nasty punishment wiped clean from Olivia's mind. Alisha hadn't tried to escape. Alisha still loved her, always had. Olivia was wrong. Alisha hadn't run, hadn't taken up foolishly with some young lover. Alisha was the innocent party in all of this, snatched right from in front of their home by this degenerate.

Knowing the real truth now only strengthened Olivia's resolve to kill the man. There could only be one surrogate. That was her, not this person. Olivia could be both a father and a mother to Alisha, if needed.

There would be some fallout. That was expected. Olivia could control that. Everything back at the house was well hidden. She'd tell the police someone had kidnapped Alisha, and that she had intervened, followed the kidnapper to his lair. He pulled a knife so she pulled a gun. Permits were in her glove box. She'd stood her ground, all legal. The courts were on her side, said so on Wikipedia. She was in mortal danger, had to shoot him. She'd find a knife in the kitchen, after he was dead, make it look convincing.

In a matter of seconds, Olivia had it all figured out.

"I'll count to five," Olivia said. "If you don't put her down, I'll put a bullet in your skull."

Ritter smirked. "What? And risk hitting your beloved whore?"

Olivia frowned at the comment. Bastard had been watching them. Pervert. Voyeur. Maybe a stalker, too.

He needed killing.

Olivia edged closer, adjusting her aim lower. "Perhaps I'll just shoot you in the balls. Maybe in the knee as well. Both of them."

Ritter could feel his anger rise. Who the hell was this little bitch that she should threaten him? He couldn't use all of Alisha's body to shield himself.

He lowered Alisha slowly to the floor, the barrel of the gun following him downward.

Alisha flopped like a corpse onto the floor. She was still breathing.

Ritter stood up. "Satisfied?" His voice aloof and arrogant.

"No," Olivia replied. "Who are you? And what the hell are you playing at?" Before she pulled the trigger, she wanted answers. Improvements needed to be made. Better precautions to be implemented. Olivia had underestimated the number of depraved people there were in the town.

Ritter said nothing. The answer to him seemed obvious.

There was an awkward silence.

Something still puzzled Ritter. Then he looked down, saw the fitness tracker on Alisha's wrist, the same rubberized band he'd seen her wear in the diner.

Olivia caught Ritter's gaze.

Ritter looked back up. "Ingenious," he finally said. This indeed was a revelation for him. "Did you make the modifications yourself or did you get someone else to do it for you? Some greasy-haired, tech-nerd who you let watch you masturbate on FaceTime?"

Olivia said nothing. He would be dead soon, so it didn't matter what he had figured out.

"So tell me," Ritter said thoughtfully, appraising Olivia in a new light, with slightly more respect. "Has she ever strayed before? You know, like a dog in heat?" Ritter wanted to unsettle Olivia. Wanted her to get angry, to make rash decisions, to let her emotions instead of her brain dictate her actions. Then she would make mistakes. He loved people who made mistakes. It was always the reason for their eventual downfall.

Choosing Alisha Myers was the gift that kept on giving for Ritter. First he discovered the young woman had dreams and ambitions. Then he discovered that she was in an apparent lesbian relationship. Now he had discovered the real icing on the cake. "Just a sex slave or a domesticated one, too?" Ritter added when Olivia didn't respond.

When Olivia said nothing, Ritter had his answer. "Domesticated as well." He laughed. "My, my, this is my lucky day," he exclaimed.

"It's your unlucky day, because I'm going to ki—" Olivia never got the rest of the words out.

It was a blur, a long vertical smudge of dark movement that drove into her.

Self-preservation made her pull the trigger, aiming at anything and everything.

The shot boomed out in the small room.

Olivia collapsed to the floor in a heap, her head smacking hard on the ground. Her jaw hung detached, dislocated. Blood dribbled from her nose and mouth.

Ritter stood over her and smiled. It was a risk worth taking.

Reaching down he pulled the gun from her grasp, rolled her over and took her cell phone from her back pocket. He stood up and studied the cell phone. A map was on the screen, a pulsing red dot in the middle, where he was now standing, inside the room, inside his cabin.

He looked at the two prone bodies on the floor. It was indeed his lucky day, despite what the bitch had said. Now he had two of them. A double hunt.

It was then he looked down and noticed a small patch of blood, slowly expanding, seeping through his shirt at the top of his chest near the shoulder.

He hadn't even felt any pain.

It was definitely a gunshot. Both Carolyn and Hodges knew it. It had come from inside the cabin, muffled slightly by the walls and by the distance. But in the still, wide expanse of night, they clearly heard it.

Carolyn and Hodges exchanged looks. A millisecond passed before they bolted to their feet, cleared the log, and sprinted across the snow toward the cabin.

They fanned out, no instructions needed, no hand signals, just an instinctual understanding between the two of them.

Hodges ran, shoulders hunched, chin tucked into his chest, eyes narrowed and up, nostrils flared, rifle angled down, but ready to be whipped up and aimed at the windows and the door of the cabin.

Carolyn was off his left shoulder, slightly ahead, but not in his line of fire. She had her gun up, pointing with one hand at the cabin, legs pumping through the snow, swearing under her breath, wishing that she was fitter.

Then Ritter's face appeared in a window next to the front door. His head turned left and right, looking outside, searching.

Fuck! Carolyn's mind screamed, her insides turning to ice. She suddenly changed direction, veered toward the carport, needing cover, Hodges right behind her.

Moments later, they found themselves in the shadows under the awning of the carport. They crouched in the darkness behind Ritter's Jeep, black and boxy, flared wheel arches.

"Wait a second—" Carolyn was breathing hard. Hodges seemed not to be breathing at all. "I don't think he saw us," she whispered between ragged breaths.

Hodges nodded. "Is that him?" he whispered.

"Yes."

"Then who did he shoot?"

"I don't know," she said. There were two cars. One was Ritter's, the other must belong to the woman Hodges had seen creeping toward the rear of the cabin.

"Maybe he shot the woman I saw," Hodges whispered.

None of this made any sense to Carolyn. "We'll wait a few moments. If no one comes out, then we'll move on the cabin," she said. "In the meantime, let's take a look."

They each edged out on opposite sides of the rear of the Jeep and slid half their faces out from behind the taillights.

The cabin seemed still. No more sound, no commotion. The lights burned brightly in the windows, and there was no movement inside. With the gentle falling snow and the slow spiral of woodsmoke twisting up into the star-covered heavens, the whole scene looked like a winter screensaver on a computer.

45

I t was a cold, dark place.

There was no boiler to provide heat. No windows to provide sunlight. The floor was rough cement, poured quick by unskilled hands. No sound was going to escape the thick, cinder-block walls. The ceiling was low, exposed beams and the occasional iron spike or shackle ring. There was a small cubicle toilet with a cheap stainless steel sink, a mirror, and a dull fluorescent tube that flickered and hissed.

It was a torturer's paradise. A room to keep people while you unleashed your deepest and darkest secrets upon them. A place well hidden from the judgmental eyes of God. But God wasn't blind as to what went on here. She just couldn't see that far into the dark. And the darkness ran very deep in this place.

But Ritter was no torturer. That wasn't him.

He had a different purpose for the room. Quite the opposite, in fact. Here he kept his treasures, safe and protected. No harm would come to them while they spent their short time here. Instead he tended to them. Fawned over them. Fed and watered them. Built up their strength, their resolve. Provided medical treatment if required.

However, there was nothing he could prescribe to calm the fear that overwhelmed them for the length of their short internment.

And for those whose fear didn't fuel their resolve, he gave them a reason to hate him.

The modifications to the basement were minor, layers of thick plastic and duct tape, a few screw-in bolts and nothing a good scrub of household bleach couldn't remove all traces of.

It took Ritter only a few minutes to truss the two women up.

He could feel the dull pain in his shoulder growing as he quickly worked. His shirt was soaked with blood, but it didn't seem to bother him. He would take care of it soon enough.

Finishing, he stood up and regarded the two bodies on the floor. Both women lay unconscious, thick black cable ties around their wrists and ankles.

He could not believe his good fortune. There would be more preparation involved, yet he relished the increased challenge. He was breaking new ground and that pleased him. This was definitely going to be his best season yet.

He went to the workbench carrying the gun, two cell phones, and the fitness band that he had ripped from Alisha's wrist. He flipped on a small lamp. Tucked into the case of the one cell phone he found an Iowa driver's license. *Olivia Bauer.*

He removed the SIMs from both cell phones, snapped them, then taking a hammer off the shelf he smashed each cell phone to pieces along with the fitness band.

An old refrigerator hummed noisily in the corner. Inside he took two vials of liquid and two disposable syringes from a large EMS hard case that sat on the bench. Inside the case was an assortment of medical supplies, surgical equipment, and drugs. Everything he needed. He brought the case with him on all his trips.

Filling the two syringes, he went back to where Olivia and Alisha lay. Olivia moaned and began to move her head side to side, blindly searching. He checked her pulse and lifted one eyelid. Her moans soon stopped as he slid the needle into the side of her neck, pushing the plunger all the way in.

He waited until Olivia settled then he felt around her jaw, wiggled it slightly, teasing it to see if she was fully unconscious. Satisfied, he leaned in, took hold of each side of her jaw with both hands, then firmly but quickly, twisted and pushed the dislocated jaw back into place. He felt around both sides of her face again, making sure the bone was seated properly then turned his attention to Alisha and gave her a smaller dose of the tranquillizer.

He checked both their vitals one more time. He wanted them to be undamaged, fully functioning for later.

He chained them both to a ringlet in the floor then carried the EMS hard case to the stainless steel sink.

The mirror was dull and hazed. The light tube blinked several times then finally came on, and a bubble of yellow light surrounded him in the gloom.

He was going to have to rely on feel and touch. The front of his shirt was damp with blood that had slowly spread out across the material.

Ritter flipped open the hard case, undid the buttons of the blood-soaked shirt, balled it, and placed it carefully in a plastic bag then sealed it.

He looked at his reflection. He saw hardened muscle, bone, and sinew, a lean, hungry physique. In Ritter's mind, it wasn't gained for reasons of vanity, but built for purpose: incredible strength, tolerance, and endurance without the cumbersome bulk.

There was a dark hole just below his collarbone, at the top of the chest muscle. Blood oozed out as he watched the fingers of his reflection press and prod around the entry wound, feeling the bullet under his skin. It was lodged in there, maybe two inches deep into the channel. Thankfully it hadn't hit bone, just muscle as it burrowed in.

He took gauze and mopped up the excess blood as it dribbled down his chest and abdomen, zigzagging through the grooves and furrows. He washed his hands, and pinkish water swirled into the drain hole.

Next he irrigated the wound, pushed a syringe filled with saline deep into the small hole. His tolerance for pain had increased tenfold in the last twelve months, thanks to a new formula he was testing. His bone density, that he diligently measured, had increased significantly as well. The typical impact shock that would break the bones of a normal person, would leave him just bruised and not damaged. Amazing as his anatomical gains were, they were yet to be fully tested.

A watery stream of pink liquid dribbled out of the wound. He wiped it away and dropped the syringe and sodden gauze into the sink. Rivers of blood, lumpy with clots, splashed onto stainless steel.

He stretched on surgical gloves, took a syringe, filled it with a local anesthetic then injected the area around the wound.

He selected a scalpel from the case. The razor-sharp blade glinted as he held it up to the person in the mirror. This was going to be a first for him.

He leaned forward, his waist pressed up against the sink and worked quickly, cutting and widening the hole, his brain thinking in opposites, left was right and right was left, deft, committed strokes, forcing himself to believe he wasn't cutting himself, but operating on the man in the mirror.

Blood flowed, thick and bright.

Satisfied, he dropped the scalpel into the sink, then took a pair of thin forceps and pushed them into the wound. His eyes watched his reflection as he twisted the forceps, searching, prodding deeper into the hole. Another stream of blood and detritus dribbled out, over the forceps, down his fingers and into the sink in big inky-red splashes. Undeterred, he pushed farther in until he felt the tip of the forceps come up against something hard, something foreign. He parted his fingers, opened up the jaws of the forceps, felt a little farther, and then closed the ends around the object.

Slowly he pulled the forceps out and held them up to the light tube. Held in their jaws was a bloody small lump of lead. He smiled.

He dropped everything into the sink, then irrigated the wound some more.

Satisfied that everything was clean, he pinched the edges of the hole together with one hand and stapled up the wound with his other.

He peeled off his gloves and washed and scrubbed his hands before applying a field dressing, securing it in place with thick strips of surgical tape.

He stood back and regarded himself in the mirror.

The day just kept getting better.

46

He injected her again, but this time it was to wake her, to bring her back to consciousness.

He had watched them both sleep, soft steady breathing. Chests rising and falling. All the time his mind thinking. Thinking about the tracking device disguised as a fitness band. Thinking about how Olivia had reacted when she saw him holding the limp, unconscious body of her partner, Alisha.

As much as he wanted the thrill, the challenge of hunting two people together, something else niggled at the back of his twisted mind.

Olivia opened her eyes, focused on the shape of Ritter standing over her. She tried kicking him with her feet, her motions clumsy and languid.

Predictable.

Ritter squatted down, just out of reach. He said nothing, just looked at her.

"Let me go," Olivia hissed, venom in her eyes. The effects of the tranquilizer had worn off surprisingly fast. She wrenched at the chains but couldn't move. "Unchain me!" she screamed.

Ritter glanced at the unconscious shape of Alisha, peacefully asleep. The drug would be good for a few more hours. Enough time to do what he intended.

Ritter turned his attention back on Olivia. She thrashed about some more, throwing all sorts of obscenities at Ritter, dropping in a few of the "c" words for good measure. But it didn't seem to bother him. In fact, it just made him more curious. The pieces of the puzzle were nearly all in place in his head. He just needed Olivia's help to complete it.

"You don't scare me," Olivia spat at Ritter.

Ritter smiled at the tantrum she was having. He flicked his head at where Alisha lay. "You chained her up, didn't you?"

Olivia stopped struggling. Her eyes continued to boil and froth with anger at Ritter.

Ritter smiled. So the jailer has now become the prisoner. "How does it feel to be chained up?" Ritter asked.

"I'm going to kill you," she whispered.

"I very much doubt that." Ritter laughed. "What was she?" Ritter needed to know. He understood their relationship, but now he wanted to know the dirty little details. "A runaway? A lonely single girl who took your fancy at a bus station?"

"You know nothing about me." Olivia's voice was low, coarse as gravel.

"Oh, but I can guess," Ritter replied with a sly smile. He knew exactly who—what—Olivia was.

Olivia glared at him. She wanted to break his neck. She was bigger than him. Probably stronger, too, she imagined. She had beaten bigger men than him, senseless, whenever they showed any interest in what was rightly hers. And Alisha Myers was her property. Now he was going to take Alisha away from her and that infuriated her.

Ritter stood up, teetering on indecision. The thought of a double hunt still appealed to him, but the attraction was fading.

He had a better idea.

What he had just learned about Alisha Myers had taken some

of the shine off hunting her. She was less appealing to him now, tainted, her life not so wonderful, not so unblemished. Ritter much preferred snatching those who were living happy little lives in their safe suburban homes, lives that were filled with joy, and hope, and promise. It meant so much more to him to tear those insulated, perfect worlds apart.

With his mind made up, he went to Alisha, took out a key and undid her padlock. He was going to create the ultimate irony. He was going to free the slave and enslave her master instead.

Olivia waited for him to do the same with her, but he never came near her. "Release me!" she hissed again. "Let me go, and see how much of a man you really are." Olivia had knocked out a two-hundred-and-fifty-pound truck driver once. The prick had come on to Alisha after her shift had ended at the diner. The jerk was waiting for her in the parking lot. Olivia was waiting in the parking lot for her, too, to take her home.

Olivia walked straight up to him and dropped him on his ass with one punch.

Ritter glanced in her direction. "Don't worry," his voice low, "I will release you. Then we'll see how fast and far you can run."

Ritter's response puzzled Olivia.

Ritter vanished into the shadows of the basement, only to return carrying a blanket. He unchained Alisha, gently wrapped her and lifted her in his arms, then looked at Olivia. "Now you be good. I won't be long."

Carrying Alisha, Ritter climbed the basement stairs and slammed the door behind him, cutting off Olivia's screams.

OUTSIDE, Carolyn pulled Hodges back into the shadows of the carport.

They watched as the front door opened and Ritter emerged. He gave a quick look around before stepping outside, locking the door behind him. He came down the steps and was heading straight toward them, toward where they were crouching behind the rear of the Jeep.

Carolyn backed out, pulling Hodges with her. All they could do was shuffle around to the other side of the metal wall, and pray that Ritter wouldn't see them.

He reached the carport and stood by the driver's side door, then paused, looking around. Carolyn and Hodges were just fifteen feet away, huddled behind the low sheet-metal wall, Hodges with his rifle pointed toward the edge of the wall, Carolyn holding her gun in both hands.

The Jeep roared to life, pulled out, and swung around the opposite side of the carport, then drove toward the house throwing up a churn of snow.

Carolyn couldn't see from where she was, but it seemed like Ritter had driven around the side of the cabin, had parked there with the motor running.

She slid along the ground to the edge of the carport.

She could see the rear of the vehicle, white vapor spiraling up from the tailpipes. She couldn't see what Ritter was doing. Moments later, she heard the clunk of the car door, and the Jeep performed a wide turn then drove right past them before turning onto the dirt road and heading back toward the main road.

They watched as the taillights glowed then finally disappeared in the darkness.

Carolyn stood up, and Hodges dusted himself off.

"Where the hell has he gone?" Hodges said.

"Don't know," Carolyn said, still staring into the darkness where the Jeep had disappeared. "But I'm not waiting for him to return." Carolyn nodded at Hodges. "Let's take a look inside. See what we can find."

They didn't waste any time. It was the opportunity they needed, to search the cabin without Ritter there. To find proof, anything that would incriminate him.

It was brutally cold, pitch black all around, with the silhouette of the mountains in the distance, and a huge heaven of stars spread out above. Hodges kept his eyes trained on the road while Carolyn checked all the windows and doors, trying to find a way in. She had to break in. The time for subtlety was over. She wanted to know about the gunshot. Clearly Ritter had shot someone. When he came out of the cabin, he didn't look injured.

She beckoned to Hodges, and they moved around to the rear of the cabin. They stood at the back where the kitchen was, a small set of steps leading up to a locked door.

"Break it," Carolyn said.

"With pleasure." Hodges reversed his rifle.

47

It was too late now; they were committed. There was no turning back.

Their feet crunched on the broken glass of the back door, the pane shattered by the butt of the rifle.

The kitchen was small, rustic, wood and stone everywhere. Carolyn had stood here just last night, stirring a pan on the stove and drinking wine with Ritter, imagining what the evening could have led to. She felt repulsed at the memory, at how she had felt when he kissed her.

Pushing the thoughts aside, she looked around cautiously, gun in hand, sweeping left to right. Ritter had gone, but they didn't know who else could be here.

A set of keys hung from a hook next to the back door. Carolyn lifted them and held them up.

"One is the key to his snowmobile," Hodges said looking at them in her hand. The snowmobile was parked in the steel carport, next to where the Jeep had been parked.

There was another key on the ring, heavy looking. Carolyn pocketed the keys and moved past the kitchen and into the passageway.

The living room where she had confronted Ritter was on the right. All the lights were on. There was a splatter of blood on the floor. She maneuvered around it, careful not to smudge it. Hodges noticed it, too, and raised an eyebrow.

Carolyn looked around the living room while Hodges stood near the archway, his ears tuned to any noise from outside, listening for the sound of Ritter's Jeep.

Carolyn walked past the bookcase, her eyes scanning every surface. But it all looked as normal as it had. She hadn't been upstairs though.

She turned and was about to walk out of the living room when her eyes fell on something, an object lying flat on the edge of the bookcase.

She backed up and looked down then lifted the strange object.

Hodges looked over. "What is it?" he whispered.

Carolyn turned it over in her hands, studying the object. It was ugly, sinister-looking, a vision of evil made from carved dark wood, hollowed out so as to be placed over the face, narrow slits for eyes to see through, eyebrows painted from burnt charcoal, chiseled hollow cheeks, tiny seashells forming a row of teeth, frozen in a hideous grin, a gaping mouth to breathe through. A wide tuft of coconut husk, stringy and yellowed crowned the head of the mask.

"It's a tribal death mask," Carolyn said, looking at the object. "South Pacific. Maybe from the Highlands of New Guinea." She had seen artifacts like this before, in strange and eclectic collections. She imagined what Ritter had used this for, to wear while he stalked his victims, compounding the fear they already felt as they stared death right in the face.

Carefully, she placed it back on the shelf. "Don't touch a thing," she told Hodges, who hadn't moved. "I'm going to take a look upstairs," she said, walking past Hodges. "Stay here and keep an eye out the front."

Hodges went to the front of the house and took up a position next to the front door. He peered through the blinds in the window but saw nothing.

Fifteen minutes later, Carolyn came back down the staircase but had found nothing. The cabin was clean. No weapons. No rope, no crossbow.

"He must keep everything in his car," she said to Hodges. Then she remembered. "Stay here," she ordered Hodges. She went back to the kitchen. In the cupboard under the sink she found the steel can she had discovered the previous evening. She pulled it out and read the label again, now knowing what it had been used for. There was no vermin in the cabin, no rats to exterminate. Carefully, she placed the can inside a plastic bag she had found in the cupboard and set it on the counter.

Carolyn checked her wristwatch. They had been inside the cabin for more than thirty minutes searching the place but to no avail. She wasn't going to give up. There had to be something here.

She went to the door next to the pantry. It was still locked as it had been last night. She fished out the bunch of keys and tried them all again. No luck. Perhaps it was just a storage cupboard with mops and brooms inside. But why lock it?

She pressed her ear to the locked door and listened.

Nothing.

She was about to pull away when she thought she heard something on the other side, distant, coming from below. Maybe the door led down to the basement where the boiler was. Maybe it was the boiler groaning.

There—again she heard it—a scream, a cry for help.

Carolyn stepped back and studied the door. It was heavyset, thick hinges, large casement lock. She needed Hodges' help to break it down. Carolyn hurried back to where Hodges was standing next to the front door.

Seeing her coming, he turned away from the window. "What did you find?"

Before Carolyn could open her mouth, slits of white cut

suddenly across their faces, and a blinding light shone through the window blinds. Then the roar of an engine came from outside.

They sprinted back along the passage, toward the kitchen and the open back door, leaving wet, muddy footprints in both directions along the floor.

In the kitchen Carolyn hesitated, looking at the door next to the pantry. There was someone down there, locked in the basement. She was certain. Wasn't she?

Swamped with anxiety, Carolyn didn't know what to do; confront Ritter or run and regroup, call in the authorities. Tell them about the dead girl in the forest they had found.

Carolyn's head swirled, the gathering wave of anxiety foreign to her. Indecision mixed with fear and apprehension.

She looked back down the passageway, toward the front door. Then she swiveled her head toward the open back door. Ritter or escape? Which one? Her or Jodie?

The rear of the cabin was open ground, smothered in darkness, maybe two hundred yards to the tree line. They could reach it—if they ran now.

Carolyn was first through the kitchen back door.

She stopped at the bottom of the steps and turned, expecting to see the huge shape of Hodges right behind her.

He wasn't there. He was still inside.

Carolyn swore and leapt up the back steps.

Hodges was standing in the kitchen. Not looking in her direction. Instead, he was staring at a small steel can he held in his hand, the can Carolyn had left on the kitchen counter.

Carolyn paused in the doorway, half in, half out, her mind screaming.

Any moment now Ritter would be coming up the front steps of the porch, put his key into the lock, and open the front door.

"Hodges," she pleaded. "We need to go." It was half whisper, half snarl.

Hodges turned his head toward her, holding up the can. "What is this?" he said, his voice low, and menacing.

Carolyn looked desperately down the passageway, toward the front door. She could see shadows pass the window next to the door.

"Hodges, please!"

Hodges didn't move. He read the label on the can, with the skull and crossbones, and the warning in big red letters.

"It's poison," he said, still holding the can, still reading the label.

Carolyn took a step forward, her mind racing. She had read the label, knew what it was, but she wasn't going to tell Hodges for this very reason. They didn't have enough evidence, nothing substantial. She didn't want Hodges to know, to get mad, not yet anyway.

It wasn't the time.

Carolyn could hear the key in the front door, the metallic click, the handle rattling.

Hodges turned toward Carolyn. His voice guttural, demonic. "Did he use this on my dogs? To bait them first before he shot them? Is that why they made no sound?"

She jumped from one foot to another impatiently, every second precious. "I don't know," she lied. "Maybe...I guess...we need to go!"

The front door slammed shut.

Ritter was inside the cabin.

Carolyn turned her head, looked down the passageway, and straight into the eyes of Dr. Michael Phillip Ritter.

48

R itter stood at the front door, looked through and saw Carolyn standing at the back door, thirty feet between them.

The space suddenly compressed like an accordion, and time sped up.

She was astonished at how fast Ritter had moved. One moment he was at the front of the cabin. The next moment he was inside the kitchen.

Carolyn barely had time to turn to face him. Barely had time to bring her gun out. No time to aim it before Ritter was on her.

The movement was subtle yet brutal. A chopping motion aimed at her wrist. Her gun tumbled to the floor.

Hodges was standing on the other side of the counter, past the edge of the doorway of the kitchen, hidden from Ritter's vision when he came through the front door.

Ritter turned and glared at Hodges. "Finally, we meet," Ritter said.

In the tight confines of the kitchen, Hodges tried to pivot, bring his rifle up and around, trying to clear the countertop with the barrel.

Ritter sidestepped, met the rifle mid-arc across the countertop with one hand, grasping the end of the steel barrel, then twisted, not the rifle, but the barrel.

Hodges felt the rifle wrench in his grip. His massive hands clamped harder, refusing to let go.

Carolyn recovered, pain searing through her wrist but she didn't scream. She didn't flinch. Her training kicked in: balls or throat, take your pick. She punched out with her left fist, aiming it at Ritter's throat, full force, expecting something to break.

Nothing did.

Ritter ducked his chin down at the last moment, and Carolyn's fist slammed squarely into his jaw.

There was no reaction. Ritter didn't move, just stood there smiling, his other hand firmly on the rifle barrel. Then he punched her in the sternum with his free hand, a restrained but harsh blow, not full force, plenty in reserve. He wanted her intact for later.

The blow propelled Carolyn backward and out through the open doorway. She tumbled down the steps before landing flat on her back in the snow. She looked up at the stars, at the dark vacuum of space above, and realized she couldn't breathe.

Ritter turned his attention back to Hodges and now grabbed the barrel with both hands and applied his full force. The barrel bent, steel kinked. Hodges stared at the end of his rifle. The weapon now useless, so he let go.

Now it was just the two of them in a small room filled with sharp objects, wooden planks, heavy cutlery, panes of glass, everything and the kitchen sink.

Ritter glanced back through the kitchen doorway, saw Carolyn outside still on her back squirming in the snow, struggling to force air back into her lungs. He calculated she would remain there, incapacitated, for a least another three more minutes.

He only needed thirty seconds to deal with Hodges.

But there was no fun in a quick kill. He wanted to spend more time with the man whose dogs he had baited with poison then killed with his crossbow. They had suffered: long, silent, and painful deaths. It was only fitting that their owner should experience the same fate.

Hodges came at Ritter, fast and low, hunkered and boiling, nothing but murder in his eyes.

Hodges was taller, wider, a hundred pounds heavier, all muscle and bone, honed from years of hard labor bending pipe and shaping steel with his bare hands.

Ritter was lean, nimble, and wiry. And something else.

They came together in the middle of the kitchen, a planet colliding with an asteroid, force on force. But science and physics had been messed with, altered. Einstein would have disapproved.

Hodges propelled forward and swung his fist, a wrecking ball-sized lump of knuckle and bone, aimed at Ritter's gloating face, everything he had behind it, full force, wanting to punch the man's head clean from his shoulders and sending it into the next zip code.

In his mind Hodges could see it happening, feel it happening, could visualize his fist pulverizing Ritter's face. A killing blow. No comeback.

Then it stopped: his fist, in midair.

Hodges looked along his arm. It just hung there, extended, ridged in space. At the end of his arm he saw the bulbous club of his own fist, Ritter's fingers wrapped around it, then Ritter's much smaller arm, and then Ritter's smiling face, still intact.

Ritter's eyes narrowed, then he squeezed Hodges' fist—and squeezed and squeezed.

Relentless, crushing pain exploded in Hodges' fist and along his arm.

Ritter didn't stop; he stood there pouring on the pain, crushing Hodges' fist even more.

Hodges felt his knees waver, the pain blinding. Desperate, he lashed out, grabbed Ritter by the throat with his other hand and lifted him off the ground. He twisted and threw him over the counter and straight into a row of overhead cabinets on the opposite wall.

Wood and glass exploded, as Ritter crashed through cabinets and slammed into the solid wall beyond.

Hodges ignored the pain he felt in his hand and turned to face Ritter. He spotted a knife block on the counter. Hodges reached for it, his fingers fumbling for the largest handle, the largest blade. He was going to gut Ritter like a deer. Hang the man's head on his wall with the other trophies.

A butcher's knife came out of the block with a zing, ten inches of glinting steel blade.

In disbelief, Hodges saw Ritter was already on his feet, unharmed. The row of cabinets hung on the wall behind him, a twisted mess of torn hinges, broken wood, shattered glass, one door hanging limp.

The butchers' knife came up, pure loathing in his face. "You killed my dogs," Hodges snarled. "You killed those women."

Ritter stood perfectly still. He seemed not to be worried by the knife in Hodges' hand. "You'll be joining them soon," he replied.

The blade came at Ritter, a straight low thrust, aimed at his gut.

Ritter reacted impossibly fast, just a sideways blur, the blade only traveling a mere few inches before bone-crunching pain vibrated up Hodges' forearm as Ritter delivered a vertical punch, straight down into the muscle then the bone. Ritter followed up with his other hand, what looked like an ordinary punch, with something out of the ordinary behind it. It slammed into the side of Hodges, cracking ribs, and driving the wind out of him.

The knife clattered onto the floor.

Hodges staggered backward as Ritter bent down and picked up the knife.

Turning the knife in his hand, Ritter regarded it for a moment.

Too easy. Too crude.

He drove the blade halfway into the wood cabinet next to him, left it there vibrating back and forth, then advanced toward Hodges.

Hodges backed up, cradling his arm. It wasn't broken. He looked at Ritter, bewildered.

Outside, Carolyn was on her side sucking in small gulps of air. Her eyes gradually came into focus. Through the kitchen window, shapes moved and bobbed.

Then came the wrecking sound of walls being smashed, glass shattering, wood splintering. There was a pause, then an unearthly scream, a howl of anguish. Carolyn got to her feet, teetered for a moment, then staggered toward the open doorway. She could see her gun inside on the floor.

Hodges needed to do something, change, transform, if he was going to live. In his mind there was no retreat, no surrender. If he didn't, then he would die and so would Carolyn.

Ritter, sensing Hodges was retreating, giving up, opened his mouth, providing the impetus Hodges needed. "I'm going to kill you like I killed your pathetic little mutts."

The words conjured up an image, raw and very much alive in Hodges' mind: four holes, four graves, dug by his own hands in the cold, frozen earth. Four friends taken from him by the monster who now stood in front of him.

A fissure opened in Hodges' brain, and an uncontrollable river of hatred and vengeance spewed out.

Hodges screamed and rushed at Ritter.

Blows rained down on Hodges, a maelstrom of pain. He ignored it and fought through until his hands found Ritter's torso. He grabbed Ritter, lifted him, and smashed him back and forth into things, anything.

First into the refrigerator. It was an old, solid thing, made from steel not aluminum, built in America during a time when men wore overalls, drank full-strength beer, wore beards not fashion statements, when things were built to last.

Then he swung Ritter into the counter, then back into the refrigerator, then upended him and brought him down hard onto the farmhouse-style sink, a heavy, thick ceramic construct that resembled something cattle would drink from.

On and on Ritter flip-flopped, a human metronome, swinging back and forth, his head, his shoulders, his arms, his torso used like a sledgehammer, battering and banging.

With his feet off the ground, Ritter's strength was diminished, he had no grounding, no connection with the earth, no pivotal torque. Physics and science playing their role. Einstein would have approved.

All the time Hodges saw nothing, just four loyal canine faces, wet noses, molten-brown eyes.

Outside, Carolyn was on her feet, had taken just one step toward the kitchen doorway when a tangled mass of arms and legs came crashing through the kitchen window and landed in a shower of glass and splintered wood in the snow.

Ritter staggered to his feet, his face a bloody mess of cuts and slices, one side of his head indented, sunken. Yet he stood there, somehow, teetering.

Ignoring Carolyn, he turned back dazed, and stared at the window he had just been hurled through. He glanced back at her, a bewildered look on his mangled face.

There was suddenly fear there, in his eyes. She could see it. Gone was the charm, the arrogance, the confidence. Replaced with the manic look of an animal about to flee.

And he did.

Limping and hunched, Ritter fled across the snow, around the side and toward the front of the cabin.

A shadow fell across the backyard and Carolyn looked up. Hodges stood there, his colossal shape framed in the doorway, the light behind him, his chest and shoulders heaving.

"Where is he?" he growled at her.

Carolyn almost didn't recognize him as he staggered down the back steps toward her. Fearfully, she stepped back.

Hodges stopped, blinked hard. His body swayed for a moment.

The river began to subside, the torrent of uncontrollable rage receding back into the crack of the fissure.

Blood trickled from his nose, his mouth, and his knuckles. Bits of glass and wood clung to his hair and were embedded in his beard.

"Where is—"

A sound came from the front of the cabin. The sound of Ritter's Jeep roaring to life.

They stood there watching as the huge shape of the Jeep, lights blazing, came fishtailing around the side of the cabin, all four tires kicking up a gush of snow.

As it barreled past them, Carolyn caught a glimpse of Ritter through the windshield, hunkered down, hands fighting the steering wheel, eyes manic and wild.

He was making a run for it, fleeing, away from town, away from civilization, into the wilderness. All the evidence she needed was in his vehicle: she was certain of it.

The Jeep swerved and careened then rushed away, in the opposite direction of the road back to the highway. Instead, Ritter was escaping into the forest, heading deep into its darkness, to hide, to recover, to regroup, then vanish completely.

Hodges hobbled back inside, before realizing that Carolyn had taken the keys to Ritter's snowmobile.

49

The devil was there, in the darkness, behind a veil of shadows, in the back row. She turned around but couldn't see him, but he was there, hiding.

He snickered and laughed, taunting her, willing her to stay, not to get off, to stay in her seat.

Then she heard her mother's voice. Felt the pain in it. Pleading, then crying, begging Alisha.

She felt her mother's hand close on hers, pulling her back.

Then the sky turned a brilliant white, before blossoming into a radiant cornflower blue.

Alisha was in the front yard of the family home, among the flowers and the bees, the air thick with the sweet smell of rose and honeysuckle.

Alisha looked down. Her mother was on her knees, bowed in sorrow at her daughter's feet, hands in the folds of her sundress, her voice sorrowful, her cheeks sticky with tears and summer sweat.

Words came but Alisha didn't care. It was too late.

Molly, her little sister, stood on the porch, and Alisha's heart went out to her when she saw her standing there, a young, innocent ten-year-old. Then a shadow passed over the sun, passed over her little sister, passed over the world.

He stood there, tall and powerful, the devil again.

Molly turned and looked up at him, then reached up and grasped her father's hand.

Frederick Myers stood there on the porch next to Molly. His shirt loose. It hung in tufts out of his trousers. Trousers that sagged without a belt, for that lay on the floor in Alisha's bedroom.

The devil on the porch snickered again at Alisha, his tongue slippery and wet, like it had been on her cheek, her neck, and then lower.

Fear filled Alisha.

Subconsciously, she took a step back, away from her mother, a step farther away from her baby sister, the chasm widening, the distance growing.

Alisha grasped her chest as her eyes found her father's. She immediately felt the stinging pain, the bruising, where cruel hands had clawed at her tender skin, her adolescence forever lost.

She had once looked up to her mother, wanted to be like her, stoic and righteous. Now she looked down at her. Her protector was gone, vanquished by her father, not even a shadow of her former self.

You knew...

Through gritted teeth, twisted pain, and tears of betrayal, Alisha watched her mother shrink into insignificance.

You knew...

Alisha stepped back farther, away from them all until they became mere specks on the horizon.

Evil is everywhere. We've just become blind to it.

Alisha turned back in her seat and looked out the window. A small bag lay next to her, a few precious things she had packed in haste as she ran from the devil.

A township came into view. Compact, pretty, pleasant faces

walking tree-lined streets, branches bent and shaded, picket fences with flowering garden beds, ribbons in little girls' hair.

Alisha stood up. She had to get off. The devil was following her.

She shuffled down the aisle, desperate to reach the doors. She willed herself not to look back, not to turn around even when the hateful, cruel snickering came again from the shadows at the back of the bus.

The scenery stopped, then came a hiss, and doors opened, beckoning Alisha to escape, to leave the stifling heat inside and step into the coolness outside. Alisha got off and stood on the side of the road, watching the bus pull away then vanish.

She was finally alone. The snickering had gone. No one else had come with her. She sighed in relief, anxiety left her small shoulders.

The devil was gone.

Then a cloud passed overhead, blocking out the sun.

The snickering returned, in her ear, from over her shoulder, behind her.

She whirled around, and an evil face filled her vision. A mask. Long drawn hideous features, with gaping slits, arched black eyebrows, sunken cheekbones, and a terrifying, heinous grin of evil.

Alisha woke startled, gasping, her hand clutching her chest, feeling pain and tenderness there, and she grimaced.

She sat up and looked around. The room was familiar. She was home, on the sofa, in the living room. The shutters were drawn. The clock on the mantle said it was just after midnight.

She felt disoriented, confused. Her mind tried to reach back, in reverse, to the last memory she had. Images slowly took shape. The diner. She saw herself walking to the car. Driving home, pulling into the driveway, then locking the car...Then she gasped. An evil hideous face.

Alisha struggled. She felt groggy, her memory doughy.

Was it a dream? Had she imagined it?

She looked around again. The house was quiet. Olivia would be

upstairs and would have seen her, watched her pull into the driveway, like she always did.

Alisha stared at the sofa, unsure as to how she got there. Maybe
she was too tired. Had come inside, sat on the sofa, took a minute to
rest. Then she had fallen asleep from sheer exhaustion. Yes, that's
how she got here.

She rummaged through her clothing, her pockets, and found a
set of keys. Her house keys. But no cell phone. It was gone. It wasn't
much use anyway. Outgoing calls were barred. Olivia had seen to
that. She was the only person who called her.

Alisha stood up, went upstairs.

Five minutes later, she came back down. She had searched the
house. Olivia was gone.

Parting the shutters, Alisha looked outside. It was dark. The car
was gone from the driveway. Olivia rarely left the house because she
worked from home. But now she was gone.

She didn't know what to do. This had never happened before.
Olivia was never not there. She was constantly with Alisha, in one
form or another. Monitoring her cell phone. Watching her on
hidden cameras. Tracking her movements with....

Alisha looked down at her wrist. It was gone. The wristband,
the anchor, the handcuff that kept her digitally tied to Olivia
twenty-four hours a day.

She looked at the keys again in her hand.

Her eyes darted to the front door. Alisha stood perfectly still,
thinking, contemplating, hoping.

She rushed to the door, grabbed the doorknob, and quickly
fumbled for the correct key. Maybe she was still in the dream,
hadn't really woken up yet.

Her wrist turned, and the doorknob rotated before she had
inserted the key.

The door opened an inch, a vertical slit of infinite freedom
beyond.

She opened the door a little more and saw the front yard, the street beyond, and nothing in her way.

Alisha rushed out, down the porch steps, then stopped suddenly, fearful that the dream would collapse at any moment, and she would find herself back in her bedroom, tracking band on her wrist, with the door locked.

But nothing faded. The scene remained intact. She was totally conscious, fully aware, coldness slapping her senses awake.

It was no dream.

She turned and looked back at the house, the door wide open, horrific memories lurking inside, in the walls, in the ceiling, down in the basement.

The basement.

She ran back up the steps.

This was no dream. But she needed to save another from the nightmare.

Moments later, they staggered out together, Alisha carrying the girl, one arm under her shoulders, holding her up, the girl leaning against her.

They stumbled down the porch steps, across the icy path. They slipped and tumbled sideways, the girl pulling Alisha down with her into the snow. The girl was weak, unsure, scared, sick.

Alisha could have left her there, in the snow, gone for help. But Alisha didn't want to leave her behind. Not for a second. The devil could return at any moment. There was no one else to help them.

Alisha screamed and pulled the girl up by her arms. They staggered on, the girl mumbling, her bare feet on the snow and ice, ankles ringed red, raw.

Together they made it to the middle of the street, the houses all around dark and ignorant.

The glow of lights appeared in the distance, an oncoming car.

Alisha turned them both to face it.

Twin bright lights washed over them, an unearthly sight, two women hunched in the middle of the street, clinging to each other, fear and bewilderment in their eyes.

50

It was not that difficult to follow Ritter. His Jeep tore a swath across the barren, icy wastelands, headlights cutting a long, wide wedge through the darkness, a huge bubble of light.

The Jeep bobbed and weaved as it plowed headlong, waterfalls of white gushing from under each tire, a madman at the wheel.

He was driving way too fast but he didn't care.

He needed to get away, to escape. Anger raged inside him as he glared through the windshield, his vision skewed, the taste of blood in his mouth as unfamiliar to him as the act of fleeing. Both were usually reserved for his victims.

One side of his skull was misshapen, caved-in and hideous.

He glanced in the rearview mirror and saw nothing but black. He stole a glance at himself and saw Picasso's *The Weeping Woman* staring back at him. His once handsome face, now lumpy and distorted, shredded and bludgeoned, irreversibly damaged. Ritter knew that no matter how much reconstructive surgery he would endure, and he would need a lot, he was condemned to a lifetime of stares and cruel, unkind whispers.

He felt no anguish. No fear. Just the burning desire for revenge.

The woman he should have killed. The man he doubted now if he could kill, unless...

His vision flickered as he drove, his thoughts jittery, intermittent signals, faulty transmissions in his brain from the head trauma. No logic. No sanity now. Just the primal, animalistic need to survive.

Hidden securely in the back of the Jeep was his hunting crossbow, the one he had used to kill all his victims. Not the decoy crossbow he had given to the police to examine, the one Carolyn had seen when she was snooping around his vehicle. That crossbow was totally different, just for show. Hide in plain sight, as they say. The decoy had different-sized bolts, different broadheads, nothing they could ever match forensically to the victim's wounds.

He had other things packed in the vehicle, too, hidden in special places. Countermeasures that allowed him to flee, to regroup, to assess and fight if needed. He would find another town, hide out for a while, tend to his injuries with the supplies he also kept as a backup.

He was taken unawares, in his cabin, by the man and the woman. Didn't think they would turn the tables and come after him.

She had balls, Ritter had to admit. If he knew, he could have prepared, taken the right doses, given the chemicals time to take affect. Then he would have beaten Hodges to a pulp. Instead, Hodges had beaten him.

A glow of light appeared in the rearview mirror and Ritter looked up.

It was a small ball of light, steadily growing.

Ritter's eye twitched in agitation.

It was them, in another vehicle. They were coming after him, maybe on his snowmobile.

Ritter floored the gas pedal. The Jeep accelerated, the snow was deep, the meaty tires not as effective. The vehicle sunk a little, the progress much harder.

His brain flickered again, and the rage increased, uncontrollable, unfathomable, the urge for revenge too much.

He jerked the wheel left, putting the vehicle into a wide turn and killed his lights. The front end of the Jeep dipped, tires groaned as a blizzard of snow and ice swamped the wheel arches. The rear end swayed back and forth as Ritter completed a partial turn, focusing on the ball of light as his reference point, a sea of darkness all around him.

He straightened the wheel. Now he was coming back at the ball of light on a diagonal, along a different path. They'd have no idea he was rushing toward them out of the darkness on their left flank, headlights off, taillights pointing away from them.

The ball of light tracked slightly to Ritter's left. He powered on, foot to the floor, heading straight at the light, judging the angle at which they would collide.

Four thousand pounds of Jeep versus four hundred pounds of snowmobile.

Only part of the mammoth rock protruded above the powdery white. Below the surface it was the size of Alcatraz Island, a behemoth lump of iron-hard stubbornness that had existed well before the dinosaurs. For millions of years it had been carried in the belly of a glacier bigger than Manhattan that had slowly ground down the state, forming lakes, rivers and valleys, crushing entire forests and grasslands in its wake.

And when the glaciers that covered Iowa finally melted, the rock was deposited here where it had sat. Partly visible in summer. Almost invisible in winter.

Ritter flipped on the headlights at the last moment, full glare, turning on the powerful LED light bar as well, wanting to blind Hodges and Ryder before he rammed into them. He didn't see the rock until it was too late. His entire focus was on the growing ball of light, lining up the hood of the Jeep toward it, so he could ram those pursuing him.

The Jeep skewed sideways as it hit a patch of soft snow, then the hood dipped down. Ritter swung the wheel at the last moment when he finally saw an apex of rock poking up through the snow. The front axle rammed the edge of the rock face then sheared away from the under chassis. Metal buckled, lights shattered, the front fender tore away, side panels peeled away. The right side of the vehicle slid sideways, dipped, dug in, then collapsed inward before the whole vehicle flipped on the diagonal.

Three, four, five times the Jeep rolled, shedding pieces of aluminum, plastic, glass, and rubber as it spun. Panels crumpled. Bolts sheared. Welding joints cracked then split completely apart.

The Jeep finally came to rest upside down and half buried in the snow, just a disintegrated, hissing, crackling, leaking, dying mess.

Dazed, Ritter released his seat belt and immediately fell onto the ceiling. He felt no pain as he scuttled sideways and climbed out of the shattered side window.

The glowing ball of light suddenly changed direction and bore down on him, and he could hear the familiar roar of a snowmobile heading straight toward him.

Undeterred, he clambered to the rear. The tailgate was crumpled inward, the rear window cracked but not shattered. Grabbing the handle he tried to wrench it open, but it was fused to the frame.

He looked up as light washed over him. The snowmobile was getting closer. The whine of its engine louder.

Ritter stood back, brought his arm up, and punched his fist into the tailgate window. Glass shattered, and he continued punching until he had cleared a wide enough hole to climb through.

In the tumbled mess of the rear cabin, his bloodied hands found the hard case he was looking for. He wrenched it out with him, placed it on the snow, then flipped the latches.

The light was stronger now, illuminating everything around him. His fingers fumbled through tiny glass vials, hypodermic syringes, auto-injectors. Hands moved fast as he pulled out four auto-injectors, tiny glass vials of blue liquid already chambered in each.

He had only ever administered a single dose at a time. That was enough.

The scream of the snowmobile grew louder, the light intensifying.

Ritter knelt down in the snow, broke the safety seal on each of the four devices, and quickly plunged each auto-injector into himself: two in each thigh then staggered to his feet.

The reaction was instant.

Blinding light suddenly hit Ritter, the scream of the engine almost on top of him. Ritter ripped away a hunk of twisted metal from the Jeep, stood, then waited like a matador.

Hodges could see Ritter's hunched shape in the glare of the snowmobile lights.

No mercy. No hesitation.

Hodges pushed the throttle to the top, and the snowmobile flew harder over the snow. Carolyn clung on for her life, and together they rocketed straight at Ritter. Hodges was going to run the bastard over.

Through the windshield, the shape of Ritter grew, until his torn-and-mangled faced filled Hodges' vision, painted deathly white in the glare of the light.

Then the world exploded.

At the very last moment, Ritter sidestepped and swung the twisted metal at the snowmobile, shattering the windshield.

Something hard and horizontal hit Hodges in the shoulder. Pain tore through his arm and across his chest. The snowmobile buckled, shunted sideways. Hodges could feel himself losing control. The machine thrashed violently under him, a mind of its own. A mad bull desperate to throw its rider. Then it flipped.

Carolyn felt like she was in a washing machine, on the spin cycle.

She tumbled through the air and landed with a jarring thud in the snow.

She staggered to her feet. Hodges had landed past her, was

buried deep in the snow, facedown, not moving. The snowmobile was lying on its side some twenty yards past where Hodges lay.

Dazed, Carolyn turned back to the mangled wreck of the Jeep. It lay thirty yards away, the front grille crumpled, skewed headlights forming a bubble of light around it.

She could see a person moving near the rear. The side of her face was wet and she felt her forehead. Her fingers came away red. She could taste blood on her lips, felt warm liquid in her eyes, blurring her vision.

She glanced back at Hodges. He didn't move.

Carolyn started toward the Jeep, her body racked with a dull pain. Drawing her gun, she pointed it at the person in front of her, just a shape, fuzzy and red.

THE PERSON WAS DOING something under the chassis, pulling, sliding, unclipping.

Then the person turned and faced Carolyn. He held something in his hands, something compact with limbs.

More blood cascaded into Carolyn's eyes. She tried to wipe it away, splattering blood onto the snow. She aimed at the person, right-handed, holding the gun as best she could with her damaged hand. It was a deliberate choice. The red-dot reticle hovered and wavered over the fuzzy shape backlit by the Jeep's headlights.

She wiped her eyes again.

Ritter came into focus.

Carolyn fired.

Sparks burst off the chassis behind him.

She fired again and again and again, driven by fear.

More sparks flew. Ritter was still standing.

The aftermath of Utah came flooding back to her once more. History about to repeat itself. Carolyn knew it. Ritter was going to escape, vanish, never to be seen again.

She settled.

Held her breath.

Aimed again.

The red-dot settled over Ritter. Center mass. No mistake this time. No repeating the past. Fist-sized holes into the motherfucker's chest. The only prison sentence he deserved.

Carolyn squeezed the trigger.

Pain tore into her and she screamed.

The bolt hit her in the shoulder.

Carolyn tilted off-balance. Compensating, she fired, wild shots, emptying her magazine, hitting nothing.

And with that, another ghost had just been set free to haunt her again for the rest of her life.

Ritter stepped forward, re-cocked the crossbow, slid in another bolt.

Carolyn sank to her knees. Her arm hung at her side, her gun held loosely in one hand, empty magazine, spent on trying to kill another monster.

She stared at the bolt in her shoulder, knew what it was, knew what she was about to become. The image of Mary Jane Westerman came back to her.

Carolyn stared down at the snow in front of her, thinking how beautiful it looked, crushed glass, drizzled in red that ran down her arm and dripped off her fingertips. The artwork spreading.

Then a voice screamed at her deep from her past. Her instructor from the academy.

Subconsciously, her left hand moved to her left hip, searching under her jacket. The right side of her shoulder, arm, and torso was numb, gone, not there.

She looked at her gun, tilted it, tried to find the magazine release, but it wasn't there. She struggled to remember where it was on the side of the weapon. It had to be there, ergonomics built into the design meant it should be easy to find, second nature for her.

Her thumb pressed and pressed at the frame, searching but not finding. Tears rolled down her face, hot and bloody. She gritted her teeth. Her brain screamed at her, drowning out the voice of her instructor.

It was too late.

She brought her left hand up, saw a fresh magazine there, in the palm of her hand, rotated and indexed perfectly.

She struggled some more. Still couldn't release the spent magazine. Her mind, not the weapon, was jammed. Jammed with rising panic. Numbness crept down her arm toward her hand. She was losing the feeling in her gun hand, felt her fingers loosen around the grip. She tried to squeeze, to not let the gun slip.

Carolyn looked up.

Ritter was closer, his face obscured. Something in front of his head again like she had seen moments before. His eye was huge, magnified through the lens.

Through the scope Ritter saw her shape, her torso perfectly segmented into four equal quarters, the crosshair over her left breast.

A quick kill. A winter's kill. The last of the season. There would be other seasons, he was certain.

The magazine slid out of her gun, and plopped into the snow.

Carolyn painstakingly slid in the new one. Couldn't raise her right arm. The feeling in it almost gone.

She swapped hands, her left hand taking the gun from her now dead right hand, like it was another person's hand, no feeling, no sensation in it.

She brought her left thumb up and over the slide, hit the slide lock of the left side, felt the welcomed thud as it shunted forward into place, feeding a round into the chamber.

She brought the gun up, left-handed.

The next bolt hit her flush in the chest, before she could fire.

Heart shot.

The killing shot.

51

Carolyn lay in the snow, on her back, arms outstretched.

Christ the Redeemer.

Wings of red slowly unfurling in the snow under her.

An angel taking flight, leaving this evil earth, turning skyward, heading toward the heavens in search of justice and redemption.

Darkness passed over her face, covering her for a moment, shrouding her body, protecting her.

Then it was gone.

Hodges didn't look down. Didn't need to. She was dead.

He went past Carolyn's body in a blur.

The world inside his head had turned white, white hot with just a single blemish of darkness at its very center.

A blemish that Hodges now ran at.

Ritter saw Hodges come out of the darkness, run past the body of Carolyn, and on toward him. Three hundred pounds of fury and rage.

Ritter reloaded then backed up fast, wanted space, widen the gap. Didn't want a quick kill this time. He was going to take his time with this one. Break new ground. Make Hodges the first male in his collection. Tyler Finch was just for fun, an experiment. Ritter testing the idea of an urban kill plot rather than a woodland one.

Skin this fucker, too. Flay him open, turn him into a human bloody canvas of skin and blood vessels.

The first bolt hit Hodges in the arm.

It didn't slow him.

He kept coming like a massive bull, all that was missing were the horns.

Ritter reloaded, took aim, fired again.

The bolt pierced the thigh this time.

Still didn't slow him.

Hodges ran faster, the gap shortening, his manic speed gobbling up the distance between them.

Ritter reloaded, mild panic rising, fluid movements practiced all summer long. But under different test conditions, alone in his lair, without the stress of another monster bearing right down on him.

Not the same.

The bolt fumbled in the flight rail. Precious seconds lost as Ritter seated it correctly.

He fired.

The next bolt hit Hodges low in the torso, a glancing shot, went in then partially out his right side.

Still didn't slow him.

He ran harder. The rage inside him molten white now, intense, inhuman, smothering everything else he felt.

Ritter stumbled backward, couldn't reload fast enough. A massive wall of hatred bearing down on him.

Another bolt into the rail. Ritter drew the cocking mechanism. Half brought up the crossbow to aim.

Then a freight train hit him.

The bow was ripped from his grasp. Massive gorilla-like hands twisted the limbs, bending metal, shattering carbon fiber.

Ritter surged forward, enhanced, powerful, his bloodstream on fire, a toxic river of synthetics flowing through him. Superhuman. The Lance Armstrong of villains.

Yet it was no match for pure human rage.

The crossbow took flight through the air, spun like a boomerang, spinning end on end, never to return to its owner.

The same hands that had shaped metal and bent steel for decades, now took hold of Ritter, lifted him off the ground by the throat, feet dangling.

Ritter struggled, kicked, and let out a gargled scream. The massive hands slowly began crushing his neck.

Hodges squeezed. Muscles bulged and strained, natural strength, conjured up from within. He looked deep into Ritter's eyes, beyond things made of flesh and blood and into a black and sinister place where the memories of dead women roamed, their screams still echoing in the dark recesses of an insane mind. The memories of his dogs also roamed there, tails wagging with fierce eyes.

Hodges saw it all, reflected back into his own mind, in his own memories. And in the moment, he did what the dead couldn't. He did it for them.

Ritter's eyes bulged as one huge hand shifted and covered his head then slowly twisted. The other vicelike hand around his throat remained in place, and began to twist as well, but in the opposite direction.

Ritter screamed again, a choking, drowning wet sound. He felt his vertebrae twisting, turning, unhinging. Cartilage separating, ligaments tearing. Blood vessels twisting, knotting, then bursting.

Ritter's head kept turning, and turning, screwing around, front to back.

Then everything snapped, and life escaped his body with a sudden jolt. All that remained was a limp carcass of nothingness.

Hodges released the body. It slumped backward and into the snow.

THE AVERAGE HUMAN body contains between nine and twelve pints of blood.

Hodges lost 30 percent of his own blood while carrying the body of Carolyn Ryder almost two miles through the snow and darkness, back to Ritter's cabin, only the tracks of the Jeep and the snowmobile as his guide.

There was finally enough signal for Hodges to use Carolyn's cell phone to call the police. The sheriff's department and state police descended on Ritter's log cabin like an invading force, and after securing the scene, they soon discovered Olivia Bauer chained up in the basement. The kitchen at the rear of the cabin looked like a wrecking ball had gone through it.

The blood loss suffered by Hodges, however, wasn't in vain. Following the blood trail, and the directions given by an almost unconscious Hodges, a separate contingent of deputies and troopers arrived at dawn to another crime scene of carnage and mayhem. They found the twisted wreck of a Jeep Wrangler, a damaged snowmobile with its track ripped from its housing, and the body of a man who, at first glance, resembled the stage prop from a low-budget horror movie.

The deputies and troopers initially thought the body of the man was lying facedown in the snow, the back of his head clearly visible with the neck twisted like a rubber band. On closer inspection they realized that from the neck down, the body was indeed facing upward, toward them, the chest and feet pointing skyward.

One young deputy retched into the snow while a trooper studied the body, thinking that bears had finally moved into Iowa.

But there was only one bear in Iowa, and after his hemorrhaging was stopped by paramedics, he was taken to the nearest hospital for an emergency transfusion, then surgery, to remove the crossbow bolts that were embedded in him.

Doctors and nursing staff were even more astounded when a

rumor circulated in the hospital that the patient had endured such wounds while carrying the body of a woman two miles through the snow to reach help.

A wider search of the surrounding forest near Ritter's cabin resulted in the gruesome discovery of the body of Madeline Bennett, a young local woman who had disappeared on the way home from work. She was another one of Ritter's victims.

Alisha Myers and another unidentified woman were later interviewed after both fleeing from a house in the town. Over the coming days, the house that Olivia Bauer had rented with her partner, Alisha Myers, was torn apart inch by inch. They found what could only be described as a detention area in the basement, the kind used to chain up prisoners. It seemed that Olivia Bauer had a history of preying on younger women, whom she groomed as domestic and sexual slaves. She would befriend young, often vulnerable runaways online or would approach those who were passing through Willow Falls. After what forensic psychologists termed as an intense period of "persuasive conditioning," the young women fell under Olivia's influence. It was something akin to brainwashing.

No sooner had Olivia's chains been removed at Ritter's cabin, police then placed another set of chains on her and arrested her. Further investigation revealed that Olivia Bauer also went under the aliases of Olive Bower, and Olander Bateman. She was wanted in two other states on social security fraud.

Further digging into Olivia's past would later reveal that she was also wanted in Michigan in connection with the disappearance of another young woman from a local government-funded shelter for abused women. Olivia, posing as a victim of domestic violence, infiltrated the shelter with the sole intent of grooming likely candidates.

52

Special Agent Dan Miller placed the paper cup of coffee down on the table and gave Aaron Wood a nudge.

Wood stirred and raised his head. With his thick black-framed spectacles askew, he looked his usual disheveled, unkempt self, but was instantly awake. Miller could see in the man's eyes that his mind never stopped turning, even while he slept, which was usually in the back of a police car, in an airport lounge, or at his office desk usually around 4:00 a.m.

Wood stretched, grabbed the coffee cup that was the size of an ice bucket, and drank half of it in one go.

Coming around to the other side of the hospital bed, Miller looked down at the sleeping form of Carolyn Ryder. "Doctors say she'll pull through. She's strong."

"She's a fighter," Wood replied, yawning.

Wood had arrived late last night, taking a chopper to the airport then the last plane out. He'd been by Ryder's side ever since.

Miller looked at her some more. Her arm was bandaged and so was her chest. Christ, she had more tubes in her than the London underground. He turned to Wood. "You got a second?"

"Sure." They left the room together, not before Wood squeezed Ryder's hand.

The FBI had taken over one of the visitors' rooms. A police guard had been placed outside Ryder's room, just as a precaution, until she was conscious and they knew more about what had happened in Willow Falls. Jodie was the only person other than Wood and the law enforcement officers who were allowed to see her.

The visitors' room was small, with a long laminate table and a scatter of worn plastic chairs.

Wood sat down and stared at the crucifix on the wall. It reminded him of the body of Clarissa Mulligan, the first victim the police had found in Willow Falls, whose pictures Carolyn had first sent him.

In the middle of the table was a large plastic evidence bag. "What's this?" Wood asked as Miller sat down opposite him.

"This is what saved her life. She must have strapped this on under her jacket before she went up to Ritter's cabin with Beau Hodges."

Inside the sealed plastic bag was the lightweight bulletproof vest Ryder had purchased at the last moment when she was in the gun store in Willow Falls.

"It's civilian issue, not law-enforcement spec, but it is still level IIIA protection. Did the job," Miller said, waking up the tablet device he was carrying.

"Can you buy these over the counter?" Wood asked, turning the vest over in his hands.

"You can in most states provided you're not a felon," Miller replied without looking up from the screen.

"Good thing she had the sense to wear it." Wood noticed a small tear in the center of the vest where the crossbow bolt that was aimed at her heart had struck.

Miller scrolled through reports on his tablet screen, crime scene photos and autopsy results. "We still can't find the crossbow." He looked up at Wood. "The one that Ritter used to shoot her and Beau Hodges." Miller folded the tablet case so it formed a stand and placed it on the table between them. "Don't really need it anyway," he said. "Found plenty of evidence in the basement of the cabin, Ritter's home in Chicago, and inside the wreck of the Jeep."

Wood leaned in as Miller began to scroll through the screen, bringing up images taken by the team who were still processing Ritter's house in Chicago. "He is Robin Hood. We have confirmed that," Miller said. "We found DNA and blood samples in the back of his vehicle belonging to Clarissa Mulligan. We also found this." Miller spread a finger and thumb, enlarging an image on the screen.

Wood squinted. "Quite a collection."

Miller nodded. "The lab guys reckon he had formulated his own performance-enhancing drugs. Some of the stuff they've tested so far is fifty times more powerful than EPO. Found a hard case full of the stuff next to the car wreck, including auto-injectors. Ritter also had a stash in the basement of his cabin. The team in Chicago said he virtually had a drug lab set up in his home. We're checking on the hospital where he worked to see if he was stealing supplies. They've gone into damage control: hospital board has called in big-shot lawyers. But we'll find out, one way or another."

"So he was self-administering the stuff, enhancing his strength," Wood said.

"Not just his strength," Miller said ticking off fingers on his hand. "Endurance, agility, reaction times, recovery times, pain tolerance, you name it."

"But it still gave him superhuman strength?" Wood asked.

"Looks like it. Initial toxicology indicates red blood cell count off the charts. The same with his testosterone levels. His bone tissue was also still regenerating. Normally at around age thirty, the bone mass stops increasing. But not in Ritter's case, they tell me."

"So he wouldn't succumb to typical bone fractures?" Wood asked.

Miller nodded. "Making him one tough son of a bitch." Miller laughed. "The lab guys just hope he hasn't sold or told anyone else about his formulations. If this stuff gets out on the open market or the black market, it will make the next Olympics look like the latest Marvel movie without the need for special effects."

"A real Bruce Banner," Wood said thoughtfully. Wood said nothing for a while, just stared at the screen, thinking about Ritter's other victims, how he had managed to simultaneously lift them up with one hand while shooting them with his crossbow with the other, pinning them to the tree.

"Here's the kicker," Miller said, a wry smile on his face. "The autopsy also revealed that it was starting to destroy his physiology, destabilize him. He was dying. Ritter didn't even know it."

"Dying?" Wood looked up. "What from?"

"From all the crap he was pumping into himself. Short-term gain for long-term pain. The side effects. It had given him cancer, lymphatic tumors, probably from all the drugs."

Wood sat back stunned. Ritter was dying, a victim of his own abuse to become superhuman.

"They gave him maybe twelve months to live by their estimates," Miller added.

Aaron Wood knew it was irrelevant that Ritter had cancer. It was cold comfort. Carolyn had found him and had stopped him. If she hadn't, then how many people would he have gone on to kill until the disease finally claimed him?

"But she got him," Wood said. "Ryder got him."

"Ryder found him, worked it out, but I think it was her companion, Beau Hodges who turned him into a human pretzel."

"So this Hodges guy," Wood asked, "what's his story?"

Miller had already interviewed Beau Hodges as soon as he regained consciousness after surgery. "He's a local hunter, someone who Ryder confided in. He says she came and saw him with this notion about someone up in the hills hunting women, capturing them, then releasing them, only to hunt them again." Miller continued to scroll through his tablet.

"So it was definitely him who killed Ritter?"

Miller nodded. "Looks that way. Killed him in a frenzy, with his bare hands, ain't seen nothing like it. But Hodges had an unfair advantage in the end."

Wood looked perplexed. "Unfair advantage? How so?"

Miller smiled and put down the tablet. "Despite all this crap Ritter had in his bloodstream, Hodges had the most powerful drug known to mankind flowing through his veins." Miller leaned forward, a knowing smile on his face. "Something capable of turning any ordinary person, man or woman, into a raging superhuman, making them capable of anything. Something we have both seen plenty of times."

Wood was truly lost now.

Slowly, drawing out each word, Miller put an end to Wood's confusion.

"Pure, unadulterated hatred."

Wood smiled, contemplating what Miller had just said. Hate was a powerful drug indeed, the worst kind known to man. He'd witnessed the horrific aftermath of its use more times than he cared to remember. "I heard local police are missing one of their own," Wood asked.

Miller nodded. "A guy called Tyler Finch, a police officer from Willow Falls. They found his police cruiser near an abandoned warehouse on the outskirts of town a few days ago. Forensics are going over the place now. Found some blood but not much else."

"Why a cop?" Wood asked, more to himself than of Miller. "Ritter hadn't killed any one in law enforcement before."

"We don't know if it was Ritter," Miller said. "We haven't found his body. But let's say, for argument's sake, it was him, that Ritter killed Tyler Finch."

Wood thought about it for a moment. There was only one motive that came to mind.

"Maybe he did it just for fun," Miller said. "Got sick of hunting women."

Wood shook his head. "That's not his style, a random kill. But you're half right."

Miller cocked his head questioningly. "Half right?"

"I think it was a test, a trial, an experiment," Wood said slowly. "Maybe he was getting bored, that he needed more of a challenge."

Miller's eyes narrowed, suddenly understanding Wood's thinking. "Christ. It wasn't random."

Wood slowly nodded. "Next season. Next year, he was going to hunt police maybe. He wanted the notoriety, the challenge, increase the risk and the thrill."

"Every law enforcement agency would have come after him," Miller said thoughtfully. "It would be a nationwide manhunt. But like you have said all along about him, he always chose the hardest path to test himself."

There was silence in the room for a few minutes.

Miller went back to his tablet. Wood went back to thoughts of Dade County, Georgia, and the aftermath of what they had found there, hatred again playing its part, or maybe it was just pure, socio-pathic enjoyment.

"Found this, too, in the remains of Ritter's Jeep." Miller held up the tablet for Wood to see again. The object on the screen looked like a handheld police radio, but with multiple stubby antennae protruding from the top.

"Portable cell phone signal jammer. Good for up to fifty yards. Jams everything, smart phones, tablets, the lot. Three hundred bucks online. Might have to get one for my teenage kids," Miller joked. "Won't put down their damn phones at the dinner table. Should put one of these on the table, make it look like an ornament."

Wood had anticipated the next question from Miller. It was only a matter of time.

"What did Ryder tell you when you spoke to her last?"

Wood rubbed his eyes. "Just that they had found the body of a woman here. She didn't say much else. And that the local police seemed out of their depth." Wood wasn't about to throw Ryder or himself under the bus.

Miller looked at Wood, not entirely convinced. "Did she mention anything about Michael Ritter?"

Wood shook his head. "No. Not a thing. But you know Ryder. She'll pursue something, won't tell anyone. If she felt there was more to it and that local police weren't capable, she'd go it alone, ignore everyone. That's how she is. You know that, Dan."

Dan Miller nodded. "A real trailblazer." He thought back fondly to when they had worked together on several cases. If it wasn't for her, and what he had learned under her tutelage, and the arrests they had made together, following instinct and trusting their guts, he wouldn't have been promoted to special agent so fast. Miller owed a lot of his career advancement to Carolyn Ryder.

Miller left it at that and packed up his tablet and collected the evidence bag. "How's Georgia going?"

"Cold and wet," Wood replied. "They can handle it for a few days without me. I'm going to hang around here for a while. See how Ryder goes."

"I saw the initial reports," Miller said. "Do you think it's him?"

They both knew who they were talking about.

"You were in Utah with Ryder, weren't you?" Wood asked.

Miller nodded. "Lost a lot of good men that day."

Wood thought about the ten red pins on the map on the wall of his office, back in Virginia. He nodded at Miller. "It's him. The girl in the cave we found, she's number eleven."

They both stood.

"Keep me in the loop if you can," Miller said.

Wood nodded.

Miller paused at the door, his hand on the handle. "I know you're still close to her; I know you've stayed in contact after she left."

Maybe this was going to turn into an interrogation after all.

Miller's face then softened. "We need her back. I'll talk to her when she regains consciousness, but I want you to talk to her, too, Aaron."

"She won't come back." Wood shook his head. "She nearly died in Utah. Nearly died here as well." Wood couldn't believe it. Carolyn Ryder wasn't even FBI anymore, and she still managed to bag one of the worst serial killers of all time. Wood knew she couldn't be replaced. He also knew she couldn't stop, couldn't let it go. It was in her blood. She was good at this, one of the best, maybe even the best. But like so many before her, she had become a casualty, a victim of those she hunted. It was an occupational hazard. The human mind gives out long before the physical body ever does.

Miller opened the door, and they walked together back out into the corridor.

"Let's just give her time to recover," Wood said.

Miller's cell phone rang. He unclipped it off his belt, brought it to his ear, nodded at Wood, and took the call.

Aaron Wood didn't get thirty feet before Miller called out to him.

Wood turned back and looked at Miller. Miller stood in the deserted corridor, cell phone pressed to his ear.

"Your cell is off," Miller said over the mouthpiece.

"I needed the sleep." Wood slid out his cell phone, switched it on. It immediately pinged with multiple messages landing.

"Well, they need you back in Georgia," Miller said, walking toward him. "They've found another body. It looks like it's the same person. Same MO. Just off the highway this time."

Wood thumbed the screen and sighed. Another red pin to add to his map.

Just when you've stopped one monster, another one jumps up to take their place.

53

The last space on the wall was now filled, occupied, complete.

It was a new addition to the collection and probably his most prized. Not to say that he didn't cherish the huge deer, perhaps the largest ever taken in the state. Then there was the massive black bear that he had taken in Wisconsin many years ago, whose dark eyes, huge snout, and snarling teeth adorned a worthy place high on his wall as well. That kill was also one of his most cherished.

And there were others too. Beau Hodges felt a deep sense of pride for all his trophies, regardless of what people thought. They had all taken immense skill, cunning, and courage.

But perhaps there was one trophy, the latest and last to be added to his collection that gave him the most satisfaction, the most pride, the greatest feeling of achievement, not as a hunter, but as a human being.

Sometimes in life we feel inadequate when we see the deeds of others, what they have achieved in the fields of science, medicine, sport, the arts, or in other human endeavors.

But now he had done something that had purpose: to him and to others in the town.

His collection was now complete, and it had given him a deep sense of purpose every time he looked at what had filled the once empty space. And what hung there was for his eyes only. And when he did look at it, dead eyes didn't stare blankly back down at him. It wasn't made from skin, hair, or bone. It was made from machined aluminum and reinforced carbon fiber.

It wasn't in pristine condition. Nor had it been lovingly restored to resemble something lifelike. It was untouched, in the exact condition as he found it when he returned and pulled it from the snow.

Its limbs were twisted, the metal scarred like a bear had clawed at it. Perhaps one had. The pulley system was cut, buckled, the draw cable snapped. The quiver remained intact. One bolt, the last of six, sat snugly in its slot.

While some may find the other trophies distasteful, barbaric, it was this trophy, the last one, his last kill, that would garner the most acceptance by all.

Everyone agreed: the townsfolk, the police, the media, the entire state, that his last act, his last kill, was his finest, and his most important.

For once, hunters and animal advocates were united in their opinion, that Beau Hodges had killed an animal that needed killing.

But Hodges disagreed.

He believed, that on that fateful day, a day he would never forget, what he killed was not an animal.

But a monster.

So in the years to come, when nieces and nephews sat in their beds at night and would look up at the bear of a man who cradled them safely in his huge arms, intently listening as he read them bedtime stories, and when they would ask him innocently, "Uncle, are there such things as monsters?"

He would put down the storybook that was filled with wild tales of witches and goblins, of angels and princesses, and answer. "Yes, there are such things as monsters in the world. I have seen one."

Eyes would go wide and thoughts of sleep would quickly be cast aside. "And what did you do when you saw the monster?" young voices eager and enthralled would then ask.

Hodges would think for a moment. Then with absolute certainty he would reply. "Well, I did what you should do whenever you see a monster. You kill it."

Turn the page to find out how you can download a FREE ebook and
A SPRING KILL,
Book #2 in The Killing Seasons
and
AMERICAN JUSTICE where you can learn more about Carolyn Ryder and her archnemesis, Sam Pritchard as she features heavily in this story.

While AMERICAN JUSTICE is Book #3 in my NO JUSTICE SERIES, it can be read as a complete story standalone and I know you will love it.

It's Spring, and a new evil has awoken.

Sam Pritchard, the Highway Killer from Utah, tried to kill her...but failed.

Robin Hood, the winter serial killer who terrorized most of the Midwest, did kill her, and technically, Carolyn Ryder, for almost five minutes, was dead.

But the woman who surgeons brought back to life on the operating table is not the same woman who was wheeled into the ER without a heartbeat.

She has changed. But one thing hasn't changed. Carolyn Ryder has some unfinished business, and it's called Sam Pritchard. She wants to find him real bad. And when she does...she's not interested in capturing him.

She's going to kill him.

A Spring Kill is available through Amazon in paperback, kindle and kindle unlimited

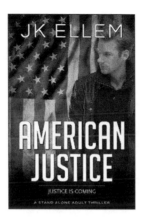

The last time Ben Shaw stepped in to help a young woman, five people died. Now he's back...
A despicable act of pure evil happens in the skies over Wyoming leaving hundreds of people dead.

A nation-wide man hunt turns up nothing for Carolyn Ryder, the FBI agent in-charge of tracking down those responsible.
But what Ryder didn't count on was Ben Shaw walking innocently into a gas station in the middle of Utah and confronting one of the perpetrators face-to-face.
Shaw sees a ghost from his past and takes it upon himself to follow the trail and exact his own form of justice. Shaw's quest quickly turns into a break-neck race across Utah with the FBI, local police and a gang of disgruntled bikers on his tail.
Can he stay one step ahead and uncover the ruthless killers responsible before they unleash their next act of evil
But there's someone else stalking the lonely highways of southern Utah leaving behind a trail of heart-broken families in their wake.
For Police Officer Beth Rimes, catching the Highway Killer has become her obsession over the years, and when Ben Shaw crosses her path, she has him squarely in her sights as a prime suspect.

Set amongst the small towns, desolate open highways and rugged natural landscape, *American Justice* is a rollercoaster road trip adult thriller.

America Justice is available in paperback, kindle and kindle unlimited through Amazon

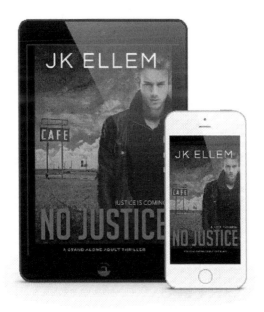

Young man helps desperate woman from being bullied off her ranch by a ruthless small-town family.

In the small town of Martha's End, Kansas, trouble is brewing. Two feuding families, the McAlister's and the Morgan's have been in conflict for generations, and Ben Shaw, a young and good looking man, soon finds himself caught in the middle.

With the Morgan family patriarch, Jim Morgan, ruling the town with his three sons, and dark and sinister things happening on the Morgan ranch, Daisy McAlister, the last of the McAlister family bloodline, is in need of help. But with his unique skillset and mysterious past, Ben Shaw may be the one to tip the balance in her favor.

Will justice be served in this town or will it take a higher power? Find out in this suspenseful thriller novel.

A PERSONAL FAVOR FOR ME!

Thank you for investing your time and money in me. I hope you enjoyed my book and it allowed you to escape from your world for a few minutes, for a few hours or even for a few days.

I would really appreciate it if you could post an honest review on any of the publishing platforms that you use. It would mean a lot to me personally, as I read every review that I get and you would be helping me become a better author. By posting a review, it will also allow other readers to discover me, and the worlds that I build. Hopefully they too can escape from their reality for just a few moments each day.

For news about me, new books and exclusive material then please:

- Follow JK Ellem on Facebook
- Follow JK Ellem on Instagram
- Subscribe to JK Ellem's YouTube Channel
- Follow JK Ellem on Goodreads
- Follow JK Ellem on Bookbub
- Visit JK Ellem's Website

Also available by JK Ellem

Ravenwood Series
Book 1 - Mill Point Road
Book 2 - Ravenwood
Book 3 - The Sisterhood
Book 4 - An Unkindness of Sinners

The Killing Seasons
Book 1 - A Winter's Kill
Book - 2 A Spring Kill
Book 3 - A Summer's Kill
Book 4 - A Fall Kill

No Justice Series
Book 1 - No Justice
Book 2 - Cold Justice
Book 3 - American Justice
Book 3.1 Fast Justice –A Ben Shaw Road Trip Thriller #1
Book 3.2 Sinful Justice –A Ben Shaw Road Trip Thriller #2
Book 3.3 Dark Justice –A Ben Shaw Road Trip Thriller #3
Book 4 - Hidden Justice
Book 5 - Raw Justice

Stand Alone Novels
All Other Sins
Audrey Kills Again!
Taxi Man
Murder School

Deadly Touch Series
Fast Read - Deadly Touch

Octagon Trilogy (Dystopian Thriller Series)
Prequel - Soldiers Field
Book 1 - Octagon
Book 2 - Infernum
Book 3 - Sky of Thorns

<u>**Boxsets**</u>
No Justice Box Set 1
Deadly Touch, No Justice, Cold Justice

No Justice Box Set 2
American Justice, Hidden Justice, Raw Justice

Ben Shaw Road Trip Thriller Box Set 1
Fast Justice, Sinful Justice, Dark Justice

Octagon Box Set
Soldiers Field, Octagon, Infernum

ABOUT THE AUTHOR

JK Ellem was born in London and spent his formative years preferring to read books and comics rather than doing his homework.

He is the innovative author of short chapter, Hitchcock-style adult thrillers in the genres of crime, mystery, and psychological thrillers which have multiple plot lines that culminate in explosive, unpredictable endings that will leave you shocked.

In 2022 he was accepted into the Curtis Brown Creative, Writing Your Novel in Six Months course which he undertook in London while working on his manuscript for future submission.

He splits his time between the US, the UK and Australia.

Made in the USA
Columbia, SC
12 October 2024

44217849R00195